Praise for *The Last Thing You'll Hear*

"A deliciously disturbing and unique exploration of the power
of music, sisterhood and finding your voice (literally!)"
Tess James-Mackey, author of *You Wouldn't Catch Me Dead*

"A stylish summer thriller. Fast-paced,
compulsive reading… A fabulous five stars"
Sue Cunningham, author of *Totally Deceased*

"A pulsing, drumming must-read for fans of festivals,
romance and fairy tales, this is also a timely critique
of toxic masculinity and the seductive power of
social media in a post-truth world"
Olivia Levez, author of *The Island*

"A fast-paced thriller set against the backdrop of a sinister
music festival, with dark Glastonbury summer vibes.
Brilliant! I tore through this in one sitting!"
A. J. Clack, author of *Lie or Die*

"Unputdownable! Find a quiet spot to lose
yourself in this high-tempo thriller!"
Lou Kuenzler, author of *Our Beautiful Game*

THE
LAST
THING
YOU'LL
HEAR

JAN DUNNING

SCHOLASTIC

Published in the UK by Scholastic, 2024
1 London Bridge, London, SE1 9BG
Scholastic Ireland, 89E Lagan Road, Dublin
Industrial Estate, Glasnevin, Dublin, D11 HP5F

SCHOLASTIC and associated logos are trademarks and/or
registered trademarks of Scholastic Inc.

Text © Jan Dunning, 2024
Cover illustration © Dan Couto, 2024

The right of Jan Dunning and Dan Couto to be identified as the
author and cover illustrator of this work has been asserted by
them under the Copyright, Designs and Patents Act 1988.

ISBN 978 0702 33293 7

A CIP catalogue record for this book is available from the British Library.

Printed and bound in Great Britain by
Clays Ltd, Elcograf S.p.A.
Paper made from wood grown in sustainable
forests and other controlled sources.

1 3 5 7 9 10 8 6 4 2

www.scholastic.co.uk

For Mum, Dad and Helen.
And for sisters and music lovers everywhere.

When words fail, music speaks.

HANS CHRISTIAN ANDERSEN

1

The sun is setting beyond the gently rolling hills, the peak of the Wrekin a looming silhouette against the shades of red and gold. I perch on the garden wall, a can of cider in my hand, shivering in the cool evening air. In the field below the house, the marquee glows blue, yellow, pink, green, in time to the throbbing bassline coming from within. It looks like a spaceship has touched down and the aliens have decided to have a rave.

Except what alien in their right mind would come to Hamlington?

I knock back my cider and wrap my arms round myself. It's the end of March and still too cold to party outside, but that hasn't stopped the entire population of Hamlington sixth form rocking up to celebrate Charlotte Jensen-Scott's eighteenth. And who can blame us? The Jensen-Scotts are loaded – no expense spared for their princess, meaning free food and booze all night. Plus, nothing interesting usually happens here.

Or that's what we thought.

I can hear her name, tossed upon the breeze. It's the only thing anyone has talked about for the past fortnight. It might be Charlie's birthday but there's another girl on everybody's lips.

Anna Walker.

Eighteen years old; the same as Lark. Only a year older than me. A "good" girl, according to the papers – a prefect at a posh private school in Shrewsbury, an A-star student who sang soprano in the Abbey choir every Sunday. That is, until she upped and disappeared from home two short weeks ago.

Vanished without a trace.

The French doors bang open and a group of girls stumbles outside. Upper sixth form friends of Lark.

"I heard she met some guy online and went to meet him in real life. The police are trying to trace him."

"I heard she met him at a church group."

"A church group, are you serious? That's it, I'm deleting Tinder. Girls, we've been doing this all wrong. Apparently, we need to get God if we want to get laid."

"Aisha! You can't say that!" They trip past, giggling in mock horror. "What if it turns out he killed her?"

"*Killed* her? I doubt it. More like she got sick of living in the back of beyond and decided to piss off somewhere else."

"Ha. Fair."

They drift towards the marquee.

"Wren!"

The voice makes me jump. My sister Lark shimmies on to the terrace, her long blonde hair glistening in the glow from the fairy lights. She looks stunning in wide-leg palazzo trousers and the fitted sequin tuxedo jacket she picked up on Vinted last week. I feel boring in comparison, with my plain black dress and mousey-brown crop.

"Why are you moping out here by yourself?" Lark swigs from a bottle of prosecco. "Come down to the marquee and dance!" She waves to her friends up ahead.

"Mmm. Later, maybe."

I frown. Lark reckons she knew Anna – knew *of* her, at least. But then, Lark knows everyone. She collects friends the way we used to collect Pokémon cards – or rather, people collect Lark. They're drawn to her. Attracted like moths to a flame.

"The DJ sounds terrible," I say, pulling a face.

"Aww, it's Charlie's brother Jem, back from uni. You're just a music snob."

"And you've got no taste." I swipe the bottle from Lark's hand, helping myself to a swig.

"Manners, little sister!" She snatches the bottle back and eyes me meaningfully. "I get it. You're waiting for Danny. Where is he?"

3

"Who knows?" I try to shrug nonchalantly. "It's not like we're joined at the hip."

"*Sure*." Lark snorts. There's another bang behind us and she barks with laughter. "Ha! Right on time!"

I spin round. Danny is framed in the double doors, looking shambolically handsome in his dad's best suit and a battered felt fedora, his one concession to Charlie's roaring twenties theme. His broad shoulders and six-foot frame are silhouetted against the kitchen lights, his face in shadow. As he moves towards us, the light hits his cheekbones. He smiles and my heart skips a beat.

"I'll leave you two alone." Lark jumps to her feet. "Don't do anything I wouldn't do!" She winks.

"For God's sake, shut up!" I hiss.

'Oh, relax!" She giggles. "He didn't hear."

It's a thoughtless remark but I glare as Lark scurries off towards the marquee. Sometimes I really *hate* my sister.

"There you are." Danny's voice is soft and deep. It sends a shiver running through me. "What's up with Lark?" His eyes linger on her disappearing form.

"Nothing." I make sure I'm facing him so he can clearly read my lips. Spiralling dark curls escape from the brim of his hat. "Just being annoying, as usual."

"Oh, give her a break." Danny's chestnut eyes sparkle. "So, are you having fun?"

"Hmm." I consider the question. Contrary to what Lark thinks, I do like parties, but this one is pretty dull. It's more like a wedding, what with the posh canapes served on silver plates and the boring speeches about how wonderful Charlie is. And now we've been herded out into the cold for some awful "disco" in a marquee – a blatant ruse so her parents and their mates can get drunk round the fireplace in peace.

I shrug. "It feels a bit wrong to be partying when a girl has gone missing, don't you think?" I frown. "I mean, I know Anna wasn't from Hamlington – and it's not like any of us really knew her, but…" I trail off. "Maybe I'm overthinking. There's probably a simple explanation."

"Yep." Danny squeezes on to the wall next to me. Our thighs touch. "Don't worry, Wren. I'll look after you. Get you home safe and sound." He slings a muscled arm round my shoulder and gives me his best ironic smoulder.

My cheeks heat up, even though I know he's only joking. Danny drove tonight because Mum insisted. She didn't want me and Lark walking home to our estate in the dark. Mum's always paranoid about safety, but since Anna went missing she's been even worse than usual.

"Well, if you're *sure* it's not out of your way?" I grin.

"Oh, it is. Miles and miles." Danny grins back. "But anything for you."

My face burns again. *I'm such a cliché.* In love with the boy next door – literally. Our family moved in next to Danny's when I was eight. My bedroom window faces his, for God's sake. I can barely remember a time when I didn't know Danny. It feels like we've always been friends.

And sometimes I think that's all we'll ever be.

A sigh escapes my lips. Luckily, Danny doesn't notice. He drops his arm and gets to his feet. I drink in the clean lines of his profile as he stares at the darkening sky.

"It's too late." He tuts. "We've missed it."

I touch his arm to get his attention. "Missed what?"

"The murmuration."

"Murmur *what*?"

He smiles down at me. The light is fading and his pupils are massive, drowning his irises in huge inky pools. "When the starlings fly home to roost, it's called a murmuration," he explains. "It happens around this time of year. Thousands of starlings, moving together as one."

I smile. It's adorable when Danny geeks out. And he's not even been drinking, obviously. He gets as high on science and nature as I do on music.

"Aww. Sorry you missed the big flock of birds."

He rolls his eyes good-naturedly. "It's not just a flock. You have to see it to believe it. Like, on their own, starlings aren't that special. But when they come together as one…" He shakes his head. "It's like magic … or art…" He shrugs, embarrassed.

"Sounds cool."

"It is." He smiles and it's like sunshine. A dimple appears in his cheek. "One day, I'll show you."

He offers me a hand and I take it, letting him pull me to my feet. His fingertips graze my skin; they're calloused from guitar-playing, like mine.

"Is that the only reason you came tonight?" I tease.

6

Danny's famously not a party person. "For the excellent bird-watching opportunities?"

"Ah, you got me." He laughs softly. "Although the views round here are also very nice."

His eyes sweep the landscape, and settle on me. We stand there, staring at each other. Still holding hands. The breeze runs fingers through my hair. The sunset is turning fiery and the night feels full of possibility. I lean closer – just a fraction – my heart thumping wildly in my chest. I hold my breath. Danny doesn't move away—

"Guys! Are you coming down?" Ruby pounces, making us jump. Isaac follows behind, like an adoring puppy. "Charlie's threatening to make everyone do karaoke. Some new business contact of her dad's gave her a top-of-the-range machine as a birthday present."

Danny drops my hand. "Did you say karaoke?" He groans.

"Yes! Come on!" Ruby urges. "We're the last ones! Wren?"

My fingers feel cold, dangling by my side. I search Danny's face, trying to read his expression. Annoyed? Relieved? It's impossible to tell. "What do you think?" I ask him.

He shrugs. "Sure, let's check it out."

My heart sinks, but I smile and nod. Grabbing Isaac's hand, Ruby leads us across the grass.

It's better this way, I tell myself. *I don't know what I was thinking.*

Danny's my best friend. I can't go messing that up.

7

*

As we peel back the canvas entrance to the marquee, the heat hits me first, followed by the pungent smell of perfume, sweat and beer. On the sawdust-strewn dance floor, dozens of bodies jostle for space, while two big sound systems pump music from an elevated stage where Charlie's brother Jem is DJing from his laptop. The makeshift bar is heaving, frazzled bartenders pouring garish concoctions into plastic cocktail glasses. A blackboard propped against an easel proclaims the night's philosophy in swirling art deco-style letters: *A little party never killed nobody!*

"I disagree." Danny grimaces, reaching under his hair, behind his right ear, to adjust the settings on his hearing aids. Loud background noise is his nemesis. "And Gatsby didn't say that, anyway. It's not in the book."

He's back to his normal, whip-smart self, acting like whatever that was, outside, didn't happen.

"I think Charlie's going for vibes, not accuracy," I shout over the din, as the birthday girl herself wafts past waving a neon feather boa. Jem's playlist is more Baz Luhrmann than F. Scott Fitzgerald-era, while the room looks like someone did an ASOS search for "flapper dresses" and decided to buy the lot.

We grab a couple of drinks – water for Danny, a Coke for me – and find a bench near the edge of the tent. I'm not feeling the music and Danny's funny about dancing. Self-conscious maybe, though I wish he wasn't. When we

8

were younger, he used to dance a lot. He turns his left ear towards the speakers.

"What's the track? I can only hear the bass."

I wrinkle my nose. "You don't want to know."

The moment I've said it, I feel bad. It's a lazy reply and it shuts Danny out, something I try not to do. Usually I'm the one calling out other people's crappy behaviour, pointing out the obvious: it's not Danny's fault he can't hear. You need to face him and speak clearly – not slowly, like some people do. His ears might not work perfectly these days but there's nothing wrong with his brain. Plus, he's an incredible lip-reader, which is a bloody difficult skill.

"Sorry. It's pretty cheesy. I don't know what it's called."

Danny shrugs it off. His eyes have found Lark. She's right in the middle of the dance floor, because *of course* she is, gyrating with her friends. Lark's a great dancer and she knows it. The only person here who could actually pass for Daisy Buchanan or Jordan Baker. Beneath the flashing lights, her hair turns pink, blue, green, lilac, then back to gold again, like some magical rainbow child.

I run my fingers through my boring crop. "Another drink?"

Danny doesn't answer; he's still watching Lark. She has that effect on everyone. It's not just the way she looks. My sister is *special* – she shines. We couldn't be more different if we tried.

A microphone screeches with feedback. Danny winces. I jump.

"OK, people! Who's ready for karaoke?"

There's a groan from the crowd, but Charlie calls birthday privileges and in seconds Jem's set has been binned. As the dance floor thins out, Charlie and her gang crowd round her phone, queuing up songs on an app. As the jerky string intro to "Toxic" kicks in, I brace myself for Charlie's Britney imitation. She throws everything into it, oblivious to the sniggers of the crowd, blowing kisses and curtseying at the end.

"Tempted?" Danny nods towards the stage.

"You must be joking," I mouth back.

"Who's next?" Charlie calls, holding out the mic.

I close my eyes. I know what's coming.

"Lark, you go!"

"Yeah, go on, Lark!"

"Lark! Lark!"

And there it is. Because if it wasn't enough that Lark is supermodel stunning, Little Miss Popular and the golden child of the Mackenzie family all in one…

My sister can also sing.

Really sing.

The X Factor. The Voice. Whatever you want to call it, she's got it. And the most annoying thing of all?

She doesn't care.

Lark's friends push her up on to the stage. Taking the mic from Charlie, the first thing she does is kick off her platform shoes. It looks cool and effortless, like everything she does.

"What shall I sing?"

"Whatever you want!" Aisha shouts, waving Charlie's phone.

Lark shrugs. "I don't mind. You pick."

A moment later, a sensuous beat kicks in and a slow guitar riff plays languidly over the top. "Dangerous Woman". Wow. That's quite a song choice. But can Lark pull off an Ariana cover?

I sigh.

Of course she can.

The second the first lyric drops, the crowd stills. Conversations hush. Everybody stares. Not because Lark sounds like Ariana – she doesn't. This is not an impression. Her voice is unique, entirely her own. Pure, clear, almost otherworldly...

And she doesn't even have to try.

Danny nudges me. "You OK?"

I nod, and plaster on a smile, shoving down the ugly thoughts that always seem to surface whenever I hear Lark sing.

Why her? Why not me?

Lark doesn't take music A level. She's never had a singing lesson in her life. *I'm* the one who lives and breathes music, who plays piano and guitar – and even the bloody violin for god's sake. I'm the one with the lyric notebook and the phone full of voice note recordings, the one who hears

11

songs in her sleep. I'm the one who dreams of playing sold-out stadiums filled with rapturous crowds singing my own words back to me.

I'm a good musician, I know that.

But Lark was born to be a star.

As she reaches the chorus, her voice soars, hitting the high notes with ease. My sister has a range to die for, seriously.

"She's killing it," Danny whispers, gaping at the awestruck faces all around. "Look at them, under her spell." I watch him adjust his hearing aids again, scowling. Even wearing them, I know Lark's singing voice is hard for Danny to hear. He struggles most with high-pitched sounds.

A breeze hits the back of my neck.

I turn to see a guy standing in the entrance to the tent. He's not from our sixth form – I think I'd remember if he was. Male model good-looking, with sharp cheekbones, a pierced eyebrow, ice-blue eyes and bleached, cropped hair, he's maybe eighteen or nineteen at most. A laptop bag is slung across his chest, and an expensive-looking pair of headphones hangs round his neck. His phone is raised in Lark's direction.

Filming her.

The song comes to an end and Lark jumps off the stage as the applause rings out. Some suck-up even shouts "Encore!" I roll my eyes. We're in a tent in a field in Hamlington, not the Birmingham O2.

There's an inevitable lull in proceedings, because of course, no one wants to follow *that*.

Aisha is climbing on stage when Charlie spots the new arrival. Her eyes widen and she pushes her way through the crowd towards him. Model Guy whispers something in Charlie's ear and she beams with delight, grasping him by the arm and leading him back towards the stage.

"Everyone, listen up!" Charlie snatches the mic from Aisha, in the middle of murdering Taylor Swift's "Blank Space". The backing track cuts out.

"Guys, you're never gonna believe this. We have a special guest! I'd like to introduce Evan… But you may know him as Spinner!"

Murmurs break out.

"Spinner is here to play a set for us!" Charlie squeals. Model Guy is already busy connecting his laptop up to Jem's controller. The marquee thrums with anticipation.

Spinner.

I mouth the name to Danny, who shakes his head. He doesn't remember, but I do. Spinner, also known as Evan Wheeler. The unassuming West Midlands teenager who went from mixing music in his bedsit during lockdown to starting a YouTube channel and DJing the Birmingham clubs.

"Whoever arranged this surprise, thank you!" Charlie gushes. "This is the most amazing birthday present ever!"

I look around, but nobody takes the credit. Meanwhile,

Spinner has finished setting up. He pauses for a moment, his right hand raised in a strangely complicated salute. Half a dozen people do it back.

Suddenly a funky beat explodes, assaulting my eardrums. It snaps and bounces beneath a jangly guitar. From behind his laptop, Spinner surveys the crowd, the light from his screen catching those chiselled cheekbones. A smile creeps across his face.

"Track?" Danny mouths, looking pained. The volume is intense. "Actually, don't tell me. I can guess."

I smile, lip-syncing along to the opening lyrics of "Last Night a DJ Saved My Life".

Danny shakes his head. "I knew it." He takes out both hearing aids and slides them into his pocket, replacing them with a pair of earplugs. The relief is immediate on his face.

Up on stage, Spinner cues up the next track, headphones hanging off one ear, apparently oblivious to the girls – and boys – dancing seductively under his nose. Lark isn't among them, I notice. She's wandered over to the bar, and I can't say I blame her. For all his good looks and undeniable stage presence, Spinner's surprise set feels a little … predictable.

I knock back my drink, wondering if it's too soon to suggest that we leave. I'm pretty sure Danny won't mind. Some bloke from his biology class has ambushed him and is shouting about Anna Walker. I can tell by Danny's polite but strained expression that the drunken rant is impossible to follow.

I'm about to interrupt when the track that's playing comes to a sudden end.

A jarring chord fills the air.

My ears prick up, my body oddly alert.

The chord fades and a beat kicks in, slow and insistent like a heartbeat. It feels like it's coming from inside me, fighting to get out.

A creeping bassline follows, dark and twisting. My foot starts tapping along.

What is this? Whatever it is, it's good.

I'm clearly not the only one who thinks so, because in seconds the dance floor is swarming. Out of the corner of my eye I see a spangle of light as Lark tosses back her drink and joins in. I find myself standing too, pulled like a magnet towards the crowd. The rhythm is intense, contagious. Impossible to resist.

A riff slides over the chords, looping and repeating, hooking my brain. I sway to the music, moving without thinking, my cheekbones aching from grinning. Everyone around me is the same. At the front of the stage, Charlie climbs on top of the biggest speaker and dances eight precarious feet above us, arms in the air and eyes closed. I laugh, but my voice is lost in the layers of sound. A strange wild energy is coursing through me. This track is *amazing*, I love it. Like, totally, one hundred per cent obsessed.

Strobe lighting flickers, making everything seem jagged and surreal. I see Ruby dancing with Isaac, and Meena too, with Jiv and Alex. Their faces are glowing and their eyes are shining bright. I wish Danny was here, dancing with me, and I twist round, looking for him, but then my attention is pulled to the stage.

Spinner – beautiful Spinner – has emerged from behind his laptop. He's lifting the microphone from its stand. And now a melody begins to play, high and pure, one short sample on repeat. Its beauty sears my brain. I stare as Spinner's mouth begins to move. My mind has gone blank. He seems to be repeating one word over and over, and I don't really understand it, but at the same time it's all I can hear, all I can think. I can't recall anything else, not even my own name. All I can do is dance, as Spinner's words fall down like rain.

There's a dull thud. Then a scream splits the air.

"Oh my god!"

The music cuts abruptly. I gasp as the crowd surges backwards, sweeping me along. Someone starts to wail. For a split second the crowd thins and I see a shape, lying in the sawdust beneath the speaker. It isn't moving.

A neon feather floats by. I feel like I'm in a dream.

"Wren!" Someone grabs my arm, pulling me out of the throng.

I blink up at Danny. "What happened?"

"It's Charlie. Didn't you see?"

I shake my head, struggling to make sense of his words. My mind flashes back to the shape in the sawdust. "She fell? Oh my god. Is she … *dead*?"

Danny shakes his head. "Jem's calling an ambulance.

Her family are coming. Let's give them space."

He takes my arm and I let him guide me. Around us, people huddle, dazed, in groups. I feel it too: the horror, the emotional whiplash. A moment ago, we were on top of the world, then reality intruded and destroyed our dream.

"That track. What was it…?" I will the riff or the melody to come back to me, to hook itself once more inside my brain. Danny doesn't reply. His face is turned away.

We join the other party guests gathered outside the marquee, the wind biting our bare flesh and the wet grass soaking our feet. Up by the main house blue lights are flashing. The dark shapes of the paramedics advance towards us.

"Where did the DJ go?" I scan the field.

Danny scowls, straining to see me in the dark. "Does it matter? Charlie's hurt." He peers closer, right into my eyes. "You're acting weird. How much did you drink?"

"Not much."

"Could someone have spiked you?"

"I don't see how." I do feel odd, though. I lean into Danny's solid shoulder. It must be the shock.

"Wren!" Lark comes over, pale and bewildered. "I can't believe it. Did you see her fall?"

I shake my head. "No. You?"

"No." She frowns. "I was dancing … I don't really remember."

We fall silent as the paramedics push past us, into the tent. Two of them are carrying a stretcher.

"We should go," Danny murmurs. "We're getting in the way. There's nothing we can do anyway. We'll hear how she is in the morning."

We trudge across the field. The night sky is beautiful, peppered with stars, but we're too stunned to speak. It's a horrible end to a party.

I climb into the car feeling empty and adrift. I don't even object when Lark grabs the front, forcing me to take the back. Danny cranks up the heater while Lark searches for a radio station to fill the silence.

Her hand pauses on the dial. A local news broadcast is coming to an end.

"And that headline once again. The body of a young female was discovered earlier this evening by a person walking their dog in public woodland near the Wrekin. The victim has been formally identified as Shropshire schoolgirl Anna Walker, who went missing from her home on March the sixteenth…"

I shiver, despite the heater's blast.

Anna Walker isn't missing. She's dead.

And they've just found her, right here in Hamlington.

2

"For god's sake, would you stop making that racket?"

Lark hammers on the paper-thin wall separating our bedrooms. I scowl at the interruption, humming louder. A fragment of a melody over the crumbs of a chord sequence, strummed on my acoustic guitar.

No. That's not how it went.

I sigh.

The day is much too warm, and I should be working on my music assignment, not trying to recall that track from Charlie's party. It's been six weeks now, but for some reason, I can't let it go. Usually I have a good memory for music, but some songs are elusive, I guess. Despite asking around, no one else from the party could remember it either. I suppose it's understandable, really. We were all so shocked by what came next.

I retune my A string, thinking of Charlie, finally back at college now, though not full-time. That first week in hospital was the worst. *A traumatic brain injury*, the doctors said. The coma was her body's way of giving her brain a chance to recover. I shiver, despite my stuffy room. Lark went to visit Charlie and said it was eerie: she looked so peaceful in her hospital bed, lying there without a single mark on her; just like she was fast asleep.

At least Charlie woke up.

Unlike poor Anna Walker.

I push away the thought and throw open a window. I need to focus on the assignment Mr Fellows set us: to write an original song. Settling back on my bed, I switch up my chord sequence, change my strumming pattern and try to improvise the skeleton of a tune.

"Wren, I mean it! I'm trying to sleep!"

I snort. It's after one in the afternoon. OK, so it's a bank holiday, but Lark should have coursework or revision or something. Her exams are literally round the corner. Still, that's her lookout. I strum harder to drown out her complaints.

My favourite daydream starts dancing in my head. I'm playing to a sold-out arena. Thousands of hands are waving in the air. Thousands of voices are singing my song back to me—

"Give it a rest, *please*!"

I snap out of my trance. I'm getting ahead of myself. Way ahead. This assignment is due at the end of term, but I've barely got anything worked out – not even the simplest verse or chorus.

And don't get me started on the words.

I lay my guitar aside and flick through my lyric notebook, waiting for an idea to jump out at me. All I can see is bad poetry, clichéd observations, and snippets of conversations overheard on the school bus.

I toss the notebook on the floor.

Why is this so hard?

I can sight-read any piece of music put in front of me. I can learn any song you care to choose. I've got melody and harmony and rhythm coming out of my ears, I've literally *pages* full of notes. And yet somehow I can't make it come together. The songs I write are … average. Underwhelming.

None of them are good enough.

I flop back on my bed. If I can't up my game, it goes without saying that my arena dream will stay a dream. But I'd give anything to write a song that *speaks* to people. A song that changes the world.

I take up my guitar again. *Perhaps I'll try a different key…*

"For god's sake!" Lark wails. "Use the cavern, Trog!"

"Dad's teaching in there!" I yell back. My irritation cranks up a notch. "And don't call me Trog!"

"Sorry, Trog."

Lark giggles and I fume. She *knows* I hate that nickname. It was Danny who discovered that the scientific name for a wren is *Troglodytes troglodytes,* but when Lark found out that 'troglodyte' means 'cave-dweller', she wet herself laughing and said it was perfect. The annoying thing is, she's right. My happy place really is a cave – or rather, *the cavern,* after the club in Liverpool where the Beatles first played – Dad's name for the makeshift music room in our garage where he teaches the local kids guitar.

"Actually, my lesson's been cancelled." Dad's voice sounds from the landing. He pokes his salt-and-pepper head into my room. "Evie's mum rang a moment ago." His nose wrinkles and I feel sorry for him. His morning has been wasted, and I know he won't charge for the lost time, though god knows we need the money.

Dad's eyes fall on my notebook. "Ah. You're writing. Dare I ask how it's going?"

"It's not." I throw down my guitar.

His smile is laced with sympathy. "What's not working?"

"Everything?" I sigh. "Especially the lyrics."

"Mmm. Lyrics are tough."

He picks up my notebook and places it gently on my bed. He knows better than to peek inside. No one's allowed to read my lyric notebook, not even Danny.

Definitely not Danny.

"Is there something you feel strongly about?" Dad leans against my desk. "Sounds like you're short on inspiration. In need of a muse."

I raise an eyebrow. "Such as?"

He shrugs. "I don't know. Love?"

"You think I should write a *love* song?" I pretend to throw up.

Dad laughs. "Love, lust, attraction – whatever you want to call it. Always worked for me."

I pull a face.

"Mac, you're here."

Mum interrupts us. Her dark-blonde hair is loosely plaited back and she's wearing a monogrammed apron ready for her afternoon shift at the café. She looks hot and tired; faint blue shadows line her eyes. She was up until all hours last night, waiting for Lark to come home from the club. Somehow Anna's death did have a simple explanation in the end – but try telling that to Mum. She's still spooked.

"What happened to your lesson?" she asks Dad.

"Cancelled."

"With no notice?" She tuts.

"They don't do it often."

Mum sighs. "Once is often enough."

"Paloma, stop worrying." He slides an arm round her waist and I blink. It's an affectionate gesture. More often these days they're at each other's throats. "You're always worrying."

"I'm just careful. One of us has to be."

He pulls her close. "Things will be different, soon."

Mum's expression shoots a warning, but it's too late.

I narrow my eyes. "What are you talking about? You're

being weird, both of you." My mind flashes back to the past few weeks – strange Zoom calls over the Easter holidays, phone calls taken into another room. "Is something going on?"

"Of course not." Mum blinks innocently, but Dad lets slip a smile.

"Come on, P. I thought we'd decided."

"*You've* decided, Mac. I still need time to think." Her slight American accent filters through, like it always does when she's worked up. The rest of the time, you'd assume she grew up right here, in Shropshire.

"Mum. Dad." I've stopped caring about my stupid assignment. "You're making me nervous. Stop with the cryptic stuff and tell me!"

"Is something going on?"

Lark emerges from her room, tousle-haired and bleary-eyed. Clearly hung-over but still gorgeous.

"Let's run it past the girls," Dad says. "See what they say."

"See what we say about what?" I press.

Mum looks annoyed, but to my relief she nods and suddenly everyone piles into my tiny bedroom. I snatch up my notebook, tucking it under my pillow, as Lark plonks herself on to my bed making my guitar bounce.

"Careful!"

"Sorry." She smirks.

There's a strange tension in the air, and it's not the unusually warm weather. An atmosphere somewhere between fear, anxiety and excitement. Mum and Dad are holding hands. They never do that. They haven't for years.

"Please tell me we're not getting a little brother or sister," Lark deadpans. "Because one: you're both ancient. And two: I'd like to return the one I've got."

I scowl, but her joke breaks the tension.

"Don't worry. It's nothing like that." Dad laughs, glancing at Mum. "OK. You remember 'Believe in Me'?"

"Your one and only hit?" Lark grins.

"It wasn't our *only* one!" Dad protests. "Our best-known song, maybe…" He can't resist. Grabbing my guitar, he starts to sing.

Walk away. Don't look back. Leave that life behind.
The truth that you've been told is laced with lies.
Walk away. Don't look back. Seek and you will find.
Put your faith in us – believe in me.

I haven't heard it in ages, but the words come back to me instantly, rising up from the depths of my subconscious and triggering a stream of old memories. We used to hear it on the radio when we were little. Lark and I would always sing along. We could never believe it was our mum singing so beautifully, and our dad playing guitar. "Believe in Me" was a hit for their band, Runaway Summer, back in the late nineties, before we were born. They released one album, *Hymns for Heathens*, played a few festivals, supported some properly famous bands. Then Lark and I came along, and things fizzled out. These days,

Dad's music lessons and Mum's Thursday night choir are the extent of their musical output.

"Yeah? What about it?" I say, when Dad finally stops singing.

He smothers a grin. "A Norwegian TV network bought the rights."

"What? When?"

"A little while back. They wanted to use it as the theme tune for the pilot of a new drama."

"For real?" Lark asks.

Dad nods. "But it gets better. Turns out, the pilot was a hit and a series has been commissioned."

"But that's … great, isn't it?" I look from Dad's sparkling eyes to Mum's tense face.

"Absolutely." Dad answers first. "Surreal, but great. And god knows, we could do with the money…"

"But?" I prompt. I can hear it, hovering in the air.

Mum takes over. "The success of the pilot has created a lot of buzz around the song. It's reached a brand-new audience – people are streaming it, there's interest in the band." Her eyebrows knit.

I can't see the problem. "Do the others know?" I ask. I mean Rob and Alys, Dad's old friends from university and Runaway Summer's other band members. There's a photo of them all on the stairs – a framed feature from the NME. Lark and I love teasing Mum and Dad about their stripy T-shirts and bowl-cut hairstyles. They're such a nineties indie cliché.

"They do know, yes," Dad says carefully. "Because we've been invited to play a few gigs. A kind of mini tour…"

"A tour?" Lark echoes.

"Yep." Dad squeezes Mum's hand. His face is flushed; it's obvious he's thrilled. "Rob and Alys are up for it, and Seb will manage us, like before. He'll sort rehearsals, liaise with the venues, do our social media and press—"

"If we agree," Mum interrupts.

"Why wouldn't you?" I still don't understand.

"Oh … reasons." She sighs. "It's ridiculously short notice for one thing. We haven't played in years. It's come totally out of the blue."

"Which doesn't mean we should pass up the opportunity." Dad scowls. He looks at Mum. "I miss the band. Don't you?"

"I miss some things." Her lips tighten. "Only, we could be opening a can of worms…" She lets this hang.

Suddenly a story comes back to me. Some guy, a stalker fan, totally obsessed with Mum. She didn't know him, but somehow he found out her home address and sent letters; horrible ones, threatening ones – all anonymously, of course. What a hero.

"That's over and done with," Dad says. "We've moved to Hamlington since then. There hasn't been a peep in years."

"I know." Mum twists a strand of hair and turns to us. "But here's the thing, girls, the part your dad's missed out.

27

The tour's not in England, it's in Norway. For twelve days in June—"

"Norway?" Lark squeals. "Oh my God, can we come?"

"You've got exams," I remind her. I can't believe she could forget. But Lark's never been too bothered about college and she didn't apply to uni. She's taking a gap year apparently, although she hasn't made any plans yet.

"Wren's right," Mum says, and Lark throws me a withering look like I'm personally responsible for setting her A levels. "What kind of parents would we be, going away during your exams?"

"I'll be *fine*." Lark smiles sweetly, perfect daughter mode reactivated. Probably planning all the parties she'll have. "I'll be done with art and drama soon. I only have English in June. This is huge. You should do this."

It kills me to agree with her, but I do.

"See?" Dad turns to Mum.

She still seems unconvinced. "You really think it's wise, Mac? To leave our daughters by themselves, after that poor girl was murdered…" Her voice trails away.

"She wasn't murdered, she died," Dad corrects, gently. "And P, that was weeks ago. It was tragic, sure. But it has nothing to do with our girls."

I nod. We all read the articles. Anna was found, still wearing her school uniform. No sign of any violence. No illegal substance in her body. No dodgy boyfriend could be traced. An undiagnosed heart problem, they concluded; though god knows what she was doing in the woods near Hamlington.

"We're not babies, Mum," I remind her. "We'll be fine. And Danny's only next door."

"That's true." Dad shoots me a grateful look. "Debs and Tayo will keep an eye. They owe us. Danny's always here." He winks and I flush.

Mum sighs. "I'm not going to win, am I?" She looks at Lark and me. "OK. But you need to stay in touch with us. Reply to my texts – no leaving me on read!" She looks us both in the eye. "Promise you'll look out for one another – be each other's support system, have each other's backs. You can do that, can't you?"

I hesitate. *Can* we do that?

"Sure," Lark says lightly. "Anything for my rockstar parents."

"Wren?"

I think. Twelve days alone with Lark. Not my idea of fun. But Mum and Dad need this trip; our family needs the money. Plus, I'll have the cavern to myself. And I'll have time too. Time I can spend with Danny.

"You should definitely go," I tell them brightly. "We'll be absolutely fine."

3

"Your parents are famous in Norway?" Danny is cracking up, wiping pretend tears from his eyes.

"Apparently. Or they will be soon. I don't know. I can't get my head round it either." I giggle. His laughter is infectious.

We're taking the short cut through the churchyard. It's another sunny, blue-sky afternoon and I've convinced Danny to walk into town after college. Not that there's anything particularly thrilling about our town centre. Hamlington, with its long, narrow high street peppered with charity shops, greasy spoons and tanning salons, definitely doesn't feature high up on the Shropshire tourist circuit. But it does have one saving grace, the reason for my regular pilgrimages.

Pet Sounds, a record-shop-and-music-store in one.

The old blue-fronted building is tucked away down a boring backstreet and has been here for ever. Dad can remember coming here to buy seven-inch records and fanzines when he was my age. The racks are brimming with plastic-wrapped vinyl, some old and collectible, some enticingly new. Ellis, the owner, always has some cool band to recommend, while their girlfriend Joss usually doesn't mind if I try out her guitar stock, as long as there isn't a serious customer in the shop.

I push open the door. Behind the till, Ellis is deep in conversation with a woman, holding a piece of paper. Joss notices Danny and turns the background music down. He smiles a thank you. That's another thing I love about Pet Sounds. Danny never has to ask.

I gravitate towards a box of seven-inches and start to sift through.

"Looking for anything?" Next to me, Danny flicks idly through the twelve-inches.

"Not really. Just browsing." I pout sadly. "Too broke."

I don't really mind. It's nice enough being here, especially with Danny. Pet Sounds is a safe space for anyone a little different, so it goes without saying that Lark has never set foot in here. She doesn't understand the appeal. She scoffed when I got my record player, the one I found at the car boot sale for a bargain twenty quid. To be fair, it's not like I play my tiny vinyl collection that much – it's easier to cue up a playlist on my phone. But I'm a sucker for records as objects. The beautiful sleeve artwork, the limited-edition inserts... To me, it makes sense that something as magical as music should be packaged like a precious artefact.

I wouldn't expect Lark to get that.

"Which song did the TV network buy?" Danny tilts his head to hear me better.

I smile. "It's called 'Believe in Me'. It was Runaway Summer's biggest hit. Your parents probably know it. Dad wrote it for Mum when they met."

"They met in America, right?"

I nod, pleased that he remembers. "Yep. In a bar in New Mexico, at an open mic night." I roll my eyes, although secretly I love this story; it's such a great meet-cute. "My mum wasn't supposed to be there. She was only twenty, not legally old enough to drink in the States. And her parents would never have let her go. She grew up in this super conservative community. Church and chores, that was it." I pause to make sure Danny's following. "That night, she snuck out with a friend and hitchhiked into the city. This weird English guy was up on stage, playing Beatles covers. And *boom*. Love at first sight." I smile.

Danny raises an eyebrow. "She left her life behind, just like that?"

"Kind of." I turn over the record I'm holding, half-heartedly inspecting it for scratches. It actually makes me sad when Mum tells this part of the story. How she tried to reason with my grandparents, but they wouldn't listen. How they issued her an ultimatum.

"She was supposed to marry within the community. When she refused, her parents cut her off. She had to walk away."

"Wow." Danny's eyes grow wide. "That's extreme."

I nod.

"Does she miss them?"

I consider. "She must have done, I guess." We move to the racks in the next section but I'm too caught up in my story to concentrate. "But this was more than thirty years ago. She hardly talks about that life any more. I'm not sure my grandparents are even still alive. We've never heard from them." I think for a moment. "She made a choice, I guess, and she's OK with it. She always says it's important to think for yourself – that you shouldn't let other people tell you what to believe. She weighed up the facts and picked … well, she picked love."

I flush. Danny is watching my lips closely. I know it's only because he's following our conversation, but suddenly I'm self-conscious.

"And now they're going to Norway, leaving you by yourself. Poor Wren. You'll be lonely."

"Hmm. Unfortunately, I'll have Lark to keep me company."

Danny's forehead furrows. "I don't understand why you hate her."

"I don't hate her." I look away. I've started noticing this recently. How Danny defends Lark.

"You used to be best mates." He nudges me. "Remember those shows you used to do?"

My cheeks grow hot. It's true that Lark and I used to be close. We'd spend hours on YouTube learning dance routines to pop songs and making costumes from old curtains, showing off for our parents and their friends. I loved it – until people began to comment on Lark's voice. It was like I suddenly became invisible.

"We were kids," I sigh. "We don't have much in common any more."

Danny shrugs. "If you say so." He wanders over to the band T-shirts. I wait for him to turn round but he doesn't look back.

He's disappointed in me.

The thought troubles me. What does he care if Lark and I don't get on?

I examine the noticeboard instead. Ads for upcoming gigs; requests for rehearsal space; instruments and recording equipment for sale.

"Hey, Wren."

Ellis has come up behind me and reaches over my shoulder to pin up a small photocopied A4 poster. In the middle is a photo of a girl, dressed entirely in black. The words HAVE YOU SEEN ME? are emblazoned above the picture.

"Do you know Mia?" Ellis asks. "Mia Hall. She used

to come in here sometimes. A little older than you. Nice kid, a bit … troubled. She was squatting round here, last I heard…" Ellis's voice trails away.

I look again at the photo. Young, thin and angry might be the best way to describe Mia. I shake my head. "She's missing?"

"Angie thinks so." I remember the woman who was speaking to Ellis when we came in. "Angie runs a soup kitchen in Hamlington. Mia used to call in regularly." Ellis frowns. "She hasn't been seen for weeks. You'll keep an eye out for her, won't you?"

"Sure." I swallow.

Another missing girl.

"Better get back to the till." Hurriedly, Ellis pins up a second A4 notice. As a sharp shaft of sunlight hits it, I stare, all thoughts of Mia banished from my mind.

In the middle of the poster is a strange illustration of a figure wearing long, flowing robes, but instead of a head the figure has one big eye. All around the figure, people are lying or kneeling or floating into space like they've fallen asleep on a cloud. The image is swirling and colourful … it reminds me of the psychedelic sixties albums that Dad inherited from his dad.

Above the image, in gold-coloured lettering, is one word:

ENRAPTURE

Goosebumps travel up my arms. Huh. There must be a draught coming from the door. Underneath the image, there's more writing:

EMBRACE THE NEW DAWN
JUNE 21

Something tugs at the edges of my brain, but I ignore it, pulling out my phone. In the corner of the poster there's a QR code and I scan it with my camera app, landing instantly on the homepage of a website. The words *Prepare to be Enraptured...* shimmer at me enticingly, along with a second command:

SOUND UP

"Ready to go?" Danny sidles up but I barely register his presence. I click on the homepage, and my phone vibrates with a jarring chord, a bit like a laptop starting up.

A message appears on the screen.

ENRAPTURE
An unmissable new music festival
Where the broken are mended
And the lost are found
Open your mind to the TRUTH

For some reason, my heart is beating fast. There's a map

at the bottom of the page, a tiny thumbnail showing a location. Tentatively, I zoom in. Whatever this festival is, it's bound to be expensive or sold out already, or somewhere miles away.

I blink.

It's happening just outside Hamlington.

"Wren! Do you wanna head off? I need a drink." Danny peers over my shoulder. His breath tickles my ear. "What's that?"

"A festival. A *music* festival." I nod at the poster Ellis pinned to the board. "Here. On the twenty-first of June."

"*Enrapture*," Danny reads and my insides flutter. "Who's playing?"

"I don't know. Does it matter?" I shrug.

A strange awareness is rippling through me. I need to go to this festival. I don't know why. It feels like fate. My fingers hover over a button at the bottom of the screen.

BOOK TICKETS

I hit the button—

"Oh." I deflate. Tickets aren't on sale yet. "Looks like you have to register," I tell Danny. "They're released in twelve days." I start to key in my details, my fingers keeping time to the tinny background beat. "I bet it sells out quickly. You should register too."

"Slow down." Danny's warm hand covers mine, stilling my fingers. It's kind of intimate, but I'm more irritated than embarrassed. I shake him off but he snatches my phone.

"Wren, I thought you were broke…" He points at the small print on the screen. "Tickets are a hundred quid."

"A *hundred quid*?" I feel it like a blow to the stomach. "Where am I going to get that kind of money?" There's no way I can ask my parents. They can't afford to help me, not before they've done the tour.

"Right." Danny hands my phone back. "So forget it. It's just a festival. No big deal." His gaze lands on Mia's poster.

"It *is* a big deal," I insist, touching his arm to draw his attention back. "It sounds amazing. *Enrapture*." The word tastes delicious in my mouth. "This sort of thing never happens in Hamlington. Come on, Danny. We have to go."

He looks at me oddly and doesn't reply. Waving goodbye to Joss and Ellis, I follow him down the high street to the Good Plaice for an icy lemonade and a bag of chips. Except … I don't taste any of it. I'm not hungry, or thirsty. My appetite has gone. Everywhere I look I see posters. On walls and lamp posts and bus shelters.

ENRAPTURE

I will go to the festival.

It's a simple statement of fact.

It feels like I'm responding to a call.

4

"The Square is the best pitch. There'll be loads of people passing through."

It's early on Saturday morning, a week later, when Danny and I get off the train at Shrewsbury station. Strapped to my back is my pride and joy; the second-hand electro-acoustic Fender I bought from Joss. It cost a year's worth of babysitting money but it's worth every penny. In my right hand I'm lugging a mic and stand, borrowed from the cavern, while in my left I'm wheeling Dad's portable battery-powered amp. I hope he won't notice it's gone.

As we head up Castle Street and on to Pride Hill sweating in the bright sun, my eyes are drawn to the dozens of Anna posters still stuck to lamp posts and papered on walls. Their edges are starting to fray.

"Strange." I turn to look at Danny. His hair is scraped back in a ponytail showing off his strong profile. "Mia's been missing for weeks, but there aren't any posters about her."

Danny's nose wrinkles like it sometimes does when he hasn't heard me, so I say it again.

"And why do you reckon that is?" He raises an eyebrow.

His tone makes me consider. Anna's disappearance made the local news every night, but Mia has barely had a mention. There was even a memorial for Anna the other weekend; donations went towards a heart research charity. But there's been nothing for Mia – no vigil, nothing.

Anna was a choirgirl. Mia lived in a squat. *Is that why no one cares?* The idea leaves a nasty taste in my mouth – but just then we turn a corner and arrive at the pretty sixteenth-century square. Putting both Anna and Mia firmly out of my mind, I lead Danny across the flagstones towards the site of the old market hall.

"Here is good."

My heart pounds as I unload my kit. I've never busked in my life. But going to Enrapture is important. More than that; it's my new obsession. Tickets go on sale a week tomorrow. I need cash fast and I'll do whatever it takes.

"Are you sure we're allowed to set up here?" Danny takes in The Square, flanked by pretty Tudor buildings. It's the weekend, and the warm weather shows no signs of abating, meaning it's a lot busier than I expected – *which is a good thing*, I remind myself. Tourists sip coffee in the café under the arches, while parents bump prams across the cobbles. Groups of girls are gathered ready to go on shopping sprees and a gang of lads is loitering on a bench. One solitary guy wearing a black beanie and mirror shades leans against a shop window, casually surveying the scene.

"Don't we need a permit?" Danny frets.

I shrug. "We wouldn't have got one in time. If anyone complains, we'll pack up. We won't be here long." I paste on a grin, more confident than I feel. "Just until we make the money we need."

"We'll never make a hundred quid."

"Anything helps," I say, lightly. "We need more than a hundred, anyway," I add, "if you want a ticket too."

There must be a breeze interfering with his hearing aids, because Danny doesn't reply.

I set up my mic stand while Danny unzips his guitar case, taking decades over it and glancing all around, his face tight and his jaw clenched. I don't understand him today. He seemed happy to come along for moral support, but I've literally had to beg him to play – which makes no sense, because he's as good on guitar as I am. Better, even. Dad taught us both. We used to play together all the time in the cavern, but over the past few years, our jamming sessions have tailed off and I miss them.

I watch as he perches uncomfortably on a bench, getting ready to tune his guitar. He wouldn't take A level music, no matter how much Mr Fellows tried to persuade him. He reckons he prefers playing for himself.

I lift my own guitar from its case and join him. Usually I can tune by ear, but the street noise is making it harder than usual. Danny's face is screwed up tight in concentration. He's got an app on his phone, a visual tuner. I don't know why he doesn't use it.

"Can you check?" As Danny passes his guitar to me I notice the lads on the next bench watching. One of them taps his ear and mutters something to his mate and they both bark with laughter.

Dickheads.

Danny looks over and scowls. A moment later he pulls out his ponytail and smooths down his hair.

"All good," I pass his guitar back, pretending not to have noticed anything. "What shall we play first?"

The question is a distraction. We discussed our set list on the train. Danny and I know hundreds of covers by heart – we're hardly stuck for choice. Our repertoire is eclectic, ranging from sixties classics like The Kinks, through brash seventies punk like The Clash, and tuneful eighties angst like The Smiths. We could plunder from the nineties with a bit of Pulp, hit up the 2000s with some Amy Winehouse, or bring things up to date with Hozier, Laura Marling, Taylor Swift… Basically, if it's a great song, at some point we've learned it.

"Let's just stick to the plan," Danny sighs, glancing at the lads again. He pulls a tin from his rucksack, chucks it at my feet and tosses in a few coins. "To kick things off."

We stand up and plug in. I take a deep breath.

We can do this … can't we?

The Square is getting busier. Dozens of people are now wandering past. I glance at Danny for a cue, but he's staring at his feet, his hair falling in his face. *Is he OK?* Maybe I shouldn't have made him do this. I know it's been hard for him since the virus, coming to terms with his hearing loss, wearing hearing aids these past four years. But deep down, he's still Danny: funny, smart, talented. To me, nothing's changed.

Finally he looks up. He nods, silent, steady.

He's fine. Everything's fine. *Stop stressing, Wren. Think of Enrapture.*

I count us in, my head nodding in time with my tapping foot. Danny's eyes are glued to my face. Together we launch into the opening chords of "High and Dry". A total buskers' cliché, I know, but I love it so much, I don't care.

Whoa… It's so different playing outdoors. A breeze messes with the acoustics, blowing the sound all over the place. It's hard to hear my vocals clearly and the subtlety of our playing is lost. I falter. When I practised this in the cavern, it sounded good, but now I'm not sure.

I mess up the lyrics of the second verse, but I plough on anyway, my voice wavering on the wind, warbly and unsure. Danny, trying his best to follow me, looks pained. I glance around. One woman is scrolling on her phone, not

43

bothering to look up, while a couple with a sleeping baby tuts and pushes their buggy away. The lads on the bench are surprisingly mute, and after a while they wander off. I decide to take it as a win. I'm sure they'd have heckled if they could. Danny's talent has shut them up.

I send him a smile. His attention never wavers, alert to my cues. A little girl toddles over and drops something in the tin. I thank her gratefully and snatch a glance. Ten pence and a loom band. Oh.

We run straight into our next song, "Motion Sickness", and Danny takes over guitar duties, leaving me to concentrate on vocals. *Why does no one stop?* They're almost speeding up instead. And nobody makes eye contact, unless I count the guy in the black beanie and expensive-looking mirror shades. He's still leaning against the shopfront on the other side of The Square, and every so often his gaze drifts in our direction.

Maybe he could spare a twenty.

I move closer to the mic. *Ouch.* The feedback screech pierces my ears. A little boy begins to cry. I sing on, starting to get desperate. *Come on people, please!*

We limp through two more songs before I dare risk another peek in the tin. Three pounds and fifty … eight pence, and most of that is Danny's.

"This is useless," I moan.

"You're doing great," he says sweetly. "But if you'd rather stop—"

"Wren!"

44

I spin round. Lark is standing there with a gaggle of friends. Charlie is among them. I've barely seen her since the accident and she looks thin, pale, washed out. A shadow of her former self.

"What do you think you're doing?" Lark hisses.

"What does it look like?" I hiss back.

"It looks like you're making a fool of yourself." Her huge blue eyes are full of faux concern.

My face flames. "Piss off, Lark."

"Sorry. That came out wrong." She backtracks. "Honest. I just meant … all these sad songs. It's not the right vibe."

"And what would you know about it?" My anger flares. More people have stopped to watch what's going on between Lark and me than they did the whole time Danny and I were playing.

Lark speaks carefully. "You need something uplifting to grab people's attention." She smiles. "Let me help."

Before I can protest, she steps up to the mic. Tossing her bag to Aisha she turns to Danny. "Dan, do you know 'Halo'? It's easy in G. There are only four chords."

I glare at Danny, willing him to say no.

The traitor nods yes.

"You too, Wren. Don't stand there like a lemon. Play guitar!"

Hating Lark with every fibre of my body, I do as she says. Although the chords are simple, I strum with hands like lead. But then Lark starts to sing, and the effect is instantaneous. Heads turn, people move closer, a crowd begins to form. Phones are being waved in our direction, set to record.

Lark, yet again, is bringing something *more*. She's not trying to be Beyoncé, although she is loving the attention, responding by improvising all sorts of high-pitched runs and trills. *Totally showing off.* The breeze has dropped now, amplifying her voice and showcasing the purity of her sound. It kills me to admit it but she sounds supernaturally good, like the gods have decided to gift her an extra level of talent today.

"Voice of an angel," sighs a passing woman. I roll my eyes.

As Lark reaches the end of the song, people whoop and cheer. Danny is openly grinning at her as she basks in the applause that rebounds off the surrounding buildings like gunshot. Mirror Shades is still there, I notice, but he's engrossed in some conversation on his phone. Lark does a little bow. Ignoring the calls for more, she picks up the tin and darts into the crowd. In a few minutes she's back, the tin now heavy with coins. I spy a big bunch of fivers, some tenners, and even a twenty sticking out. Maybe still not enough for two Enrapture tickets, but *a lot*.

"Lark, you're a legend!" Danny breathes.

She laughs. "Yeah, not too shabby, hey, Wren?"

I don't answer.

Lark looks hurt. "So what's this in aid of anyway?"

"None of your business," I snap, but Danny speaks up.

"Wren wants to go to Enrapture."

"The festival?" Her eyes suddenly sparkle. "I know, right? It's going to be amazing. Charlie's dad's company is one of the sponsors." She waves to her waiting friends, by now tapping their feet, getting bored. "He's getting us complimentary tickets."

So, Lark is going for free. I sigh.

"Lark, come on!" Aisha whines.

"Catch you up in a minute!" she calls back. "I'd better go," she says to us, pulling an apologetic face. "This was fun. Wish I could stay and do another."

"It's fine." I keep my eyes fixed on the ground. Even though she hasn't asked for a share of the money, I can't bring myself to thank my sister. Danny does it instead, going totally overboard. I turn away. The crowd is starting to disperse now the show is over. Knowing when I'm beaten, I start to pack up.

"Excuse me." The voice startles me.

It's Mirror Shades. I blink. His tight V-necked T-shirt shows off muscular arms and well-formed abs, and his jeans fit far too well to be anything less than designer. High cheekbones, smooth tanned skin and an even distribution of stubble complete his model good looks. But he's also standing a fraction too close for comfort.

I take a step back.

"I heard you play." He pulls off his beanie and rubs a gold-ringed hand over the pale, close-shaved fuzz of his head.

"Right." I don't know what else to say. I stare at the

pendant round his neck. A leather string, hung with a golden eye.

Danny and Lark turn round. I sense them tuning in.

"You sounded impressive." The guy pushes his sunglasses on top of his head. Ice-blue eyes bore into me and a gold piercing glints in the light.

A flash of recognition hits me. "You're…"

"Evan Wheeler." He extends a hand, his grip firm, intense. "But people call me Spinner," he adds in a whisper. Danny and Lark have joined me now, but he doesn't shake hands with them.

"Spinner…" Lark echoes, bristling when he ignores her. His gaze is fixed firmly on me.

"You're the DJ," I murmur.

"Correct." He looks around almost furtively, as though he's expecting to be ambushed. And it's true: people are staring. The gang of lads is back, openly gawping in our direction. One of them lifts a hand in a strange salute. Spinner acknowledges him with the same salute back.

His dazzling blue eyes turn back to me. "Can I ask you something? Have you heard of Enrapture?"

A yearning fills my body. I nod. "Yeah, of course."

"Cool." Spinner smiles, slowly. "The promoter is a friend of mine."

Lark jumps. "Really?"

"So what?" Danny steps forward, a little in front of me. It might seem protective, but I know he's just following the conversation.

"He's kind of a mentor, yeah?" Spinner ignores both Lark and Danny and continues to focus on me. "His name is Adam Webb. He's a music producer from the US; he's worked with loads of famous artists."

My ears prick up. Lark edges closer.

"Adam's a generous guy," Spinner goes on. "He likes to support young musicians. He's always looking for new acts." He winks and my stomach flips. "He's putting on a stage at Enrapture, for emerging local talent."

It takes a second to process his words. *A stage at Enrapture. For emerging local talent—*

"Auditions are next weekend." Spinner leans close, his voice low. Danny's nose wrinkles with the effort of listening, or maybe it's a reaction to the scent of Spinner's expensive cologne. It's making me feel light-headed. Spinner taps his nose. "This is not public knowledge, know what I'm saying? No running to tell all your friends. Adam is a *private* guy, yeah? He's choosy about who he works with. You get a chance like this, you don't go blabbing. And you definitely don't turn it down. Understand?"

"Yeah. Of course." I nod.

Spinner roots in his pocket. "Here's the address. Next Saturday, at twelve." He hands the card to me. "You'll be there."

He doesn't wait for a reply. Out of the corner of my eye, I see a car, a silver Tesla with blacked-out windows, pulling silently into Market Street. Heat shimmers from the roof as it pauses, like a cat about to pounce. Sliding his sunglasses back on to his nose and pulling on his beanie, Spinner strides towards it. The teen boys track him with their camera phones.

It's only as the car pulls away that the memory hits me.

The set Spinner played at Charlie's party.

I should have asked about the name of that track.

5

"*You'll be there.*" Danny murmurs. "What a dick."

I squint in the sun. "That's a little harsh."

Danny's eyes narrow. "I don't trust the guy."

"Why?" I start to laugh, then stop when I realize he's not joking. "Is this because of Charlie's party? Danny, come on. That was an accident! It wasn't Spinner's fault Charlie got hurt."

"He didn't stick around."

I screw up my face. "Well, whatever you think of him, he just dropped some massive news. Didn't you hear what he said? There's going to be a stage for local talent at

51

Enrapture! He's friends with the promoter-producer guy, Adam Webb."

"I *heard*." Danny shoots me a look. Totally unimpressed.

Lark has been silent until this point, but now she grabs the card from my hands. "Let me see that."

"Hey!" I snatch the card back. "He gave it to me!"

"He gave it to *all* of us," she corrects.

"No." I stand my ground. "He approached *me*. He spoke to *me*." I still can't quite believe it. "He was watching us for ages before you turned up."

Lark raises an arched eyebrow. "He came over after *I* sang."

"Stop!" Danny steps between us. "Does it matter? You're not serious about this?"

"Why not?" I gesture at the tin, my brain buzzing. "This isn't anywhere near enough money to buy Enrapture tickets. But we wouldn't *need* tickets if we were playing the festival instead!"

"Wren, I…" Danny wipes the sweat from his forehead. He looks tired, and a baby is crying loudly nearby. "We can play covers, but we're hardly a band…"

"We could be!" I bounce on my heels. Adrenaline is fizzing in my veins.

Danny sighs and turns to Lark. "What do you think?"

"No!" I break in before she can answer. "We're not auditioning with her."

Lark's face twists. "Wren…" Bright spots of colour dot her cheeks. "Don't take this the wrong way, but I'm not sure you'll get far without me."

52

"How d'you work that out?"

"Well, think about it." She glances at Danny. "Who drew the crowd just now? You're a great musician," she adds quickly, "but you need someone who can *perform*."

My mouth falls open. "You're *so* out of order!" I turn to Danny to back me up but he won't meet my eye. I move into his line of vision. "Aren't you going to say anything?"

He winces. "She has a point. You'd be stronger together than alone."

I can't listen to this. I spin back round to Lark. "I can't believe how selfish you're being! You can go to Enrapture with Charlie, you don't need to audition. You're only doing this to spite me, because you can't stand that – for once – someone was interested in *me*. If you really cared about singing – about *music* – you'd be studying it at college. Are you even serious about *anything*?"

Lark looks hurt, but I steam on regardless. "This could be my big chance. But no, it has to be *The Lark Show*. It's always *The Lark Show,* and everyone else has to play second fiddle. There's no way I'm auditioning with you."

"Good. The feeling's mutual then," Lark shoots back.

"Guys, please!" Danny holds up a hand. "I can't... Where does this leave me?"

"On my side, obviously." I look him square in the face. "Auditioning with me."

"*Now* who's being selfish?" Lark throws a possessive arm round Danny's shoulder, draping herself over him. "Danny's my friend too. You can play guitar, Wren. It's not like you need Danny to accompany you. You can audition by yourself."

"It's not my fault you didn't learn!"

"Would you stop!" Danny looks anguished. He's right, we're making a scene, and we're not even supposed to be talking about this. Spinner said it isn't public knowledge. "He did this on purpose, I reckon," Danny continues. "For some reason he wanted to make you two fight." He pushes the hair out of his eyes. "If you ask me, this whole festival is sus. No bands are confirmed, we hardly know anything about it. I don't get the appeal." He pauses. Lark and I are silent. "But … if you're both set on auditioning, and if neither of you will listen to me, I s'pose there's only one solution."

"What?" we chorus.

Danny sighs. "I'll audition twice."

Three minutes later everything's decided. Danny and I will audition together, then he'll play guitar for Lark.

"You and your sister are unbelievable," he complains, as he and I start the hot walk back to the train station. "If you ever did join forces, no one would be safe. I couldn't give a toss about Enrapture – I don't want to go; I don't want to play. But thanks to the pair of you –" he sighs another deep sigh – "I'm doubling my chances of doing both."

The next week passes excruciatingly slowly. The upcoming audition is at the forefront of my mind and the hardest bit is that, apart from Lark and Danny, I can't tell a soul. Every day is a struggle to contain my nerves and my excitement, but it's pretty obvious from the buzz at college and the way our music class group chat keeps blowing up that I'm not the only one preoccupied.

Enrapture has got its claws into everybody. Festival fever is taking hold.

Ruby

So tickets go on sale next Sunday at 7pm.

Has everyone registered?

Meena

I have

Alex

Me too

Jiv

And me

Ruby

Isaac?

Isaac

You know I have

Ruby

Just checking 😊😬 Tickets are gonna sell fast!

Alex

Hell YES! What else is there to look forward to?

Ruby

OK. We need a strategy. I have an idea

Isaac

Wow. Bossy much???

Ruby

Excuse me, what?!!

Isaac

Don't be touchy. It was just a joke

Ruby

Well it wasn't funny

Meena

Guys, chill. What sort of strategy, Rubes?

Jiv

Like logging in on multiple devices?

Alex

And booking for each other, so we have more chance?

Ruby

EXACTLY! Is there a limit on ticket numbers?

Meena

Don't think so

Ruby

Cool. Let's do it. We stay in contact on Sunday. If you get through to the booking page, let the whole group know

Meena

Wren, are you in?

Alex

Hasn't she replied?

Ruby

Where are you, Wren?

Wren

Sorry. Count me out. Too broke ☹

I close the chat before they start feeling sorry for me. I promised Spinner we wouldn't breathe a word and I can't jeopardize my chance to play in front of a big music producer by blabbing. I have to smash this audition. I can't be the only person in Hamlington to miss out.

Putting my song-writing assignment on hold, I spend

every spare minute in the stuffy confines of the cavern running through all the songs I know. I need to choose the perfect one for Saturday. I just wish Danny was as invested in our success. Whenever I text him song suggestions he replies with a vague "You choose", and when I book the college practice room at break time either he's conveniently forgotten to bring his guitar to school or he fobs me off with some other excuse. He really does seem to be the only person in Hamlington immune to Enrapture's allure.

Unless he's secretly practising with Lark?

The thought sneaks in like a slippery green-eyed monster, rearing its vicious head. I shove it down where it belongs. I know it's not possible that Danny and Lark are practising together. Because true to form and bang on brand, Lark isn't doing *any* practice.

There's no need to practise when you're as talented as her.

"See you later. Don't wait up!" Lark grabs her jacket from the back of the kitchen chair and breezes past Mum and me to the hall, where Aisha is waiting for her.

I look up. "You're going out?" It's Friday night. Tomorrow's the audition. Surely she hasn't forgotten?

"Only to the pub. To celebrate finishing art. I am *never* lifting a paintbrush again!" She tosses her head, dramatically. "Well, not unless I'm doing my nails."

"Lark?" Mum twists round. "Make sure you and Aisha walk back together, OK? Stick to the main roads. Or even better, get a taxi." She shifts uneasily. Mia still hasn't turned up, and the story finally made the local news last night, although the coverage was nowhere near as extensive as for Anna.

"Yeah, yeah, I will." The front door slams and I scowl. Lark, out partying without a care in the world, while I'll be spending the evening rehearsing in the cavern. Again. It says everything about how much Lark wants this. How much she cares.

"People deal with things in different ways," Mum murmurs.

I shoot her a glance. It's like she's read my mind, though as far as I know Lark hasn't said a word about tomorrow's audition, and I know I haven't. Mum liberates a bottle of wine from the fridge and pours herself a generous glass. "Your sister keeps promising to revise, but I haven't seen much evidence of it so far." She sighs. "I won't be able to nag her from Norway."

I pour some cold juice for myself. "I bet she'll still pass," I say. Lark is lucky. She's never failed anything in her life.

"You're probably right." Mum's face softens. "She's like Mac – so laid-back and trusting. Always sure things will work out." She smiles at me. "Some of us need to prepare."

I hear the implication in her words. *Lark's talent comes naturally to her. Poor Wren needs to work.*

"I'm glad the band has got this time to rehearse." Mum's eyes flick to the calendar on the kitchen wall, carefully marked up in Sharpie. Plans have come together quickly since the day they told us about the tour. Seb has booked practice studios in Birmingham for the whole of May, Dad's already found a sub to cover his lessons, and Mum's agreed a sabbatical with the café.

"How are rehearsals going? Are you feeling more excited?" I ask. "You're not really worried about that stalker guy crawling out of the woodwork, are you?"

Mum's eyes dart unconsciously to the black mirror of the kitchen window. "God, no." She knocks back her drink with a laugh. "Your dad's right – that's in the past." She frowns. "It was nothing. Just a pathetic little man with a grudge."

"I thought you didn't know him?"

She blinks. "I didn't. I don't. I'm just guessing. Gosh, it's warm this evening." Blowing her hair out of her eyes, she pours another glass of Pinot. "Am I excited about the tour?" Her face lights up. "I think so, yes. The performance bug hasn't gone away. I'd forgotten how freeing it feels, being up on stage…" She grins a gap-toothed smile that knocks ten years off. "When everything comes together and the audience is singing your songs, you feel … I don't know, invincible! Like you could change the world."

I smile. Her enthusiasm is infectious.

"God, listen to me!" She giggles self-consciously. "That's two glasses of wine talking. But I'm right," she adds. "You'll see one day."

I'll see when I play at Enrapture. Then I correct myself: *I'll see if I play.*

A sigh slips out. It's not fair: Lark doesn't revise, Lark doesn't practise, Lark doesn't care about anything … but

Lark is special. So Lark will be chosen anyway.

It's happened before. I let myself remember.

There was the primary school nativity, when Lark was picked to be the Angel Gabriel, with a tinsel halo and long white dress. I was a camel in a brown velour hoody with a pillow stuffed up my back. When Lark sang her solo she totally stole the show – even though everyone knows that Mary and Joseph are the main characters in the nativity and, what's more, Angel Gabriel was a boy.

Then there was the time when Mr Smythe, our horrible music teacher at junior school, decided the right way to select his new choir was to poke the weak or quiet singers with his bony finger. Lark, of course, escaped a prodding. I was the one sent back to class.

My sister always gets chosen.

But … then there was the time we went camping. It was late and the two of us were lying in our tent sharing headphones, one earbud each, a random playlist shuffling on my phone. "The Sound of Silence" by Simon and Garfunkel started to play. As we lay there listening in the night, the song's melancholy beauty cut through me, right to my core, stirring a thousand emotions and sending a scattering of goosebumps down my arms. It was a magical feeling, like the music was speaking my language. Like it had chosen *me*. When I told Lark this, she laughed, like she couldn't quite believe it. And then she admitted that music had never given her chills, not once.

I felt sorry for her.

61

So would I rather be her, or me?

"You've gone very quiet. Is everything OK?" Mum lays a hand on my arm. I look into her face. *I can tell her.* Music is her magic too. She'll know what this means to me.

"There's an audition," I say. "Tomorrow. Me, Lark and Danny, we've all been invited to go." And I tell her about Enrapture, Adam Webb, and the local talent stage. "I didn't mention it before because…"

I pause. Spinner's warning plays in my ear. *Adam is a private guy. You get a chance like this, you don't go blabbing.*

I shrug. "Well … because it probably won't work out."

"You and Lark are doing this together?" Mum's eyes are misty.

"Not together." I see the disappointment in her face. "Lark doesn't even want this, not the way I do." I rest my head on my hands. "But she's the one with 'natural talent', so she's bound to be chosen."

"Not necessarily," Mum soothes. "You're both talented in different ways. If this Adam … Adam Webb… If he's an experienced music producer, he'll see that." She frowns.

Nice try, Mum. She can't even convince herself.

I head to the cavern for another hour. I *have* to smash this audition. Not only would I get to go to Enrapture – and the need to go is overwhelming – it would also prove to everyone that I can be just as special as Lark.

My parents will see me differently.

Danny will see me differently.

I'm sick of living in my sister's shadow.

6

Saturday morning rolls round.

I wake from a restless sleep with a churning gut and clammy hands. As I tune my guitar for the hundredth time and test out a few tentative chords, my fingers slip on the frets. I clear my throat and try a few vocal exercises to warm up my voice, but only a thin, wavering sound comes out.

I groan. The nerves. They're getting to me.

I lay down my guitar and wonder how Lark is feeling. Probably still sleeping like a log. But I'm going to mess up big time if I don't do something to calm myself down.

I reach for my phone and find the playlist, the one I

made exactly for times like this, times when I'm anxious or tense. I shove in my noise-cancelling earbuds and sink back on to my bed. Pretty soon, the sound of melodic guitar and soothing vocals floats over me, washing the stress away.

That's better…

Music is medicine. It's always been like that for me. As my heart stops pounding and my breathing slows, I marvel at how amazing it is, that music can have so much power over the way I feel and think. How can a beat, a rhythm, a chord progression … the simple rise and fall of a melody – how can it all affect me so profoundly? How does it lift me up and energize me, fire me with passion or with anger, drown me in sadness or despair? All I know is that no other art form feels so … *powerful*. Books, paintings, poetry, films – I like them well enough. But music hits different, it speaks to something bigger: some instinct deep in my bones.

Mum sticks her head round the door.

"I did knock," she says, as I pull out my earbuds and hoist myself up on my elbows. "Danny's downstairs. Dad says are you ready?"

"Two minutes."

She ducks out again and I get up and slide my guitar inside its case. A last-minute wardrobe change, then I slick on some mascara and try to coax my pixie crop into a style that looks … a little less librarian maybe, a little more punk.

"Is that what you're wearing?" Mum says, waiting outside in the hall. My T-shirt is an old one of hers: Belle and Sebastian. Runaway Summer supported them once on tour.

"Do you mind?"

"Of course not." She grins. "It's lucky."

"Then I'll definitely wear it." I grin back. She kisses my cheek and I head down the stairs.

Danny is leaning against the front door, scrolling on his phone and jiggling his foot like he always does when he's tense. In faded jeans that fit him perfectly and a simple slim-fitting black shirt, he looks so handsome my heart almost stops. He looks up at my approach, pushing the hair back from his face. His eyes meet mine.

"Wren. Wow. You look great." He coughs.

I flush at the compliment. "So do you."

It's warm in the hall. We smile at each other, strangely shy.

"Where's Lark?" Danny asks. Cold water douses the flames.

"She stayed the night at Aisha's." Dad appears, jangling the car keys. "I gather they went clubbing after the pub."

Clubbing! Typical.

"She says she'll make her own way there."

"Then what are we waiting for?" I open the front door and the baking sun hits me. If Lark wants to be casual about the chance of a lifetime, that's her lookout. "Let's go."

The satnav plans a route that takes us right round the Wrekin and all the way to the other side, following a network of winding country lanes. Dad turns the ignition, scowling at the map.

"Weird place to have an audition. You're sure they didn't hire a place in town?"

I check the address on the card Spinner gave me.

OVERLOOK STUDIOS
WREKIN EDGE FARM
WENLOCK LANE
TF6 5BC

"No, this is right."

We pull away. Dad makes eye contact in the mirror. "Your mother said this promoter guy used to be a music producer?"

I nod. "His name is Adam Webb." Danny shifts beside me in the back seat, turning side on to hear me better. "He's from the US," I carry on. "Apparently, he's very successful."

Dad shrugs. "Don't recognize the name."

I laugh. "That's because you're old and out of touch."

Danny chews his lip. I'm not sure he heard Dad's comment but it's clear he's got the gist. "Actually, Wren, I looked him up," he says. "Adam Webb, I mean. There's nothing online. Well, there are thousands of Adam Webbs, obviously. But none of them are successful music producers."

I shrug a so-what? "Maybe he worked for a studio. Not everyone is internet famous. Producers work behind the scenes. They're more under the radar, right?"

Danny doesn't answer. He stares out at the patchwork of fields.

66

"Oh no, this isn't good." Dad brakes suddenly, and the car slows down. We're approaching the reservoir on our left, and the cool water shimmers invitingly. Ahead of us, two police cars are blocking the way, their blue lights flashing intermittently. An ambulance is parked on the verge. A police officer is standing in the road, waving the traffic slowly through.

As we crawl by, I crane my head round, staring back over my shoulder. At the far edge of the reservoir is a small white tent. A group of people in high-vis vests are standing on the bank, while three figures, clad in black, are slowly entering the water.

The car is hot, but I shiver. "What's going on?"

Nobody answers. The rest of the journey passes in a sombre silence, my excitement somewhat checked.

The road begins to climb, hugging the forested edge of the hill.

"Here we are. Wrekin Edge Farm. This is it." Dad pulls up at a pair of stone gateposts flanking two large, wrought-iron gates. Beyond them, a long gravel road winds through an avenue of trees. Dad leans out of the window to press the button on the post, and the imposing gates slowly open inwards.

Wow.

We emerge from the avenue of trees on to a large circular driveway, complete with conspicuous stone fountain in the centre. An enormous old farmhouse lies beyond. It reminds me of the type of place that rich families renovate for millions on the programmes my parents love to hate-watch on TV. Danny and I exchange a glance.

Is this Adam Webb's actual house?

Dad whistles. "I take it back. He must be successful if he can afford to live here."

"Look!" Danny grabs my hand, taking me by surprise and making my tummy flip. He points past the beautiful farmhouse. Nestled into woodland, right on the edge of the grounds and overlooking a steep escarpment, is a modern timber building. With two floors and a deeply pitched roof, it looks like a cross between a church and a luxury cabin. Enormous windows interrupt the wood cladding, filled with what I suspect is sturdy, sound-proof glass. My hunch is confirmed by a small sign on the driveway pointing in the building's direction: OVERLOOK STUDIOS. A paper notice is pinned underneath. It reads: *Auditions this way.*

"Want me to come in?" Dad asks. "Or shall I wait outside?"

"We'll be fine." I say it carelessly, but my nerves are back with a vengeance. "You don't need to hang around. I don't know how long we'll be."

Dad looks dubious. "I should probably meet the guy."

And talk about music for hours.

"No, it's fine," I say again. "We've got each other." I flush as I catch Danny's eye, but he smiles on cue.

"Well, OK. I do have to run into town …" Dad runs his fingers through his hair. He glances again at the sleek lines of the studio building. "I'm sure everything's above board, but call if you need anything. I'll be back soon."

We haul our gear from the boot and watch the car drive away. Tiny dots of perspiration prickle my hairline and my fingers are clammy on the handle of my guitar case.

Are we about to meet the real Adam Webb?

Spinner did say that Webb likes to support young musicians, but I didn't think we'd be going to his home. I thought a successful music producer like him would hire someone else to programme the local talent stage…

It's so quiet here.

There's nobody around. In the midday heat, the light seems extra bright and the air strangely still. As we walk towards the studio building, my mouth feels dry and the crunch of gravel sets my teeth on edge. I hope I'm not getting a migraine. They come on sometimes when I'm dehydrated, or stressed—

A shrill scream pierces the air.

I freeze, my heart thumping in my chest like a tom-tom. "What was that?"

Danny is still. He must have heard it too. We stand there like statues, but nothing happens. No movement, no panic. No signs of life in the studio or back at the house.

A second piercing cry splits the air, louder than the first.

I clutch Danny's arm. "It came from over there." I point beyond the studio, towards the woods.

It sounded like a girl.

Danny follows my finger. Suddenly he doubles over.

For a split second, I'm about to panic, then I realize – he's laughing.

I look back. A peacock has landed on the studio roof. It perches on the guttering and peers down at us with disdain.

"Bloody bird!" I huff. "It nearly gave me a heart attack!" I look at Danny, who's still giggling. "Like I'm not nervous enough."

"Poor Wren, come here." He puts down his guitar and pulls me in for a hug. Wrapped in his arms, my insides flutter. He pulls back to look at me, pushing a strand of hair from my eyes. "You don't have to be nervous. It's only an audition. You're amazing. I mean, you'll *be* amazing…" He clears his throat.

I blink at him. "Um … thanks. And thanks for doing this. I know you didn't want to." He doesn't answer and I peer closely at him. "Aren't *you* nervous?"

"About the audition? Not exactly, I…" Danny glances over my shoulder. "I don't know. It all just feels weird, I guess."

He pulls out of the hug and turns towards the studio building. The door is slightly ajar so we walk straight in, pulling the door closed behind us. A large and cool reception lobby greets us, with a swanky kitchen bar in one corner and two plush velvet sofas facing each other in the middle of the room. A glossy coffee table sits between them, piled high with music magazines. To our right, a polished oak staircase spirals up to the second floor, while an open door on the far wall reveals a corridor leading deeper into the belly of the building. Glancing down it, I see a door at the end with a sign above it: RECORDING IN PROGRESS. The sign is unlit.

Lark isn't here, then. The mean part of me celebrates.

You snooze, you lose, sister.

Maybe she won't turn up at all. Then a doubt creeps in. If no one else is here, is this some kind of trick?

"It feels like we're trespassing," Danny whispers.

I nod. "I know."

The sound of footsteps makes me look up. A familiar figure is standing at the top of the stairs.

"You came. Truth."

Spinner pauses, waiting for a response, but I find myself suddenly speechless. It's an odd thing for him to say, and yes, he's incredibly attractive, but there's more to it somehow. Like Lark, he has an undeniable presence. It's no wonder I've been seeing more and more mentions of him on my socials lately. Spinner this, Spinner that.

He walks down the stairs, his arm stretched out towards us. I wonder briefly if we're supposed to hug him, then I realize he's doing his weird salute. I wave instead. Danny merely nods.

"Sit. Chill." He gestures at the sofas. I find myself doing as he says, putting down my guitar and sinking into the plump cushions. Danny follows my lead. Spinner stays standing, leaning against the bar.

My eyes flick to Danny, trying to read his face. I know Spinner said that Adam Webb was a friend of his, but I didn't expect Spinner to be here at the audition too, let alone acting like he owns the place. He can't be much older than Lark. How long has he known Webb? And how did a teenager like him get to be friends with a big US music producer in the first place?

"Adam's in the studio." Spinner picks up some papers from the bar counter. "He'll be out in a minute." He blinks. "Where's the rest of your band?"

"This is our band," I tell him. "Just the two of us. It didn't stop the White Stripes." *God, why am I babbling?*

"There were three of you before. Where's the other girl?"

I stare at my hands, a sinking feeling in my belly.

"She's coming," Danny says, giving my arm a squeeze.

"We want to audition separately," I squeak. "If that's OK?"

Surprise registers briefly on Spinner's face, then he shrugs. "Yeah, yeah. Whatever you want."

Behind us, the main door flies open.

"Sorry! I'm not late, am I? Have the auditions started?"

Danny's face lights up as Lark steps into the room. She's wearing a pale blue belly top that displays her evenly tanned midriff, along with a pair of expensive-looking cargo pants that I assume belong to Aisha. Her make-up is immaculate and her hair is artfully pinned up, a few loose tendrils framing her face. She looks every inch the stadium-filling star – an almost perfect body double for Taylor Swift on her *Eras* tour. I pick at a hole in Mum's vintage indie tee, the one that made me feel so confident – even *lucky* – this morning. Now all I feel is scruffy and out-of-place. Lark looks like she could be headlining Wembley in half an hour, while I'm not even cool enough to be her warm-up act.

Spinner's sculptured features form a smile. "You're right on time, sweetheart."

"*Not* your sweetheart, but OK." Lark saunters over to the kitchen and helps herself to a glass of water. "Ugh, it's too hot, and I am *so* hung-over."

Danny grins. His eyes are still glued to Lark so he doesn't see how Spinner's lips tighten at Lark's burn. Touching the eye pendant round his neck, Spinner fans out the papers in his hand.

"Fill in these forms first, yeah? Nothing to worry about, just a waiver. Name, date of birth, artist name, contact info, socials if you're on them. And adult consent, if you're under eighteen."

No! Why did I tell Dad to go? Danny frowns, but Lark speaks up.

"I'll sign for everyone. I'm eighteen."

She digs in her bag and pulls out her college ID. Spinner looks at it carefully, taking his time. "Yeah, that should work," he says eventually, waiting a beat before giving it back. "Your hair looks better down, by the way." He thrusts the forms at her and turns away.

Lark blinks, like she's not sure if she's been complimented or insulted. I'm not sure I know myself.

"Er, whatever," she manages, flopping on to the sofa next to me and Danny. I watch as she scrawls her neat signature at the bottom of each form, adding her phone number and email underneath. She passes one to me and another to Danny. Danny thanks her politely, but I complete my form without a word.

"Who else is auditioning?" I ask Spinner, who's now sitting on the arm rest of the other sofa and flicking idly through a music magazine. "Where's everyone else?"

"Adam's seeing people all weekend," he answers smoothly.

"When do we find out if we've got through?" Danny adds, tying his hair back with a band.

Spinner doesn't reply. He's looking at Danny oddly and it takes me a second to work out why. Danny's question … it came off a little loud. He misjudges volume sometimes, it's no big deal. And it's what Danny says that matters, not the way he says it. But that doesn't stop some people being assholes.

"Wait…" Spinner has spotted Danny's hearing aids. "Are you…?" He looks quizzically from Danny to his guitar. "How can you even—"

"Yeah, when do we hear back?" I repeat Danny's question, cutting Spinner off before he properly embarrasses himself. It's so lazy to assume that Danny's hearing loss means he can't – or shouldn't – play guitar. He got that a lot after his illness – people saying what a shame it was that he'd have to give it up. It wasn't true; he just had to adapt. It's different for him, that's all.

"You'll know when you know." Spinner says dismissively, throwing the magazine aside and collecting up the forms. "Who wants to go first?"

"We will." I jump in before Lark can speak.

"Fine." Spinner gets to his feet. "I'll let Adam know. Warm up, tune up, whatever. The studio is fully equipped." He raises a pierced eyebrow at my beaten-up guitar case. "But you can use your own gear, if you prefer."

He strides off down the corridor towards the recording studio.

"Gosh, what a charmer," Lark quips, and I smile inwardly because for the first time in ages we actually agree on something. At least Spinner's weird brush-offs aren't getting to her. She digs an elbow in my ribs. "You can thank me later for signing your form, Trog."

And then she has to ruin things again.

"Good afternoon."

We all look up. A tall, bearded stranger is standing in the doorway to the corridor. He's dressed in long, brightly coloured robes and his dark hair is pulled back into a loose ponytail. I blink. I've never seen anyone quite like this man; somewhere between a druid and a priest. He could be forty or sixty, it's impossible to tell. There's an ageless quality to him. His posture is as striking as his clothes – he stands as if he owns the room. Which I suppose he does. Because this has to be Adam Webb, super-successful music producer from America, looking every inch the creative guru. Even Spinner seems to be in awe of him, hovering behind him like an overkeen sidekick.

The stranger smiles broadly.

"Thank you so much for coming. Allow me to introduce myself. My name is Adam Webb, but you must call me Adam."

His voice is smooth and rich like chocolate cake, and his grey eyes are warm and welcoming. Instantly, I relax. It's like sunbathing on a deserted island, basking in his glow.

"And you three young people are…?" He peers at the forms Spinner hands him. "Daniel Akintola. Wren *Mackenzie*." He stumbles on my surname and I put it down to his accent, a soft American twang. "And last but not least, Lark *Mackenzie*."

There it is again.

"How very serendipitous!" Adam smiles widely, looking between Lark and me. "A pair of musical sisters. How wonderful." He seems genuinely thrilled by our presence, and I'm charmed. "It's a great pleasure to meet you. Follow me."

7

Adam turns, his long robes fanning out behind him like a psychedelic bride. As his ponytail swings to one side, my eye is drawn to his neck. At the base, staring back at me, is a tiny tattoo of a bird.

A dove for peace, I think to myself.

He disappears down the corridor.

"Ready?" Danny whispers.

I pick up my guitar case, taking a deep breath to calm my nerves.

"Good luck!" Lark calls after us. "Break a leg!"

I don't bother to reply.

We follow Adam, Spinner bringing up the rear like

a security guard as though we might suddenly run off to explore. It is tempting, I'll admit. As we head down the corridor, I stare, intrigued at the pictures on the wall. Instead of the gold and platinum discs I would have expected a music producer to have, there are black-and-white photographs featuring stern-faced people wearing old-fashioned clothes. Another frame holds a faded map of a town. The caption reads TRUTH OR CONSEQUENCES.

Adam is waiting for us outside the recording studio door. Hanging to his right is a print that makes me do a double-take. The image depicts hundreds of people rising into the sky on a beam of light, like they've been sucked up by a gigantic UFO.

"Like the festival posters," I mouth at Danny.

"I see you're admiring my art." Adam blesses me with a wide, indulgent smile and I stand up straighter, like I've been awarded a gold star. "Do you know what that image represents?"

"Not really," I admit.

"It represents The Rapture." Adam bows his head.

"'*En*rapture'?" A thrill zips through me. "You mean, the festival?"

"Not quite." Adam smiles again. "Although, my festival will be a life-changing experience for those who attend."

I smile, not quite understanding.

"For millennia," he goes on, his voice soft and melodious, "people have prophesied a once-in-a-lifetime event. A gathering of truth-seekers who will meet their messiah and create a new kingdom together. Unbelievers will be left behind." His eyes close, and even Spinner has a faraway look on his face. I glance at Danny. Is he following this strange conversation? His creased forehead tells me that he is.

"What's that got to do with the festival?" Danny asks.

Adam's eyes pop open. "Do you ever feel lost, young man?"

Danny shrugs. "Um, sometimes, I guess."

"Of course you do." Adam's face floods with sympathy. He places a hand on Danny's shoulder. "Lost, broken, confused…" Danny starts to interrupt, but Adam goes on. "It's natural. And it's not your fault. The world has taken a wrong turn. But there is a different way. After you."

He opens the door and I stop trying to process his words. All I can do is gape.

I'm staring at the recording studio of my dreams. It's airy and open, with a high ceiling and wooden floor, and dotted around the space is an array of the most incredible instruments I've ever seen. I recognize a Steinway grand piano, a Pearl drum kit, even a Hammond organ, as well as a beautiful golden harp and a range of eye-wateringly expensive guitars, both electric and acoustic. In one corner, there's an isolation booth for recording vocals, while to my right is a control room full of monitors, computers and the most complicated mixing console I've ever seen. The equipment here is mind-blowing, ranging from analogue vintage to brand-new state-of-the-art.

"*Wow.*" Danny looks like he's changed his mind about the audition. His eyes are out on stalks.

"Make yourselves at home." Adam ushers us in.

An enormous set of glass doors fills the end wall, and I walk over to them. The recording studio is snugly nestled right on the edge of the hillside and the view from up here is incredible. I'm looking down on a verdant, bowl-shaped valley scattered with woodland and rolling fields.

"Isn't it beautiful?" Adam comes to stand next to me. "The local name is Devil's Dale. So quaint!" He taps on the glass. "Work will be starting imminently, but luckily we won't be disturbed. We're completely sound-proofed up here."

"Work?" I echo.

"Devil's Dale is the site for Enrapture."

I twitch involuntarily. "I can't wait."

Adam looks delighted. "I'm glad you feel that way. I must say, I feel the same. I come from very humble beginnings, Miss Mackenzie, but I learned early on how powerful music can be. How persuasive and influential. It's always been my goal to harness that power, to share it with people and use it for the good of the world."

I smile and nod. *We're kindred spirits, Adam and I…*

"Where should we set up?" Danny interrupts.

I turn, feeling guilty. We left Danny out of the conversation and he missed Adam's inspiring words.

"Wherever you like," Adam replies. "Take your time, get settled in. I shall listen from the control room."

He slips into the room-within-a-room and settles behind the mixing desk. I'm surprised to see Spinner in there too, leaving Danny and me alone in the intimidating performance space.

"This is wild," Danny whispers, plugging in his guitar lead and pulling up a stool. "I'd kill to try that Les Paul over there but I'm scared I'd break it."

"I know what you mean," I say, strapping on my guitar. Despite the offer to play one of Adam's beautiful instruments, I feel better using my own.

"I don't get it." Danny says, his voice still low. "Why would a massive music producer invite a couple of random kids into his own private recording studio and give them free run of his equipment?"

I shrug. "Who knows? But I'm not complaining." I grin as I check my tuning. "He seems…" I glance at Adam, putting on headphones behind the screen. "Nice? A bit eccentric, maybe."

Danny raises an eyebrow. "A bit?"

"Wren. Daniel. Can you hear me?" Adam's voice crackles over the intercom. "Ready, whenever you are."

My eyes meet Danny's. *OK?* Sitting across from me, guitar at the ready, he nods. I step up to the mic and clear my throat.

Here goes.

I nod to count us in and we break into the opening of the song we've chosen. Or rather the song *I* chose. Hozier's "Take Me to Church". I still remember the first time I heard it. It floored me that a song could be so simple and strong, so fearless and honest. And while a voice like Lark's would really make it shine, I'll try to do it justice.

Miraculously, I manage the first verse without slipping up, and as I reach the slower "Amen" section just before the chorus, I put everything I've got into my performance. Lark may have purity, but I have passion, at least.

Danny's on form too. The acoustics are great here, which helps. We're tight and in sync, perfectly tuned in to one another's movements. As his eyes lock on to mine, I can almost feel the sparks fly.

We sound good together.

We are *good together.*

Adam is watching intently from the control room window, his face an unreadable mask. I try not to let it put me off. Taking a deep breath, I launch into the chorus. He *has* to let us play at Enrapture. I don't care if it's the tiniest stage at the festival, the crappiest slot on the bill. All I want is the chance to—

"OK, thanks." Spinner's voice crackles through the speaker, bursting the bubble of my dream.

I stop playing, glancing at Danny in confusion. "But we haven't fini—"

"It's fine," Spinner interrupts. "We heard enough."

No. I grip the neck of my guitar. We were good, I know we were. Frustration ferments in my stomach. I turn to look at Adam, but he's busy writing something in a notebook.

"Sorry," Spinner adds, like an afterthought. "Adam's pushed for time. He has other people to see."

I gape. *What other people?* Lark is the only person out there.

"Mr Webb." Danny has stepped forward and is speaking into my mic. "You should hear us to the end. You need to give Wren a chance to show what she can do."

I could kiss him for trying, but it's pointless. I stare hopelessly at the floor. Somehow we've blown the audition. It's over.

"Young man, you're right."

I look up. Adam has come out of the control room and is walking towards me. "Wren, before you go, I'd like to try something, if you don't mind?" His eyes dance. "Will you indulge me?"

Still hot with humiliation, I nod.

"Can you read music?"

"Yes."

"Good." Adam walks over to the grand piano and picks up the sheet music lying on top. He motions for me to come forward. "Leave your guitar; you won't need it. Daniel, you've done an excellent job. You can wait outside."

Danny shoots me a questioning look. Adam's face was half turned away and Danny always complains that beards make lip-reading harder.

"Adam wants me to stay," I say, my stomach squirming. It feels wrong to leave Danny out.

"Only for a moment," Adam adds, placing his notebook

carefully on top of the piano. "I'd like to hear Wren sing alone. Unaccompanied. She'll join you in the lobby shortly."

Danny looks uncertain, but I nod to let him know I'm fine. It's me that Adam's not sure about – Danny's already proved he can play guitar. And if it means salvaging this shit-show of an audition, I'll try anything.

Reluctantly, Danny puts down his guitar and leaves the studio.

As soon as he's gone, Adam passes me the sheet of music. It's been folded so that only the top two lines are visible, and I see that the notes are written by hand, neatly formed in black ink. I start to smooth out the paper, but Adam stops me.

"Just those top two lines. Don't worry about the rest."

I frown. "There aren't any words."

"That doesn't matter, either." Adam chuckles softly. "You can hum, or sing '*la*'. How is your pitch?" He presses a piano key. "This is your starting note. Don't look so worried! Think of this as an experiment. I want to hear your tone, your range. It's the raw material I'm interested in. What do you say?"

"Um … OK."

I peer at the music again. It doesn't look too difficult: two lines of a melody in the treble clef. But the notes are high. *Super* high. Fine for a soprano, but that's not me. Lark is the one with the range.

Don't think about Lark.

I push the thought away and note the time signature, the key. Then I try to hear the tune in my head.

"Ready, Miss Mackenzie?"

"I … yes, I think so."

I stumble at first, fluffing badly, my voice hesitant and apologetic. I feel silly singing *'la'*, and I'm sure I've got the rhythm wrong. Cheeks burning, I race to the end, trying to get it over with. I haven't salvaged this audition at all. If anything, I've made it worse.

"Not bad," Adam says kindly. "Have another go. The same two lines. But when you reach the end – *da capo* – repeat. Sing until I ask you to stop."

"OK."

I stand up taller, determined to make a better impression. On the second run through, I still make mistakes, but by the third time, I've pretty much nailed it. My tone is thin and weak, because the pitch is too high for my voice, but I've got the notes in the right order and the melody is falling into place. It's lovely, actually – sad and sweet … and slightly familiar, I think I—

I stop, grabbing the piano like an anchor. "Sorry," I mutter. My head feels strange, spaced out.

Adam's grey eyes survey me. "Everything all right?"

"I … I don't know."

In the control room, Spinner stares stonily at me.

"I'm really sorry, I think I might be getting a migraine."

My head doesn't hurt yet, but I do feel dizzy. It must be the stress. Tears prick my eyes. *Such crappy timing.*

"Not to worry, Miss Mackenzie. You did wonderfully." Adam scrawls something in his notebook and smiles kindly at me. "Thank you so much. Rest assured, I'll be in touch. You can go now, but do send Daniel and your sister in."

I pick up my guitar and drift towards the door.

Danny is in the hallway, silently studying Adam's art. His forehead furrows when he sees me. "What's the matter? Did something happen?"

"I messed up." I rub my eyes. "Got a headache coming on."

"Oh, Wren." His face fills with sympathy. "Do you need anything?"

"No, I'll be fine. I have painkillers in my bag."

"You want me to stay with you?"

Yes.

"No." I nod at the studio door. "Adam's waiting. Stay and play for Lark. She'll never forgive me if you don't."

Lark leaps up as I enter the lobby. "You're out. How did it go?" She touches my cheek. "You look peaky, are you OK?"

"I'm fine," I snap, throwing down my guitar and pushing past her to the sofa. I need to sit down. "Everything was good. Great, actually. Danny's waiting. Adam said to go through."

The minute she's gone, I dig in my bag and pop a painkiller. My head feels fuzzy but it isn't hurting yet. With migraines, as long as I act quickly I'm usually OK.

I glance around, looking for a cloakroom where I could splash some water on my face. There isn't one. My eyes stray to the spiral staircase. There must be a bathroom or something upstairs.

Sure enough, when I reach the top, I find one next to a bedroom suite. An open door reveals a glimpse of unmade bed. The bathroom itself is luxurious, with a claw-foot bath, designer handwash and fluffy towels. As I splash my face with cold water, I happen to glance into the mirror.

Behind me, above the toilet, is a wall full of platinum discs.

I smile. *OK, so he hangs them in his bathroom.* Adam certainly is an oddball – but he's a modest one at least. Shaking my head, I pull out my phone. So much for Danny's online stalking skills. It's pretty hard to dismiss Adam's credentials when faced with evidence like this. Quickly, I snap a photo, then I head back down to the cool, air-conditioned lobby where I sink into the soft velvet sofa and wait for Danny and Lark to reappear.

"Wren." Danny touches my shoulder, making me jump. "We're done. Your dad's on his way."

I blink. "Sorry, I was in a daze."

"How's your headache?"

"Fine. Must have caught it in time." I look over his shoulder. "Where's Lark? How did she—"

"She's coming now." Danny's face is unreadable. "You can ask her yourself."

Lark appears in the lobby, with Spinner by her side. Adam is nowhere to be seen.

"Help yourself to water." Spinner slides an arm round Lark's waist, steering her towards the bar. "It gets pretty hot in there."

"I'm fine. I'm not a delicate little flower." Lark disentangles herself from Spinner's grasp. "I told you: I've just got a raging hangover."

I don't get a chance to ask Lark anything, because at that moment, from outside, comes the sound of wheels crunching on gravel and the blare of a car horn. Dad.

I sink into the back seat, feeling hollow; I guess the tension of the day has finally caught up with me. Dad asks questions, but all I can do is shrug inarticulately, and after a while he gives up. In the front passenger seat, Lark is quiet too, her blonde head resting on the glass. Only Danny is sharp and alert. He swivels in his seat and I follow his gaze to see the recording studio, receding into the distance. The horrible peacock is gone, but Spinner is standing in the doorway watching us, one hand raised in a salute.

I rest my head on Danny's shoulder.

It's over. But were we good enough?

I would do *anything* to play at Enrapture – but the only thing left to do is hope.

8

Waiting is hideous.

It's literally *one day* after the audition, and already I'm driving myself round the bend. I honestly can't remember being so preoccupied by anything before. I mooch round the house in a horrible state of limbo, analysing the audition over and over. We didn't get to finish our song. I messed up my weird singing test... But then Adam told me not to worry and said I did "wonderfully".

Is that true, or was he only being nice?

I wish I could talk it through with someone, but Danny's gone to Telford to hand out leaflets for the local conservation trust, and Mum and Dad are at yet another rehearsal and won't be back till late. I consider texting Ruby and the music gang from college, but I'm still not sure if they're allowed to know, and the last thing I want to do is piss Adam off.

Lark is at home, supposedly revising for Monday's drama exam, but when I peek round her bedroom door I find her on her phone.

"What do you want, Trog?" She barely looks up from the screen.

"Nothing." I hover on the landing. "I was just … thinking about the audition. How did yours go?" I affect an air of casualness, but Lark isn't buying it. Her eyes narrow.

"It was great. Why?"

I grit my teeth. "No reason. When do you reckon we'll hear?"

"Couldn't say." Her voice has a patronizing tone and it grates on me. "I'm sure Adam's a very busy man, but when he gets in touch I'll let you know."

"You'd better," I growl.

It's beyond irritating that Lark will hear from Adam about both of us – but she signed the waivers, her contact details are on the forms. Like a small blonde Simon Cowell, she's going to be the genie who grants my wishes or the demon who destroys my dreams.

"Is that all?" She smiles sweetly.

I shut the door before I strangle her.

By evening, I've worked through all my favourite playlists but none have made a difference to my mood.

My concentration's so shot I can't even play guitar. At ten to seven, with nothing else to distract me, I lug my laptop down to the kitchen, where the Wi-Fi signal is strongest. The cat blinks, silently judging me.

"Stop looking at me like that," I hiss, as I do the one thing I promised myself I wouldn't.

I log in to my Enrapture booking account.

WELCOME USER:
LITTLE BROWN BIRD

A chiming chord greets me and my heart rate shoots up. As the BUY TICKETS holding page loads, a bass-heavy background beat, vaguely familiar, throbs like a pulse, adding to the tension.

By five to seven, my phone is blowing up.

Ruby

Me and Isaac are ready to go. How's everyone doing?

Meena

I have 5 tabs open. Is that enough?

Jiv

I'm here with Alex. Let's do this!

Ruby

OK, it's nearly 7. GOOD LUCK EVERYONE!!!

I can't bring myself to post a comment. Not even to wish them luck.

At exactly seven o'clock, the holding page updates. Now I'm staring at a shimmering rainbow-coloured digital clock display. The digits change hypnotically as the clock counts down from twenty seconds before starting all over again, numbers synchronizing to the pulsing beat. Every time the clock reaches zero, I hold my breath as the page attempts to connect me to the booking portal – with no success.

Clearly everyone for miles around is trying to do the same.

Staring at the screen like a zombie, I start refreshing the page every few seconds instead. It's a pointless activity because, even if I manage to get through, I don't have the money for a ticket. And yet somehow I can't stop myself. Maybe I like torturing myself. Maybe I'm in denial.

Maybe some small, sad part of me is hoping for a miracle.

At 7.22 p.m. my phone pings, breaking my trance.

Jiv
Woo-hoo! Alex is on the booking portal!

Meena
Whaaaaat???

Ruby
OMG OMG… Update ASAP!

Five minutes later, it pings again:

Alex

Stand down, gang. WE HAVE 5 TICKETS!!!

Ruby

You are amazing 🖤🖤

Meena

Enrapture here we come!

Waves of celebration emojis follow.

I scowl at the screen. I know I should write something charitable, something *nice*. But I can't find the words. As if to rub salt into my wounds, the countdown on my laptop disappears and the page updates with a flash:

TICKETS FOR ENRAPTURE ARE SOLD OUT

Twenty-nine minutes. That's all it took. With a deep sigh I mute the group chat.

Lark breezes into the kitchen. "Wow, you look terrible. Who died?"

"Tickets for Enrapture sold out." I snap my laptop shut. I don't expect Lark to care. She can go with Charlie no matter what.

Surprisingly, she passes up the chance to crow. "Already?

93

That was fast. I'm not surprised, though. Everyone's talking about—"

She's interrupted by the front door banging open. Snippets of strained conversation drift towards us from down the hall.

"… not safe to leave at a time like this…"

"… being paranoid … an accident, that's all."

The front door slams. Our parents appear in the kitchen, red-faced and tight-lipped. Lark and I exchange glances.

"What's going on?" Lark asks.

"Nothing." Mum puts down her bag.

"Then why were you arguing?" I ask.

"We weren't," Dad says.

"You were," Lark retorts. "We heard you."

Dad falls silent and Mum takes a deep breath. "They found a body. That poor girl, Mia Hall. It was on the radio today, at the studio."

My skin feels cold. "Where was she?"

Suddenly I know I don't need to ask. My mind flashes back to the little white tent. The oil-skinned divers entering the water.

Mum shudders and Dad takes over. "They think she went swimming in the reservoir. Got into trouble and drowned. Remember the road block yesterday?" He grimaces. "Alys and Rob knew a little more. Their son used to play in a band with Mia a couple of years ago. Bit of a sad story, really. She ran away from home, fell in with a bad crowd. Apparently she'd been squatting outside

Hamlington with a bunch of junkies."

Mum scowls. "That's irrelevant, Mac. She didn't deserve to die."

"I didn't say she did!" he barks angrily. "But you can't deny it, Paloma – that kind of lifestyle … it comes with risks. It was an *accident*, but you're acting like something sinister is going on—"

"Two missing girls in three months!" Mum's hands tremble as she takes off her coat. I've never seen her so shaken up. "I used to think Hamlington was a safe place."

"It *is*. Girls, talk some sense into your mother." Dad turns to Lark and me. "She wants to cancel the tour. After all our hard work, the rehearsals… We're supposed to leave in three weeks' time, but your mum thinks the pair of you aren't safe. All because of two tragic accidents. Two totally different sets of circumstances. Two totally different girls."

"They were only eighteen," Mum murmurs.

"And that's *all* they had in common. Nothing else!" Dad sighs with exasperation. He shrugs off his jacket and stomps upstairs.

"Dad's right," Lark says, hugging Mum. "Don't worry. It's sad, but it's just a coincidence."

I stare at the ground, thinking.

First Anna Walker, now Mia Hall.

Two teenage girls with nothing in common.

Except for the fact they're both dead.

*

95

I drag myself out of bed. Monday mornings are always rough but this one is particularly unappealing. The air is muggy and uncomfortable, and I know that college will be full of gossip about yesterday's grisly discovery, not to mention an added dose of drama about Enrapture.

Breakfast is a subdued affair. Runaway Summer have a rare day off and Mum is scrolling on her phone while her coffee goes cold, trying to pretend she isn't reading long threads about Mia on the local neighbourhood chat.

Dad scowls and heads to the cavern to dig out lesson plans for the substitute teacher, muttering under his breath about "herd mentality" and "echo chambers". I'm not totally sure what he means, but it's true that he's never had any time for rumours or conspiracies. I would have expected Mum to agree with him, what with her "think for yourself" mantra, but I guess the problem with a small town is that news gets twisted quickly. People jump in with their theories, regardless of the facts. It's easy to get sucked in.

But it's still not worth cancelling their tour.

I cram some bread into the toaster. My parents have to go to Norway; I can see how much they need it. Yes, the recent deaths are unsettling – especially coming so close together. But in the cold light of day, I'm with Dad. They're unfortunate, *unconnected* events. Lark and I really couldn't be safer – life in Hamlington is normally so boringly predictable – and the past few weeks with the band have had such a positive effect on our parents. While they've been rehearsing they've been different people, happy and relaxed. It's obvious that being in the studio is good for them, that the act of making music together has given them a new lease on life.

Lark swans in ten minutes before the bus leaves. She spies my breakfast.

"Ooh, can I have some? I'm *starving* and I'm running late."

I scowl. "It's mine. Make your own."

"That's not very nice, little sister. I've got an exam, remember?"

"So?"

Lark's eyes flick sideways. "So ... you wouldn't want me to get too hungry and forget to tell you any *news*..."

I spin round. "You've heard from Adam?"

"Wouldn't you like to know!"

She flutters her eyelashes and I want to throttle her. Reluctantly, I surrender my toast.

"Thank you." She leans casually against the kitchen counter, chewing. "I did check my emails this morning ... but, sadly, nothing's come through yet. Although I have had a few messages from Evan." She smiles to herself.

"Who's Evan?" Mum looks up from her phone.

"Just a DJ." Lark tosses her head.

I frown at her. "He's not 'just a DJ'," I correct, for Mum's benefit. "His stage name is Spinner. He's friends with Adam Webb. He's the guy who invited us to audition."

Lark smiles innocently. "That's right. He's only nineteen but his career is going really well."

"Mm…" Mum nods slowly. "I think I've heard the name."

I raise an eyebrow. *My* mum *has heard of Spinner?*

I turn back to Lark. "Why are you messaging Spinner anyway? I thought you didn't like him."

"When did I say that?" she shoots back. "Anyway, I told you. *He* messaged *me*. He was sweet, actually, asking how I was after the audition. You know, because I felt faint?"

"Faint?" Mum echoes. "You never said."

Faint. I eye my sister suspiciously.

Mum's phone rings. She picks up with a sigh. "Seb. What a surprise. Been speaking to Mac by any chance? Hold on a second … yes, it's boiling, we're all getting very fractious here …" She takes the call out of the room.

"You weren't 'faint'! You had a hangover," I huff at Lark. "That was your own fault. I had a migraine. Did he ask about me?" I shove my books into my bag without waiting for a response. This is typical. Attention-seeking Lark acting the diva. Again. Changing her tune about *Evan*… I know exactly what she's up to.

"Evan isn't involved in the selection process," she says, reading my mind. "Apart from talent-spotting, obviously. Adam is programming the local talent stage. *He's* the one who decides who gets to play. Evan can message anyone he wants." She blows a golden strand of hair out of her eyes. "He was telling me how he got into DJing. It was actually really interesting—"

I snort.

"It was! Before the YouTube stuff, he started out with vinyl. He's got some old decks – you know, turntables—"

"I know what *decks* are," I snap.

"Oh, right. Like your old record player."

"Yeah. I seem to remember you mocking me about it."

Lark ignores this. "He wants to teach me how to do it. He's coming round tomorrow at seven and bringing his gear." She swings her bag over her shoulder. "We'll need the cavern, by the way."

I stare at her. "But Danny's coming over tomorrow! He said he'd help with my assignment." I sigh. I'm still not making any headway with my piece. Plus, I was secretly hoping Danny and I might jam together, like we used to. I cross my arms. "We need the cavern. Why can't you go to *Evan's* place?"

"He doesn't have his own place right now," Lark replies. "He's staying with a friend, not that it's any of your business. All his stuff's in storage."

"Except, conveniently, his decks."

She turns on me. "Wren, why are you being so difficult? You could easily rearrange your plans. You can see Danny *any* day."

"What's going on?" Mum comes back into the kitchen.

"Wren thinks the cavern belongs to her. I'm never allowed to use it," Lark whines.

"You've never wanted to!" I snap.

"But now, when I ask – politely – if I can have it for a couple of hours tomorrow night, she gets all possessive…"

99

"Danny and I have plans!"

Mum sighs. "A couple of hours isn't long, Wren."

"I need to work on an assignment!"

"Could Danny do another night?" she suggests, gently.

"Why are you automatically on Lark's side?" I cry. "We can only do tomorrow. Danny's busy tonight and he's got some hospital appointment later on this week."

Mum frowns. "Debs didn't mention it."

"Well, it's probably just a check-up." I brush it away. Danny has lots of hospital appointments, regular audiology consultations. "The point is, why should I rearrange my life just because Lark wants time alone with her new *boyfriend*?"

"He's not my boyfriend!"

"Not yet. But isn't that the plan?"

Lark blinks. "What are you trying to say?"

"Stop!" Mum sinks into a chair. "I don't know why I let Seb talk me round. First those missing girls, now this." She glares at us. "You *promised* to have each other's backs. But how can I believe that when you're always fighting?" She lets out a deep sigh. "I don't know if I can—"

"Mum." I stop her, guilt churning in my belly. Putting an arm round her shoulders, I shoot daggers at Lark over her head. "Don't cancel anything. We're fine. *Everything's* fine." I take a deep breath. *I'll be the bigger person.* "Danny can come round tomorrow at six. We'll be done in time for Lark to use the cavern." I smile at Lark: *Your turn.*

"Fine," she manages.

"Thank you," Mum murmurs.

I snatch up my bag and run for the bus stop. But as I slide into the seat next to Ruby, Lark hisses a reminder in my ear.

"Don't forget, Trog. Tomorrow. Seven. *Sharp.*"

9

The atmosphere at school is strange. *Feverish* is the only way to describe it. With the novelty of the heatwave, excitement about Enrapture tickets and the shock of Mia's death, high drama has descended on sleepy, boring Hamlington and the gossip is out of control.

Literally everyone seems to have an opinion on Mia, regardless of whether they knew her or not. A group of girls in my tutor group are huddled together crying, but there's a self-conscious element to their tears that makes me uncomfortable. Mia wasn't our age. She didn't go to our school.

Did any of them actually know her at all?

I look for Danny at break, but he's got a meeting with Anna, the specialist teacher who drops in to support him. As I walk, alone, into the sixth form hub, I regret it immediately. It's stifling, and the rumour mill is in full throttle, impossible to tune out. Isla Ashcroft is holding court on a sofa, loudly telling anyone who will listen about how she saw someone who looked exactly like Mia kissing an older guy and getting into his car. Someone else chips in to say that Zaina Ratcliffe's brother's best friend sold Mia ecstasy and weed. I'm not sure how any of it has a bearing on why Mia's body was discovered in a reservoir.

At lunchtime, it's the same in the canteen. As I queue to buy a sandwich, more rumours reach my ears. It's not difficult to see what is happening. Slandering, victim-blaming – Mia is being painted as a bad girl, like that's an explanation for her death. Nobody is asking any real questions – everyone's just joining in. My sandwich tastes dry in my mouth. It's chilling how quickly people will believe the first thing they hear, how they jump to conclusions without knowing or asking for the facts. "What do you think, Wren? What do *you* think…?"

It's all anyone wants to talk about.

That and Enrapture.

Enrapture.

The word cuts me every time I hear it. Everyone has tickets to the festival, and I mean *everyone*. Apart from Danny and me, not a single person seems to have missed out. I slide into a seat next to Ruby and the rest of the music gang. They're not talking about Mia, thank goodness, but their eyes are shiny and unfocused and their movements are giddy and twitchy. Either the heat is sending them delirious or they're all still high on the triumph of scoring tickets last night. Ruby's in such a good mood she doesn't even blink when Isaac pulls her roughly on to his lap and forces a kiss on her in front of everyone. Usually Ruby hates PDAs, so I can't help being surprised.

Enrapture, Enrapture… The chatter goes on.

I turn away, consumed with envy, ramming my headphones in my ears.

It's the only way to drown out all the noise.

On Tuesday evening, the cavern is more like an oven. I wait impatiently for Danny, practising fingerpicking patterns on my guitar. My stomach keeps twisting, oddly tense. It's partly because it's been ages since Danny and I played in here together, just the two of us, making music.

But it's also because I'm brooding about Lark.

Normally, I couldn't care less about her social life, but the idea of her meeting Spinner winds me up. It feels unfair. Lark may claim that Spinner has no say in the results of the audition but, if that's true, why was he at the recording studio on Saturday? Why did Adam let him stay to hear me and Danny play? And how does Spinner know Adam anyway? He said they were friends, but Spinner is only nineteen. Adam's old enough to be his dad.

A tap at the side door makes me jump. Danny's head appears.

"Sorry I'm late."

"You're not." I smile as he comes in. He looks nice, in denim cargo shorts and a soft grey T-shirt bearing a faded logo of a fox. He drops into the ratty swivel chair Dad uses for teaching and idly pulls a loose thread.

My heart sinks. "You didn't bring your guitar."

"Oh, I didn't think I needed it." He nods at my lyric notebook lying closed on top of a plan chest. "I came to help you."

"Yeah. No. Of course." Disappointment crushes my chest. "It's fine. It's good. I need all the help I can get." My cheeks heat and I grab my notebook, suddenly self-conscious. "You're a lifesaver, you know that?" *Why am I jabbering?* "I don't know what I'd do without you—" *Ugh. That came out too intense.* I cringe.

Danny looks confused.

"What I'm trying to say is … thanks. You're a mate." *Stop talking, Wren.*

"Oh. Yeah. No problem." Danny goes to say something, then stops.

And now this is awkward.

"Did you hear that Enrapture tickets sold out?" I fill the silence. "In less than half an hour. And Lark still hasn't heard back from Adam."

Danny doesn't reply. He swivels round to face Dad's keyboard, his fingers playing a chromatic scale. I pull

105

my stool over to his left side, making sure that he can see me.

"I said, Lark still hasn't heard from Adam."

"Yeah, got it." Danny scowls. I'm not sure if he heard the first time or if he doesn't care.

We should be getting on with my assignment, but the question bursts out of my mouth: "Tell me the truth. How did her audition go?"

Danny stops playing and looks at me, hands fidgeting in his lap. "Didn't you ask her?"

"Well, yeah. She just said it was great."

"Hmm." He blinks. "I wouldn't say that."

My selfish heart lifts. "Why?"

"Because…" He shrugs. "It was strange."

"Strange? Strange how?"

"Well…" He plays the scale again, slowly and deliberately. "It started off like ours. Playing for Adam. Lark sang 'Halo' again."

"The whole way through?"

He nods. Bitter fingers twist my gut. "Then what happened?"

A pause. "Adam wanted her to sing by herself, like you did. But he told her to go into the isolation booth, that little room in the corner."

"He didn't ask me to do that." The fingers in my gut twist harder.

"He gave her the same music," Danny goes on.

"Lark can't sight-read," I say, smugly.

106

Danny nods. "Adam didn't care. He said he'd play it for her."

I frown, taking this in.

"She went into the booth," Danny continues, "and Adam went into the control room – along with Spinner – he didn't send me out this time. I think he forgot I was there." His fingers drum on the sides of the keyboard. "And I couldn't hear, but I could see." He pauses to look at me.

"You mean you could lip-read?"

He nods. "A bit. I think Adam must have played Lark the tune from the control room, because she started singing and Adam and Spinner were listening through headphones…" He hesitates, like he's afraid his next words will hurt me. "I saw Adam say something like "perfect", and a little red light came on."

"They recorded her." The monster in my gut grows claws.

Danny nods.

"Well, what's 'strange' about that?" I ask bitterly. "He recorded her because he thought she was great."

Danny shakes his head. "It was while she was singing … She was singing, but then she sort of staggered."

"Staggered?"

"Yeah. I went to check on her but Spinner got there first. He helped her out of the booth."

I shrug. "Spinner said something about it being hot in there." *Or Lark just did it for attention.* "She seemed totally fine afterwards. Did Adam say anything?"

"That's just it. He didn't seem bothered, or surprised." Danny's gaze drifts off. "How does Lark seem now?" The concern in his expression rankles me.

"She's fine, I told you." It comes out snappier than I mean it to. "She'll be here soon anyway, so you can see for yourself. Spinner's coming round at seven, to teach her how to DJ."

"Spinner's coming *here*?" Danny's shoulders stiffen. "Is that a good idea?"

"I know, right?" *I knew Danny would understand.* "They've been messaging each other. It's so unfair."

Danny frowns. "I didn't mean—"

"Ugh." I'm looking at my phone screen. It's twenty to seven already. "We don't have much time," I sigh. "We should make a start on my assignment."

"Sure. Right." Danny seems relieved. He turns the swivel chair round, so he's sitting directly opposite me. "OK, so … play me what you've got so far."

Our knees are touching.

I turn up the volume on my amp and move it closer. "Um … I don't have much worked out." My face grows warm. "I've been messing around with some chord progressions, and I, um … I quite like this…"

I clear my throat and start to play.

D minor. B flat major seventh. C major. A minor. I work through the sequence, picking arpeggios with my right hand.

Still touching… Should I move my legs? Leave them where they are? Danny doesn't seem too bothered. He leans

108

in, nose wrinkled, listening intently. Close enough that I can breathe his scent. I drink it in; a mix of earth and musk and woodsmoke.

"That's nice. I love that." His eyes meet mine. My right hand fumbles and I lose my rhythm. Danny sits back. "Sorry, I put you off. What about a melody? Are there meant to be lyrics?" His eyes flick to my notebook.

"Yeah, but like I said, nothing's working." I flush.

"No worries. Let's focus on the chords."

I start again.

"Wait." Danny leans forward again and reaches out, stopping my left hand on the frets. Rough fingertips brush my skin but his hand is warm. My heart starts beating madly in my chest. "Maybe…. move the B flat chord to second position?" He slides my hand gently up the fretboard, repositioning my fingers one by one. Our foreheads are almost touching. His breath is soft on my face. "How does that sound?"

I test out the sequence. "Mm, it's better." I smile. His eyes are like fiery autumn leaves. A tingling warmth creeps across my chest. The air seems to crackle as we look at one other. "You should take music, you know," I murmur, flustered. His face is so close… "You're better than anyone in my class."

"You're mumbling," Danny whispers. His eyes are on my mouth. Instinctively, I wet my lips.

The side door flies open and we jump apart.

"Sorry, am I interrupting?" Lark pokes her head into the

cavern. "It's nearly seven. Evan will be here any minute."

She bounces in without waiting for a response. In tiny shorts and a green tank top that hugs her curves, she looks even more stunning than usual, her golden locks rippling down her back in waves.

"Hey, handsome!" Lark ruffles Danny's hair and throws herself on to the sofa. "God, it's roasting in here. Has Wren been serenading you with love songs?"

Danny smiles and doesn't reply. I think – hope – he missed her comment; her face was turned away. Normally it bothers me when she forgets, but for once I'm grateful. There's no time to say anything anyway, because just at that moment, a car screeches noisily into the street. The engine cuts abruptly and a car door slams. A moment later there's a rap on the side door. Lark springs up to open it.

"Well, well, well. This is very cosy."

Spinner stands in the doorway, his headphones round his neck. He throws us a brisk salute. His ice-blue eyes scan Dad's makeshift music studio before coming to rest on Lark. "Not quite up to my usual standards, but I can work with it."

Lark blinks.

Spinner smiles. "I'll get my gear."

"I'll help." Danny jumps to his feet. I'm a little surprised, although I don't mind if he wants to hang around. I wouldn't trust my sister as far as I could throw her. Someone needs to keep an eye on Lark.

We follow the boys outside, to where a sporty black

BMW convertible is parked halfway up the kerb.

"Be careful with these." Spinner pulls a pair of speakers from the small back-seat space and passes one to me and one to Lark. "These monitors are state of the art. Try not to drop them, ladies." Lark raises an eyebrow, but Spinner ignores her, opening the boot. Nestled inside is a large black console with two turntables and a mixer. Danny leans in to lift them out, but Spinner holds up a hand and speaks loudly.

"I've got it. No offence, but these girls are precious. If they get damaged, they cost more than you could afford to replace."

He dumps a tangle of leads in Danny's hands instead.

"'*Girls*'?" Lark shakes her head. "Are you referring to your decks?"

"Don't be jealous," Spinner says with a wink. "It's not a good look on you. I learned on these babies. They're responsive to my touch."

Lark says nothing, lost for words.

We follow Spinner into the cavern, where he clears a space on Dad's workbench and starts setting up. Lark tries to help, but he fobs her off.

"It's cool, babe. I can do it. The set-up is pretty complicated. Your sister's the musician in the family, right?" He nods in my direction and I smother a smile. "Don't you worry about anything. Just relax."

Lark looks unhappy. She perches on the sofa next to Danny.

111

I wander over to Spinner. "So, how did you learn to DJ?"

"Pretty much taught myself." He bends to adjust the arm on one of the turntables. "Left home at fifteen. Family problems – you know. I was staying with a mate. His older brother had a set of decks and I used to watch him play. When he went off to college, he gave them to me, said I could keep them. He was a good guy. Shame his family kicked me out."

"Oh. That sounds … tough." I didn't know this about Spinner. I think about how lucky Lark and I are to have the cavern … and music lessons if we wanted them, our parents' support.

"I've moved around a lot." Spinner's expression hardens. "Learned to back myself, you get me? If I didn't, no one else would. School was a waste of time. The teachers were useless. They couldn't see my potential. Their minds were too closed, know what I mean?"

I nod, but I don't really understand.

"I got into boxing for a while…" He makes another trip to the car and comes back with a slim black record box. "Could have gone professional." He heaves the box on to the table, flexing the muscles in his biceps.

"Why didn't you?" I ask. Danny, leaning forward to follow the conversation, rolls his eyes.

Spinner runs a hand over his stubble. "I got scouted by a bunch of model agencies. They wanted me to move to London. Most of my exes are models." His eyes flick to Lark.

She blinks, inspecting her nails.

"You turned down London for Hamlington?" Danny says, incredulous.

"I turned down modelling for music," Spinner corrects. He stops fiddling with a cable to shoot a long, cool stare at Danny, and strokes the sleek black kit in front of him. "This is my calling. Spinner is on the rise."

Danny snorts, and I frown. OK, Spinner's a little arrogant, but why shouldn't he be? He's had a tough life and he's had to work hard. If things are on the up now, good for him. I shoot Danny a look that says *Behave*. Spinner is tight with Adam. If we wind him up, it could ruin our audition chances.

I smooth things over. "Sounds like your career is going well."

Spinner grins and stands up taller. "I knew you were a smart girl. Maybe I should teach *you* to DJ—"

"It's so hot in here," Lark interrupts. "Shall I get us something to drink? I think there might be beer, back at the house. What would you like?"

"Yeah, anything." Spinner waves a hand.

"I'll come with you," Danny offers as Lark jumps up.

My eyes narrow, watching them go off together. But, bonus track: now I've got Spinner to myself. Time to do some proper digging.

"So, when did you and Adam meet?"

Spinner thinks. "Beginning of March? He turned up at a gig. Said he'd just moved here and offered to mentor

113

me." He shrugs, mock-modest. "He said he could use talent like mine."

"*Mentor* you? What does that mean?"

"It means he's nurturing my talent."

"How?"

"I told you." Spinner looks me in the eye. "Adam's a generous guy. I get to use his studio, his gear. He's letting me stay with him, until I get a place of my own."

So that's who sleeps above the studio...

Spinner shrugs. "He believes in me. I already had a following, but Adam reckons it could be bigger. *Much* bigger. We're talking massive, yeah? We've been writing stuff together – Adam's guiding me. We're a great team."

"You played a track at Charlie's party." I lean forward. "Do you remember? Just before her accident. Was that one of yours?"

"Party?" Spinner flicks carelessly through his record box. "Oh yeah. We were trying something out."

We? I think back. Adam wasn't there. "What was the track called?"

He frowns. "It doesn't have a name. It's a … whaddya call it? A work in progress."

Lark breezes in with a four-pack of beers, Danny bringing glasses in her wake.

"You're an angel." Spinner takes the beer she offers him. Catching the crook of her elbow, he plants a kiss on her cheek. She seems surprised and her cheeks flush.

"Is it time for my lesson?" she asks.

"Go on then," Spinner says, lazily. "Choose a record. I'm all yours."

Lark throws me a look: *Bye-bye, Wren. Time to leave.* I glance at Danny, but he's staring at the decks.

"So how do you do this then?" he asks Spinner. "Is there a skill to it?"

Spinner snorts. "Well, sure. Not any idiot can do it." He's speaking slower as well as louder, and I cringe with second-hand embarrassment. "No offence, yeah, but you'd find it way too difficult." He taps his ear, like Danny could have possibly missed his meaning. "To be honest, it would take a *normal* person years to become half as good as me."

My mouth falls open. Danny is very still. I expect Lark to say something but she seems to have tuned out the whole exchange, focused as she is on flicking through Spinner's record box. She turns round.

"What?"

I put my hand on Danny's arm. "Let's go."

"Hey, there's no point being modest." Somehow, Spinner has misread the situation. "Modesty gets you nowhere. I speak as I find. Don't fear the truth. When you're good at something you should own it. Adam says this thing: 'It's our duty to use our gifts to help others.' That's what we're doing. We're building a platform, to share my gift with the masses." He laughs. "And if it happens to make me rich and famous? Oh dear, what a shame."

"Danny…" I pull at his sleeve.

"It's OK." He shakes me off, eyes still fixed on Spinner. "I want to stay."

"Of course you do." Spinner slugs his beer. "You're getting a Spinner masterclass for free." He beckons Lark over. "Found a track you like?"

"This one?"

She passes him a record, smiling when he nods. He steers her into place beside him and slips the vinyl from its sleeve. "Watch and learn."

He lays the record on the left turntable and sets it spinning. Then he takes the little arm with the needle mounted in its head, and drops it deftly into a vinyl groove. A blasting dance track fills the studio. I jump and Danny winces, quickly adjusting his hearing aids.

Spinner grins. "Now we find a mix."

Expertly, he cues up a second record on the right turntable, headphones hanging off one ear. "I need to hear both tracks at the same time." Satisfied with the mix, he holds the second disc still. As the first track comes to an end, he lets the second turntable spin and slides the cross-fader, taking the new track in and the old one out.

"See?" Spinner glances at Lark.

She nods, watching closely.

"Aww. You're cute when you're concentrating." Her face breaks into a smile. "The trick is learning to read the audience. You have to give them what they want – but not right away."

"Basic psychology," Lark murmurs.

"Right." Spinner raises an eyebrow. "You're smarter than you look."

I blink, and look at Danny. Bizarrely, Lark seems pleased.

"You have to tease people, build their expectations, make them wait. That's what Adam says. '*Until they lose their tiny minds*.'"

She's nodding again. "Can I try?"

"Be my guest, princess." Positioning her body in front of his, Spinner lifts his headphones off his own ears and places them over hers, taking longer than necessary to adjust their position. Lark seems unbothered, swaying to the track. "Mix it with this one." Spinner plucks another record from its sleeve and Lark drops it on to the turntable with a clatter.

"*Careful!*" Spinner reins his temper quickly back in. "It's fine. Cue it up, slowly. You need a steady hand when you drop the needle."

"Like this?" Lark lifts the arm of the turntable by the handle.

"That's it. Nice and slow. Don't scratch the vinyl."

"I'm scared!" she squeals. "When do I drop it down?"

"Don't be scared. I'll help you." Spinner moves closer, his head next to Lark's. Closing one hand over hers, he brings the needle to a hover over the spinning grooves. "Now."

The turntable arm jerks. It slips out of Lark's hand and the needle drops heavily, skittering across the record.

"Ouch!" She jumps back, her finger in her mouth.

"You broke the needle," Spinner growls.

"It broke me!" Lark cries. "Look, I'm bleeding!" She holds her finger aloft and I squint. It's the faintest of scratches; a miniscule bubble of blood.

"Poor baby." Spinner smiles slowly. Taking her hand, he lifts it to his face. "Want Spinner to kiss it better?"

I wait for the torrent of sass, but it doesn't come.

Lark giggles as he puts her finger to his mouth.

10

I brush my teeth too hard and make my gum bleed. The bright red droplets on the cold, white porcelain immediately remind me of Lark pricking her finger on the record needle, and her helpless-maiden act last night.

Fury fizzles in my gut.

She was so shameless – flirting with Spinner to get herself into Adam's good books. She wasn't interested in him before.

I rinse my mouth, but the salty taste still lingers. *Spinner.* I'm starting to see why Danny doesn't trust him. His charisma is undeniable, but he's such a bag of contradictions – a weird mixture of pent-up resentment and fervent self-belief. He looks like a powerful Greek god, but the things he says and does make him seem like an insecure little boy.

I cringe, remembering how he spoke to Danny. The way he implied that Danny could never DJ – that Danny's not *normal*, whatever "normal" means. It's ignorance, that's all. Spinner doesn't know Danny. If he did, he'd never have made those comments. He didn't seem to realize what he was saying, so I doubt he actually meant to cause offence. Adam believes in Spinner and Adam is a nice guy – a generous man, an intelligent man, *choosy* about the people he works with. Adam must see something worthwhile in Spinner to go to the effort of nurturing his career. And Danny did claim that he was fine...

I sigh at myself in the mirror. I'm probably getting worked up over nothing.

By the time I need to leave to catch the bus, Lark still hasn't surfaced and I don't bother waiting. I stand at the bus stop, grumbling at the lack of shade, and scroll social media on my phone. Someone in my history class has invited me to join a new group chat called "Memories of Mia". At least half the sixth form has joined already, judging by the list of members.

I hesitate.

It feels wrong to accept. I didn't know Mia, and the last thing I want is to be a tourist, gawping crassly at someone else's grief. But I'm worried that the rest of the group will see if I decline and judge me as rude or disrespectful.

As soon as I accept the invitation I regret it. Scrolling down through the so-called memories, I see that the chat has already splintered into two distinct camps: people who genuinely knew Mia in one; horrible, trouble-stirring trolls in the other.

KeeleyS

Mia was my best friend in primary. RIP 4eva xox

Eliza123

miss you so much mia

FlossF

Still remember how we rocked Battle of the Bands 🖤

TamS

you were so talented. drugs waste lives 🙁

RichW

Mia – amazing bass player, awesome vocalist 😁

HAM666

Mia Hall was nothing but a skanky drug addict

SpiderSTAN

They used to drown witches just sayin

I feel ill. A longer message makes me pause:

LilyM

I actually knew Mia, unlike some people here. Mia had her challenges but she was NOT an addict. When the autopsy report comes back, you'll see. STOP with the gossip and leave the investigating to the police. People spreading lies should be ashamed.

I mute the chat, feeling grubby.

At lunchtime, I go to the canteen, trying not to inhale the gross scent of overcooked carrots and keeping an eye out for Danny. I drop my bag on the stool next to me, saving him a place at our usual table. The rest of the music gang are here already. They're not as hyper as yesterday; in fact they're mostly engrossed in their phones and there's none of the usual banter – no whinging about assignments, complaining about orchestra practice, or comparing Spotify discoveries.

Huh. *Strange*.

"Hi, guys."

Nobody answers me. They don't even bother to look up. I guess it's stuffy; the air is pretty close. Ruby is staring at her screen, earbuds in, drumming rhythmically on the table; Isaac has one arm slung round the back of her chair, nodding along to some unheard track; Meena is scrolling with a faraway look on her face; while Jiv and Alex are sitting with their heads pressed together, sharing headphones, one earbud each.

"What's everyone doing?" I pull my stool up next to Ruby.

She flinches. "Wren! I didn't see you."

"What's going on?"

"Oh." She blinks. "We're just looking at the app."

"App?"

"The app for Enrapture."

The word jolts something inside me. "Enrapture has an app?" I snatch up my phone. A quick search and I've found it. The icon is a gold eye on a swirling rainbow cloud. My foot taps impatiently as I wait for it to download. When it finally does, my fingers race to open it. The screen erupts in a kaleidoscope of colour.

ARE YOU READY FOR A NEW DAWN? ENTER THE STATE OF ENRAPTURE

"Press enter," Ruby urges, but I'm already doing it.

A chord chimes. I feel it in my bones.

The sound has an effect on the rest of the group too. Chins lift, eyes squint up at me.

"Wren, hey. You got the app."

I nod.

"Jiv and I just checked, but they still haven't confirmed the line-up," Alex says.

"Who cares?" Jiv laughs. "We're still going, right? I mean, it's not Glastonbury, but it's the closest thing Hamlington is gonna get."

"Enrapture could be bigger than Glastonbury one day," Meena murmurs, her eyes wide.

Ruby whoops. "Can you imagine? Hamlington! Music capital of the world!"

There's a hysterical edge to their laughter which I put down to heat and excitement. The buzz is contagious; it's impossible not to join in. Only Isaac is silent, smiling enigmatically at his phone.

"It's only one night," Alex complains. "Why is it only one night?"

"Who do you think the headliner will be?"

There's a flurry of suggestions, from the spectacular to the bizarre. Suddenly everyone's talking over one another, super animated.

"I hope it's someone good," Meena says.

"It bet it won't be." That's Jiv.

"Why do you say that?" Ruby demands.

"Because, er, this is Hamlington?"

"So?" Meena challenges. "It depends what they're getting paid."

"There's definitely big money involved." Alex taps his phone, fidgety. "The tickets all sold out, right? And loads of businesses have agreed sponsorship deals." He shows his screen to Jiv. "Look. Jensen-Scott Enterprises is one of them – that's Charlie's dad's company. He's loaded."

"Who is the promoter?" Ruby asks.

I freeze, wondering if I should reply. How much am I supposed to know? Spinner's words echo in my ears … *Adam is a private guy, yeah?* I'm saved from deciding when Isaac speaks up:

"Some American music producer, apparently. His identity isn't public knowledge, but he's worked with loads of artists – major household names. He just moved to England and lives somewhere outside Hamlington. That's what I heard."

"Why would anyone move here?" Jiv mutters.

Alex rounds on Isaac. "How do you know?"

"I follow Spinner." Isaac makes a gesture with his hand but nobody else seems to notice. "It was on his socials." A smile creeps slowly across his face. He waits a beat. "So … Spinner is confirmed to play. The news officially dropped –" he checks – "five minutes ago."

"For real?"

"You're kidding."

"No. Way."

I stare in surprise – but not so much at the news that Spinner is playing. He's friends with Adam, I guess it was to be expected. I'm more astonished by my friends. They seem to be losing their minds. I had no idea they were such big Spinner fans. A few months ago he was barely on their radar.

"You'd better not be winding us up," Alex says to Isaac.

"Nope." Isaac smiles again. "Spinner speaks the truth."

It's an odd thing to say, but no one questions it.

"Oh. My. God!" Ruby clutches Meena's arm. "This is amazing. I don't know how I missed the notification. I've been following Spinner for weeks."

"I know!" Meena squeals. "I follow him too!"

"You do?" I ask her.

She looks at me, strangely. "Of course. Isaac got us into him."

I sit there, silent. They're all glued to their socials again, earbuds in and faces rapt.

"Enrapture will be more than a music festival," Isaac intones. His voice sounds oddly robotic. I don't think I've ever heard him speak so much in the whole time we've been in sixth form. We couldn't believe it when he got together with Ruby. She's so loud and *out there*, he always seemed so shy. "It's going to be a life-changing experience," he declares.

"God, I hope so," mutters Jiv.

"Hey, look at this!" Ruby interrupts. "This is on the app. Read the section called 'Our Mission'."

Obediently, we tap in sync. The moment the page opens, a pulsing beat begins to play. *The same one from the ticket site*, I think vaguely. I find myself nodding along.

There are six lines of text on the screen.

The world is broken.
You're lost and alone,
Searching for something to believe.
Open your mind.
Return to simpler times.
At ENRAPTURE, we will heal.

Everyone has fallen quiet.

Jiv is the first to come round. He blinks slowly. "OK, I'm sold."

"Me too." The beat is still pulsing in the air and Alex's leg jiggles as he speaks. "It's true, the world is going to shit. The news is always depressing, everything's messed up. Sometimes I worry about the future. Like, is there actually anything to look forward to…?"

"Or anywhere to belong…" Ruby's fingers drum the table.

"It sounds so nice," Meena says, nodding vigorously, her eyes unusually bright, "going back to simpler times…"

I smile and nod along.

"Or … it *could* be a load of horseshit," a voice rumbles in my ear.

Danny is reading over my shoulder. "Don't fall for the hype, Wren." Before I can stop him, he snatches my phone from my hand and shuts the app down.

The beat stops abruptly.

I blink up at him. "Someone's in a good mood."

He raises an eyebrow in reply.

Waving goodbye to the others, I join Danny in the queue for the snack bar outside. He's hungry, that's all. *Hangry.* Once he's fed his sausage roll addiction, no doubt he'll snap out of … whatever it is that's bothering him.

It's cooler in the courtyard and quieter too, away from the clattering noise of the canteen. Danny turns to look at me. "Wren, I'm not joking. Don't you think something feels off? Nobody knows anything about this festival, but it's all anyone's talking about. Just now, in biology, some kid mentioned Spinner, said he's been confirmed to play." His eyes narrow and he looks into the distance. "The reaction it got – like it was the announcement of the century. Like Spinner's some kind of god."

"Ruby and the others, they all like him too," I say. "I knew he was popular, but … even my mum's heard of him."

"The guy is everywhere." Danny shakes his head. "He wasn't joking last night when he said he was 'on the rise'."

I'm quiet as I consider. "Spinner's… complicated," I say finally. "I mean, yes, he's a little arrogant, but I don't think he's all bad." I shrug. "It's not really my kind of music."

"It's not his music that bothers me…"

Danny's voice trails off. I follow his gaze. On the other side of the courtyard, a group of year nine boys are hanging around outside the maths block. As the lower school bell rings they part company, signing off from one another with a salute. Danny shakes his head.

"It's just a gimmick, the salute thing," I say, drawing Danny's attention back to me. Spinner's remarks must have hurt him more than he let on. "It's harmless. Just a silly thing to – I dunno, to show who you're into, or whatever. Like wearing a badge, or a band T-shirt." Ruby's comment suddenly springs to mind. "To show that you belong."

"'*Belong*'? Belong to what?" Danny purses his lips. We reach the front of the snack bar queue and he pays for his sausage roll, biting it so savagely anyone would think it had personally insulted him. "Spinner's influential, Wren. People listen to him. He's got thousands and thousands of followers."

"He's good at self-promotion. So?" I walk side-on so that Danny can see my face, leading the way across the playing field towards our favourite bench.

"It's not the self-promotion. It's the rest of his content." Danny's forehead knots and his eyes cloud over, dark and serious. "You should check it out, Wren. Lark is your *sister*."

I slow to a halt. It's the look on Danny's face. He's genuinely rattled, genuinely concerned.

About Lark.

And then I think.

The way he smiled at her when we were busking. The way he asked about her after the audition. The way his face lights up like a beacon every time she walks into the room.

He's jealous of Spinner.

I stare at the ground, at the cracked, sun-baked earth. My words have dried up too.

Danny likes Lark. He likes her. It all makes sense.

"Wren, are you OK?"

I try to speak, but I'm too hot, I'm finding it hard to breathe. *I think, deep down, I've always known.* I've just been in denial.

This explains everything – the way he's always watching her, defending her, looking out for her. Making excuses for her behaviour and telling me off for mine, trying to persuade me to be nicer to her. It even explains the awkward moments the two of us keep having, where he seems to be on the verge of telling me something. And it definitely explains his instant dislike of Spinner and Enrapture.

"Wren?"

"I ... um ... I need to get a book from the library," I croak.

I rush back across the playing field, fighting tears.

I'm in love with Danny.

But Danny's in love with Lark.

11

As soon as the bell rings I stomp home over the meadows, not bothering to say goodbye to anyone. The heat is stifling and I can't face the school bus and its lingering, stale smell of sweat. Maybe some fresh air will clear my head.

Danny's in love with Lark.

The thought swirls round and round my head, taunting me. I stumble along the path without paying attention, stamping down bright feathery dandelions and crushing delicate globes of clover beneath my heel. My sister is always the chosen one – the one who gets everything handed to her on a plate, without any effort at all. Things she doesn't deserve. Things she doesn't even want. I know she doesn't do it on purpose, but if she really cared about Danny she wouldn't be so thoughtless around him, so careless of his needs.

I sigh. Yet again, Lark breezes through life, winning everything, while I'm the one who gets hurt. Danny only sees me as his friend. He wants to cut any association with Spinner and he'll ruin our chances of playing at Enrapture because of a pointless, unrequited crush.

I take a shortcut through the wood, desperately trying not to cry. *I don't even know why I'm surprised.* Everyone likes Lark, especially guys – she's never had any problems there. And Danny's known her for ever; as long as he's known me. The three of us used to play together all the time, jumping through the sprinkler in our garden or riding our bikes around the estate – until Lark went off to secondary school, leaving Danny and me behind in year six.

Poor Danny. Stuck with the wrong sister. Worshipping the other from afar.

"Wren! Slow down. Wait up!"

I turn to see Danny coming towards me, heaving his bike clumsily over the lumpy ground. Scrubbing my eyes with my sleeve, reluctantly I slow down.

"Why did you race off?"

I shrug. "Thought you were cycling. And don't you have a hospital appointment?" I'm improvising, flustered and uncomfortable.

"It's tomorrow. In London. We're going down tonight."

"*London?*" I didn't know. "Oh. Right."

132

I wait, but Danny doesn't elaborate and we walk side by side without speaking. *Another awkward silence.* Except this time it feels more like a gaping chasm between us and I don't how to close it.

Eventually he clears his throat. "Look, I'm sorry I upset you. I know how much Enrapture means to you. I just think Lark should know who she's getting involved with…"

My lips tighten. *Here we go again.*

"And Adam's kind of weird too. With his creepy art and funky robes…"

If he's trying to make me laugh, it isn't working. I can feel myself getting cross.

"There's just something odd about him," Danny persists, "don't you think?"

That does it. "No." I stop walking. "I don't think so. He's American, he's rich. He's not like anybody we've ever met. That doesn't make him weird." I root in my bag and pull out my phone. "He's a genuine music producer. I can prove it." I scroll through my photo reel looking for the picture I took in the bathroom, the wall of platinum discs. I turn my screen round to show Danny. "There. I've sent it to you. See for yourself."

Danny barely glances at the photo.

I sigh, hot and bothered. "Adam's … what's that word? A philanthropist. He's financing a huge music festival. It's going to be amazing for Hamlington. He could squirrel all his money away, keep it for himself, but instead he's investing it here, supporting local artists. He's mentoring Spinner and his career is taking off. What else do you need, Danny? He's a good guy."

I pick up the pace again, striding ahead.

"Wren, I know you want this –" Danny has to jog to catch me up – "and you deserve it. But don't let it stop you—"

I spin round. "Stop me what?"

"From seeing red flags."

"'*Red flags*'?" The sun beats down on me, relentless. I'm losing patience. "What *red flags*?"

Danny looks down. His hair falls into his face.

"What?" I repeat.

He lifts his chin. "Check your email. You're on the Pet Sounds mailing list, right? They sent something last week. It went into my junk mail so I only saw it this afternoon. It's about Enrapture and the emerging artists' stage."

"So?"

Danny takes a deep breath. "The stage is sponsored by Hamlington Music Trust. They're running a competition. The artist with the best original song will get a development grant and fully funded place at a summer music school."

"You're joking!" My mouth has fallen open. Then I frown. "Wait. Best *original* song?"

Danny is silent.

"I don't get it. What's the issue?"

His chestnut eyes meet mine. "Wren, the Trust are selecting the musicians. *They're* the ones programming the

134

stage, not Adam. Official auditions were last night, in the town hall. *Last night*," he repeats. "When we were hanging out with Spinner."

I stare as Danny's words sink in. "Then what did we audition for?"

"The rock star returns."

Lark is lying on the sofa watching TV when I get in. For some reason, she's cocooned in a blanket, even though it's suffocatingly hot. As she hoists herself up on to her elbows, I notice she's still in pyjamas.

"You didn't go to college?"

"I'm on study leave now, remember?" She smiles mistily. "I'm revising at home."

"Oh yeah. Looks like you're working really hard." I raise an eyebrow. The screen is paused and I recognize the movie she's watching: *Frozen*. An ethereal Elsa is caught mid-spell, her crystalline ice palace just starting to bloom. God, we used to love that film so much. We'd spend every weekend acting out the scenes. Naturally, Lark was Elsa and I was Anna, while poor Danny ran himself ragged playing all the other characters, from evil Prince Hans to good-guy Kristoff – even Olaf the snowman and Sven. I smile at the memory. He did make a very cute reindeer.

The scent of roses hits my nostrils and I turn to see an enormous bouquet spilling out of a vase on the table, dwarfing everything else around.

"Aren't they gorgeous? Evan sent them this morning,"

Lark's cheeks flush pink. "But never mind that." Her lips purse mischievously. "Didn't you hear what I said?"

I re-wind... She called me "*Rock Star*". Not Trog.

"You've heard from Adam!" Any doubts about our audition are instantly cast from my mind.

"I *may* have received an email this afternoon..." Lark throws off the blanket and stretches like a cat. Her eyes flick to her phone resting on the edge of the coffee table.

I move but she pounces. "Shall I read it to you?"

"I'd rather read it myself." I don't know whether to trust her. This could be a wind-up. She could be raising my hopes for her own petty entertainment before dashing them on the rocks.

"No can do, little sister. The email was sent to me." Lark twists a glistening strand of hair. "We should probably get Danny here. Do you want to message him or shall I?"

"He's gone to London."

"When will he be back? Tomorrow? It can wait another day..."

"*Lark!*" I launch myself at her.

Her shouts of protest bring Mum running. "Wren! I was on the phone to Seb. What's going on?"

"Lark's heard from Adam about the auditions, but she won't tell me what he said!"

I can hear myself whining and I hate myself for it. I sound more like seven than seventeen.

Lark rolls her eyes. "Oh, for god's sake, Wren. Don't be so dramatic! I was messing around. Of course I'll tell you.

Let me dig out the email." She takes her time, scrolling on her phone. I have to dig my nails into my fists to stop myself from strangling her. Mum hovers, tense.

"OK, here it is." Lark clears her throat.

Butterflies flutter in my belly. As she reads, I picture Adam in his long, priest-like robes, and hear his soft, mellow voice.

"*Dear Lark, I want to thank you for coming to audition for me last weekend. It was a pleasure to meet you, your sister and your sister's friend. It's clear that you come from a musical family.*"

Mum smiles.

"*I promised to let you know my decision, and here it is. I would be delighted to invite…*" Lark pauses for effect and I almost stop breathing. "*… Daniel Akintola and Wren Mackenzie to appear at Enrapture on June twenty-first, performing on the emerging artists' stage.*"

Lark stops.

"*Me?*" I'm struggling to form words. "Me and Danny? He picked us? Are you sure?"

Lark nods, her expression hard to read.

"Wren!" Mum resembles a goldfish, her mouth opening and closing. "This is… Wow! I can't believe it. What an achievement!" She smothers me in a hug. "I'm so proud of you. Wait until your dad hears!" She looks genuinely stunned, and I can't say I blame her. I'm astonished too.

"Yeah, congratulations, Wren."

I break free of Mum's embrace. Lark looks solemn and small on the sofa, her knees hugged into her chest. My delight abruptly dies. This is what I wanted – for me to be chosen, just once, instead of her – but it's not quite as satisfying as I expected.

Mum rushes to Lark's side. "Oh, sweetheart, I'm sorry. Auditions are brutal. They're so subjective. You must be disappointed."

She shakes her head. "I'm fine, honestly. Wren deserves this."

"Thanks." I blink. She's being so nice about it. "Are you *sure* you don't mind?"

"I'm sure." The corners of her mouth twitch. "I didn't finish reading. Do you want to hear the rest?" She settles back into the sofa. "OK. The next bit is details … someone will email through your passes the day before the festival, blah blah blah…" She pauses.

"Go on."

Lark smiles and becomes Adam again:

"My dear Lark, I expect you were hoping to perform on the same stage as your sister. However, I wonder if you will consider a slightly different opportunity. You have a unique vocal talent, which could, in my opinion, be remarkable, with nurturing and guidance. As you may know, I have been mentoring Evan Wheeler for some time, and his career is on an exciting trajectory. I would now like to offer my services as a mentor to you. If you are amenable, our work together would commence immediately, and, should our collaboration prove fruitful, there may be an opportunity for you to perform at Enrapture as a guest vocalist for Spinner, during his set. Please let me know if you accept, which I

hope you will. I can then arrange for our sessions to begin. Yours in anticipation, Adam Webb."

"Gosh!" Mum looks completely shell-shocked. "Let me get this straight. Wren is performing at the festival with Danny, and this Adam person wants to mentor you?"

"Yes!" Lark shrieks, bouncing up and down.

"Wow." I lean against the wall, speechless. My mouth hasn't caught up with my brain. It does make total sense that Adam would want to mentor Lark. Her voice is unbelievable, that's never been in doubt. Suddenly Danny's account of her audition makes sense. That's why Adam recorded her. As for my audition… Well, Danny and I have lucked out. We've managed to bypass the official selection process and make the final cut. So what if it was a little *unorthodox*? Who's going to argue with Adam? Adam is the promoter. Adam is the boss.

I grin. It's a good outcome – a great one! The main thing is, I'm going. *I'm going to Enrapture!*

My head buzzes and I almost swoon. I'll be up on stage, playing my guitar in front of a real, live audience. And if Lark ends up singing backing vocals for Spinner? That's just karaoke, performing to a track.

"Well done," I tell my sister, and I mean it. She beams.

Mum laughs with relief. "You know, I was so worried this would be another thing to come between you two. But as long as you're both happy, I'm happy." She turns to Lark. "Your exams, though – they come first. You've still got two left. And at some point I want to meet this Adam

Webb and have a proper talk about his plans for you." She breaks into a smile. "It's so exciting! June the twenty-first is perfect timing. We're back from our tour on the twentieth. We'll be able to see you both perform!" She pulls us both into a hug like we're little kids again.

Lark's eyes meet mine over Mum's head.

"Happy?" she mouths, her eyes dancing.

"Happy," I mouth, smiling back.

12

The celebrations continue into dinner. Dad cooks his special chilli while Mum runs to the shop to get a cheeky bottle of bubbly. I bask in the glow of their pride like a cat on a sunny garden wall. Lark is looking at her phone. I glance sidelong at her. She seems strangely blasé about Adam's news, but then I guess she's used to being chosen.

It's a brand-new feeling for me.

At college, I'm walking on air. Suddenly I'm an insider instead of an outsider – a legitimate part of festival fever – and it feels amazing. When I tell the music gang my news, they seem genuinely thrilled. Jiv and Alex have also got a slot, and so has some band in the upper sixth. When Jiv frowns and asks why I wasn't at the town hall auditions, I hesitate for a second, wondering whether to mention Adam. But in the end I simply say that Spinner scouted me. Jiv's eyes widen, then he nods and says, "Truth," so, luckily, it doesn't seem like a big deal.

At lunch, Ruby, Meena and I spend the entire time browsing on the Enrapture app. Somehow an hour passes in five minutes, even though there's barely any content there. We're so absorbed we lose track of time and end up being twenty minutes late for last period. It earns us an after-school detention but I'm too hyped to care. Adrenaline pulses through my veins, pumping in time to the app's steady background beat. I seem to hear the sound everywhere, even when my app is closed, and although I know it's just the sound of other people's phones, or the heat messing with my mind, it punctuates my every word and thought, making it difficult to concentrate. The only thing I can think of is Enrapture.

It feels like it's tattooed on my brain.

After detention, I wander home in a daze, desperate to see Danny and tell him the news. *When will he be back from London?*

I turn into our estate, and the sight of his empty driveway makes me sigh. The urge to message him is ridiculous, but somehow I manage to resist. This is the kind of news that needs to be delivered in person. I want to see his face when I tell him. I know he's had doubts, but I also know his feelings about Lark are colouring his feelings about Spinner. When it comes to Adam and Enrapture, everything adds up. The jigsaw pieces slot together perfectly. When Danny hears we've been chosen, he'll cast his doubts aside.

At seven, the growl of Debs' car pulling on to next door's driveway makes me jump to my feet and throw on my shoes. I give Danny ten minutes to get inside before I can't wait any longer.

"Wren, love! Come in." Debs hugs me as though I'm her long-lost child, not the girl next door she's known for years. "Danny's in the kitchen. Tayo warmed something up. There's plenty if you want to help yourself."

I breathe in the delicious aromatic smell of onion, tomatoes and spices.

"Amazing, thanks."

I find Danny sitting at the kitchen table. He has his back to me and next to him is an untouched bowl of chicken stew and jollof rice. He's watching some mindless reality show with the sound down and the captions on.

"Hey."

He doesn't turn round so I put a hand on his arm. He jumps. "Wren. You scared me."

"Sorry."

"It's OK." He plasters on a smile. I notice it doesn't reach his eyes.

O-kay… Another awkward pause. I push it aside and dive in.

"Guess what? Lark got an email. We did it. We're playing at Enrapture!" My body thrums with pleasure and glee spreads across my face like an oil slick. I look at Danny, waiting for his expression to mirror mine.

His shoulders stiffen. "We got in?"

"Yes!" I move to hug him but, at the last second, I pull back – I'm not sure why. We've always hugged, we do it all the time. I've never second-guessed it before.

"Well done, Wren," he says, finally.

I frown. "What do you mean? It was both of us."

"You sang for Adam," he says softly.

I open my mouth to argue, but he gets in first. "How did Lark take the news?"

My glee takes another nosedive. Sliding into the seat opposite him, I relay the details from the email: how Adam wants to mentor Lark and how there's a chance she might be a guest singer during Spinner's set. "She's happy," I say. "Everything's worked out perfectly." I search for the spark in his eyes.

"You didn't look, did you?" Danny's voice is flat.

"Look at what?" I'm lost.

"At Spinner's socials. The things he posts online." He reaches for his phone and scrolls, tight-lipped. Finally he hands the phone to me.

I stare at the dense grid of images. Most of them are close-ups of Spinner. He's fond of posing for moody selfies, his god-like features strategically lit so that he looks more like a Renaissance painting than a nineteen-year-old boy.

Lots of photos have been taken in the gym and feature Spinner pounding a punchbag or lifting a tower of weights. The sight of his sculpted bare torso and glistening six-pack makes me blush. And then there are the nightclub shots, with Spinner looking every inch the superstar DJ on the podium underneath the lights. One of these images accompanies his announcement about Enrapture. The post has tens of thousands of likes. The profile picture on Spinner's account is an after-party outtake; he's chilling in some lounge bar with an anonymous girl on his lap. Her face is obscured by Spinner's hand, raised in that trademark salute.

Danny is waiting for my reaction. I pass his phone back, pulling a face.

I get why these pictures wind him up. Danny is the polar opposite of Spinner – equally talented and attractive, but inherently allergic to posturing and showing off. Idly, I wonder if Lark has seen Spinner's socials. I suppose she must have – who doesn't online-stalk their crush? Then, I frown. The Lark I know didn't have a crush on Spinner. The Lark I know would have laughed at these images.

Has she really changed that much?

Danny pushes the phone back to me. "Read the captions."

I click on an image to humour him. I notice there's a track embedded – one of Spinner's, I presume – and I unmute Danny's phone to hear it.

I startle as the chord rings out. Danny raises an eyebrow,

but I can't help it. I've been hearing this all day: a beat pulsing steadily over a slow and sinewy bass.

"It's the music from the Enrapture app," I explain. "It must be sampled from one of Spinner's tracks."

Danny's nose wrinkles, trying to tune in. "So what?" He taps the screen impatiently. "Never mind the music. Read what he says."

I try, but it's difficult to concentrate. The music is messing with my brain. It's tinny and faint and coming out of a phone speaker, but something about it is addictive. My leg jiggles and my head nods.

I force myself to focus.

The caption for the image is long – a stream-of-consciousness rambling similar to Spinner's monologue the other night. It starts with how difficult his life has been, the struggles he's had to overcome, then it moves on to him bragging about his talent and his career. A meandering section follows and I skim that quickly – something about being strong, successful, a *real man*. To be honest, I'm not taking it in. It's hot in the kitchen from Tayo's cooking and my head feels foggy and unfocused. I skip to the end of the caption. There's a hashtag: *#SpinningTheTruth*.

"Do you see what he's saying?" Danny jabs the screen. "He reckons he's some kind of role model. That if you learn from Spinner, you could be rich and powerful too. He's offering a load of extra content for anyone who subscribes to his channel – tips and tricks for 'taking back power', whatever that's supposed to mean." Danny scowls. "And it's all packaged up like some big 'truth'. No one is calling him out on it. Look at the comments. His followers lap it up – even the girls." He shakes his head.

"I'm not sure…" My mind feels dull. I need time to digest this and it's hard to think clearly with that track looping over and over…

"Wren!" Danny barks and I jump. He looks so serious I almost want to cry. I miss his sunshine smile, so to bring it back, I say what I know he wants to hear.

"I'll talk to Lark."

The relief on his face is instant. "You promise?"

"I promise."

He closes Spinner's socials. Abruptly, the track cuts out.

I shake my head, trying to recapture my good mood. "Look, let's forget about Spinner. *We* don't have to work with him. We don't need to see him at all. We've got our own set to think about." I pause, waiting for Danny to react. *Nothing?* "We should make a rehearsal plan. Do you think we need a name? We should probably have a name…"

I'm rambling, but I can't help it. *Why doesn't he say something? Why won't he look at me?* "What's the matter? I said I'd talk to Lark."

He stares at his untouched meal.

"Hello?" I peer under his hair, wriggling into his sightline, so that he has no choice but to face me.

"I don't want to do it," he mutters.

"What?"

"The gig. I'm sorry."

I blink. I can't believe what I'm hearing.

He shifts. "I … I think you should do it by yourself."

"*By myself*?"

"I'll only let you down." He looks away.

Let me down?

I touch his cheek, turning his face back towards mine. "Why would you think that? Bloody hell, Danny. You know you're better than me."

And you have to work fifty times harder.

He shrugs. "Embarrass you, then."

I take this in. "Wait. Is this about those idiots when we were busking? And the things that Spinner said?" When he doesn't answer, I reach across the table. "Talk to me. Where is this coming from?"

Silence.

Then my eyes land on something; a glossy leaflet, sitting on top of a pile of papers on the table. On the front is a photo of a teenage boy laughing with his friends. The boy's face is in profile and on the side of his head, embedded in his hair, is a small disc, like a flat pebble. A wire links the disc to a device behind his ear. I pull the leaflet towards me and open it. Words like *life-changing* and *transformational* and *unbelievable* jump out.

"What's this?"

Danny draws a breath. "An implant. A cochlear implant. We went to see a specialist." His voice is small. "My parents want me to consider it. I think they think it will fix me."

"'*Fix*' you?" I don't like the word and what it implies.

148

"Wren, you know I miss things. I get stuff wrong and make mistakes." He says it tonelessly. "It's true. An implant could help."

"'But'…?" I can hear it coming.

He sighs. "It's not that simple. It would mean surgery." He rubs his eyes. "And it's different to a hearing aid. An implant doesn't amplify sound, it stimulates the nerve and sends signals to your brain. I'd have to start over, relearning how to hear."

Relearning how to hear. Put like that, it sounds huge. Then I think of how resilient Danny is, how adaptable he has to be, especially with music.

"Would it help you play guitar?"

He shrugs. "Maybe, maybe not. Sound is … different with an implant. *Music* sounds different. Maybe too different. It's a risk…" He lets this hang. "Music is part of who I am – I couldn't lose that. And…" He looks at me. "It's probably hard to understand. Being deaf is part of who I am now too. The last few years have been tough, but … I dunno…" He swallows. "I was starting to like who I am."

"I like who you are too." The words fall out of my mouth before I can stop them.

Danny blinks.

"I mean…" My cheeks burn. "You know what I mean." There's a pause. Danny says nothing. Inside, I'm dying.

I try again. "It doesn't matter what other people think," I say, trying to cover up my embarrassment. "That's their problem, not yours."

Danny's eyes grow huge and shiny. "I just feel like everyone feels sorry for me. Or else they expect me to mess up. And if I do, it will prove them right." He looks so miserable, all I want to do is throw my arms round him, but … I don't know if I should.

"I can't get up on stage," he says. "Not in front of loads of people. Busking in The Square was bad enough. I don't mind playing guitar at home, or even in the cavern with you. But I'm not going to play at *Enrapture*." He spits out the name with contempt.

My eyes narrow. "And this has nothing do with Lark?"

"Lark?" Danny stares at me, bewildered. "No, of course not!"

I'm quiet, not sure what to believe.

"I don't want to do it without you," I say eventually.

"Well, you have to." He turns away and I know what that means. He won't talk about it any further. Whatever the real reason behind his decision, that's the end of it.

Danny won't play at Enrapture. His mind is made up.

13

Half term arrives the following week, and I spend it playing emotional tug-of-war. Every morning I wake full of glee about playing at Enrapture, then five minutes later I remember that Danny won't do it with me and my sunny mood deflates. It kills me to think he cares so much about other people's opinions – that's not the Danny I know.

What's the real reason he won't play?

Whatever it is, one thing is for sure: music-making has climbed to the top of the agenda for the Mackenzie family. Mum and Dad are barely home. With their flight to Bergen only a week away, they're constantly in the studio rehearsing. At least it leaves the cavern free for me. I'm down there every spare minute I get. Enrapture is in a mere three weeks and, Danny or no Danny, I need to practise.

And then, of course, Adam wants to begin his work with Lark.

I find her one evening in the bathroom, leaning over the sink, applying smooth strokes of eyeliner to her eyelids in dark, precise flicks. The evening sun slices sharply through the slatted blind, still warm. I watch quietly for a moment unseen. She's wearing a tiny, white, figure-hugging minidress. Next to her, a pair of strappy-heeled sandals lie discarded on the floor.

Lark spies me in the mirror. "I'm using the bathroom. Go downstairs."

"Are you going out?"

A languid smile crosses her lips. "It's my first mentoring session tonight. Adam sent a schedule." She glances at her phone, which rests on the edge of the sink. It's open on the calendar app. Sensing she won't object, I pick it up.

I whistle. "Bloody hell. He needs you every day?"

"You don't become as successful as Adam without working hard." Lark frowns into the glass. "He's nurturing my voice. It takes time."

"Doesn't he know you have exams?"

"It's fine." She tosses her head carelessly. "How I manage my time is my own business." She slicks a smear of sticky pink gloss on her lips and frowns into the mirror. "Do I look OK?"

I hesitate, considering how to answer. Not because it's a

difficult question, but because it's so unusual, coming from Lark. She never asks me stuff like this. In fact, she doesn't obsess about her appearance much at all, probably because she doesn't have to. She's less high-maintenance than most people expect, and she's not particularly vain.

"You look good," I tell her. "But you don't need to dress up for a rehearsal. Did Charlie lend you that dress?"

"This?" Lark twirls. "Actually, Evan sent it."

I blink. "He *sent* you a dress?"

"I know!" She laughs. "He said as soon as he saw it, he could imagine me wearing it. How cute is that? He guessed my size, but it fits like a glove. Do you like it?"

I bite my lip. The dress is nice enough, but Lark is choosy about clothes. She stopped letting Mum dress her when she was four, and she's more of a quirky vintage trouser suit and trainers kind of girl. "Do *you* like it?" I ask instead.

"Mmm…" She dabs some colour on her cheeks. "It cost a fortune – he left the tag on by mistake." It doesn't really answer my question. I think of the promise I made Danny to talk to Lark about Spinner, but before I can open my mouth a car horn blasts outside in the street.

"Ooh, that's Evan now. He's giving me a lift." Lark snatches up her sandals and flies downstairs.

I follow her down to the hall. Mum is peering out of the window at Spinner's black BMW, blocking the street.

"Wow." Mum blinks when she catches sight of Lark. "That dress is really … something."

"Evan got it for me." Lark tosses her head.

"He did? How kind." Mum's face doesn't quite match her words. "Sweetheart, I've been thinking. It's wonderful that this Adam Webb person has shown such an interest in your voice, but…" She falters, watching Lark strap on her flimsy sandals. "I know he's very busy, but it would be good to meet him before we go to Norway. Don't you think so, Mac?"

Dad has appeared in the hall and Mum looks to him for backup.

"I'll suggest it." Lark cuts them both off with a sharp peck on their cheeks. "But you're right. He's busy with the festival. You'll meet him there anyway. I'll get you both backstage."

I marvel at how confidently she throws this out. *She hasn't even had her first mentoring session.*

"Don't worry," Lark continues. "I know what I'm doing. And I've got Evan looking out for me." A smile drifts over her face.

The car horn blasts again.

"He's getting impatient," I say, surprised she isn't annoyed.

Dad frowns. "Why doesn't he ring the doorbell? We don't bite."

"Will he bring you back?" Mum frets.

"*Yes!*" Lark slicks a final coat of gloss on her lips. "I'll be back before midnight, just like Cinderella. No pumpkins here. Stop stressing!" The door slams and she's gone. Off to meet her handsome prince.

Mum and Dad exchange a glance.

"Mind if I use the cavern?" I ask Dad.

"Be my guest." He roots in his pocket and tosses me the keys. "Danny coming over?"

"No, he's … um … busy." I'm aiming for casual but my face heats up. Quickly, I slip out of the door before any more questions can be fired my way.

The sultry night air hits me. As I slide the key into the lock, my head is crammed with conflicting thoughts. *Do I want to see Danny, or not?* We would usually spend half term together, but he's been weirdly distant since the evening he told me he wouldn't play the festival.

And I've not been in a hurry to make plans.

I shut the cavern door with a sigh. The truth is, I don't know how to act around Danny any more. Not now that I know about his feelings for Lark. It feels like everything has changed. For years, our friendship has been easy; a boat sailing on the calmest of seas. And while I guess I knew it couldn't last for ever, that one day the wind might change and a wave come along, in my braver moments I thought I might summon that wave myself. That one day I would work up the courage to tell him how I feel. *Or that he might even tell me.* Only, now it's too late. Because while I was waiting, floating happily in those calm, flat waters, a tsunami came along in the shape of my sister and smashed our boat on the rocks.

Tears prick my eyes, but the cavern is quiet and calm and as soon as I pick up my guitar and plug in my amp I start to feel a little better. I warm up with a few finger exercises, banishing everything but Enrapture from my mind. It doesn't matter if the local talent stage is the tiniest stage of all. It doesn't matter if my slot is only fifteen minutes long. I need to be good. I need to stand out. And if I'm going to be in with a chance of winning this competition, I need something else.

An original song.

I flick through my lyric notebook, searching for a starting point, but my mind stubbornly draws a blank. My pencil stutters, blocked. *What's wrong with me?* Playing at Enrapture is the most exciting thing to happen in forever, but my mind is in tatters, my creativity stumped.

Because I'm doing it on my own.

I push the thought away, bringing my focus back to my guitar. The chords come easily enough. My fingertips fly over the frets, exploring the sequence that I worked on with Danny. I start to hum gently, trying to shoehorn a melody over the top, but it's no good. Everything feels forced, and, when I try to improvise some lyrics, what's left of my inspiration dies a death.

Why can't I make it come together?

A knock at the side door makes me jump.

"Mind if I grab a few things?" Dad pokes his head round the door. "Seb needs to send our gear ahead of us." He grins. "You know the dates are sold out?"

"Really?"

"It's going to be our big comeback."

"Don't turn into a diva, Dad." I smile. "We've got enough divas in this family."

Dad pauses, a box of cables in his hand. "Don't be jealous of your sister." He sinks into the swivel chair. "It could be good for her, being mentored by this producer. She's a bit lost, this could give her some direction."

I consider this. I've never thought of Lark as lost, but now that Dad's said it, I can see what he means. I've got drive, but my sister ... drifts. I'm good at one thing, she's good at everything. Perhaps it makes it hard to choose.

"And you can do something she can't," Dad goes on.

"Like what?" I scoff.

He nods at my guitar, my notebook. "Write your own stuff."

I groan. "Except I can't. Nothing's working."

"Oh, we all have those days. You need to push through. Play me what you've got."

I pull a face. "Do I have to?"

"Go on."

Flushed with embarrassment, I play sixteen bars of the chord progression that Danny and I worked on, improvising a vague sort-of melody over the top.

"OK..." Dad motions for me to stop. "Interesting. Not bad. I like the mood, kind of melancholy ... but optimistic. That's a nice contrast. Unpredictable, in a good way..."

"Come on, Dad. I hear a 'but'..."

He leans back thoughtfully. "The best songs, I think, connect with people. They make us feel something."

157

"OK, but how do I do that?"

He tilts his head. "I suppose … by feeling it yourself. Your chords are nice, your playing is great, the melody's not bad – you can work on that. Do you have any lyrics in mind? What's your song *about*?"

I sigh. "I don't know."

"That's the problem. You need something to say." He sits up. "Want to play together?"

"Er, OK…" I hesitate. We haven't done this in ages. "Like what?"

"Nothing like a classic." He digs in a box on the shelf and pulls out a battered chord book. I smile. His beloved Beatles. He flicks through the pages for a while. Finally he props the book up on the keyboard stand. I glance at his song choice: "Yesterday".

A shiver runs through me. The title alone gives me chills. I remember the first time Dad ever played "Yesterday" to me. I was only six years old, and I thought I'd never heard anything so beautiful in my life.

He unclips his guitar case.

"What should I play?" I ask, scanning the music. It's a guitar score, but I could improvise on keys.

"Just sing." He glances at me. "Let yourself feel."

So I do.

The moment Dad plays the opening chord, I give into the music, for once not worrying whether my voice is as powerful or as special as Lark's. I let my body absorb the melody and think about the words I'm singing, letting myself feel them, deep in my bones. It's a song about a guy whose girlfriend has walked out, and how he wishes he could go back in time and put things right. And while I can't relate to that exact scenario, while I'm singing I think about my own life, about how all the relationships around me are changing too.

Mine and Danny's.

Lark's and Danny's.

Mine and Lark's.

Things used to be simple, but now they're not.

All of a sudden, the words from the Enrapture app pop into my head: *Return to simpler times.* I totally get it. I wish I *could* go back in time. My life feels so confusing now, so complicated.

I reach the last line and choke up. "Sorry."

"No need to apologize." Dad lets the closing chord ring out. "That was powerful. You were feeling it."

"It's a good song," I manage.

"McCartney said the melody came to him in a dream." Dad laughs. "He woke up with it in his head and had to get it down."

"Huh. I wish that would happen to me."

"He wrote a bit like you, actually. Mood first – chords and melody – then he found lyrics to fit."

"The lyrics are sad."

"They weren't at first." Dad chuckles again. "It was called 'Scrambled Eggs' before it became 'Yesterday'."

"You're winding me up."

"It's true! All I'm saying is, there's not one way to write a song. It's a kind of alchemy I guess. Melody, harmony, rhythm, lyrics – you need them all, but they don't have to be complicated, and it doesn't matter what order you put the ingredients into the mix. It all turns to gold if you're saying something true. Trust your instincts, your emotions – say what's on your mind. Let it rise to the surface. And things will come together."

"Is that how you wrote 'Believe in Me'?"

"Pretty much." Dad's eyes go distant, faraway. "To be honest, that song flew out of me. Your mum and I had just got together. Her parents disapproved and she felt guilty. They wanted her to marry the son of their church leader – they were devastated when she broke off the engagement."

"Mum was *engaged*?" My eyes widen. "She never said. What was his name?"

Dad shifts. "I never met him. For obvious reasons. Anyway, it was her life, her decision to make. And I wanted her to know that I would always listen to her – that I'd give her the life she wanted, if she put her trust in me."

"Aww, Dad."

"It's a simple song." Dad's fingers dance around the fretboard as he talks, playing it silently in his mind. "Some of the best songs are. People love them because they feel true." He lays his guitar back in its case. "Don't overthink things. Write from the heart. Everything else will fall into place."

14

A week into sweltering June, Mum and Dad leave for Norway. Their departure couldn't be less rock'n'roll. There's no swanky tour bus, only Seb's battered blue minivan, which swerves into our cul-de-sac at a quarter to nine in the morning, ready to take the band to Birmingham airport.

"Hope that thing's got air conditioning," Dad quips. "But I'm not holding my breath."

Lark and I watch from the front doorstep as Alys and Rob spill out of the van and rush to hug Mum and Dad. Their excitement is palpable, just like the unspoken connection between the four of them.

Music brings people together.

I shoot a mournful glance at Danny, standing on his own front doorstep with his parents. It's sweet that they've come out to wave goodbye. Danny's only just got up, judging by his mussed-up hair and his T-shirt, which is inside-out. He looks so adorably dishevelled, I want to jump the garden wall and hug him, but I restrain myself. We still haven't hung out properly since that night.

His eyes meet mine. I give a muted wave.

"Oh my God, just go already!" Lark mutters over my shoulder, glancing at her phone. Her first English exam is tomorrow at nine, and Aisha's coming over to cram last-minute *Othello* quotes.

"Remember to stay in touch!" Mum moves back towards the house and I spot the look of panic in Dad's eyes. If she's going to start listing all the meals in the freezer again, they'll never make their flight.

"We will!" I can practically hear Lark's eyeballs rolling.

"Paloma, relax. They'll be fine." Dad catches Mum's arm and plants a kiss on her cheek. He looks younger – they both do – and it's nothing to do with his new haircut or her salon-fresh highlights. *They need this trip*, I remind myself, trying to calm the butterflies fluttering in my belly. There's no reason to feel anxious. Mum's nerves must be rubbing off on me, plus I'm bound to be stressed about Enrapture. It's unfortunate timing, their going away now, right before the festival. But it's only for twelve days, then they're back.

"Wren?" Mum suddenly pulls me close. She whispers

in my ear. "I'm worried about Lark. Promise you'll look out for her?"

I gape, taken aback. I barely have time to nod before she lets me go and turns to hug my sister. There's no chance to ask her what she means. The van doors slide open and Dad bundles her inside. Then Seb fires up the engine and they're gone.

I stand there for a minute, staring into space.

Lark's phone pings, breaking the silence. She checks the screen. "Evan's on his way. We're going out." She touches her hair self-consciously.

"You're what?" I stare in disbelief. Our parents have literally just left. We're both too old to need a babysitter, but Mum's parting words have unsettled me.

"I'm worried about Lark."

"I thought Aisha was coming round."

"I cancelled." Lark shrugs. "Aisha won't mind. Evan cleared his diary just for me."

"Gosh, how nice of him."

She nods, missing the sarcasm completely. "Yeah. So anyway, don't wait up. I'll probably be back late."

My mouth falls open. "The night before an exam?"

Lark isn't listening. I follow her gaze to see Spinner's glossy black BMW turning into our road. *Like he was lying in wait.* Out of the corner of my eye I notice Danny hovering by his door. His parents have disappeared back inside. When he spots Spinner's car his expression clouds over.

The BMW screeches into our drive, thumping bass pumping from within. Spinner rolls the driver's window down. The noise feels obscene in our quiet residential street.

"Ready to go, babe?"

"I'll grab my bag." Lark moves to go inside the house but Spinner's face hardens.

"You're not wearing the necklace."

She stops, her hand jumping to her throat. "Oh. It doesn't really go with my—"

"Put it on," Spinner commands.

I wait for Lark to object, but she just scurries into the house. I glance at Danny but with the pounding music, I doubt he caught the exchange. He must pick up on my unease though, because he steps over the fence between our gardens and joins me to wait for Lark. She reappears in a moment, a shimmer of gold round her neck.

Danny and I stare.

"Do you like it?" she asks us, fingers playing with an eye-shaped pendant hanging from a chain.

Just like Spinner's.

Danny's face is stony. He's recognised it too.

"Hey! I didn't get it so you could show off to other guys," Spinner calls from the car.

"Don't be silly," Lark giggles. "It's only Danny!"

"Stop wasting time. Come on, get in."

She runs obediently to the car.

"Lark, wait. Where are you going?" I call after her.

No answer. Ten seconds later, they're gone.

Danny's face is like thunder, but I don't know whether it's because of Spinner, the necklace, Lark's casual burn – or a combination of all three. He kicks at a stone on the path.

I try to lighten the mood. "So… You do realize your top's on inside out?"

"What?" Danny looks up and I point. "You can't change it now, it's bad luck."

He smiles. "Good job I'm not superstitious…" Without warning, he grabs his T-shirt by the neck, in that weird way boys do, and pulls it forward over his head. I catch a swift glimpse of taut stomach and smooth, toned abs before I make myself look away. My face flames, and it's got nothing to do with the heat. By the time he's turned the T-shirt round and pulled it back on, my cheeks have barely cooled down.

"So anyway…" He shuffles, awkward. "You busy?"

"Right now?" I hesitate.

Danny takes advantage. "I need to talk to you about something. There's something you need to see."

I look up at him, trying to read his face. I should be rehearsing, working on my song, but even with Dad's advice progress has been slow. Bordering on non-existent if I'm honest. Putting it off for a few more hours won't hurt. Plus, I can't avoid Danny for ever. We're friends. It's not his fault he's in love with my sister. It's my problem. Much as it hurts, I need to learn to suck it up.

I shrug. "I guess I have time."

"Amazing." His smile blinds me and the dimple appears in his cheek. "Meet back here in five? And don't forget your bike."

I stare after him. "My *bike*?"

Fifteen minutes later, I'm wobbling down a sunny country lane outside Hamlington, doing my best to stay upright. It's been years since I rode a bike, as Danny knows full well. I grit my teeth, trying to focus on the road rather than on whether my brakes work properly, or how disgustingly sweaty I'm getting, or the muscular outline of Danny's arms as he overtakes me with ease.

"Not far now. You're doing great."

I'm concentrating too hard to reply. It takes another ten minutes before I can relax enough to look around. Cycling is hard work but it's pretty here, with the ever-present Wrekin watching over us in the east. For a few moments I can put aside all the things niggling at me: Mum and Dad's departure, Lark disappearing with Spinner, even Danny's feelings for Lark.

"This way."

Danny swings off the road and pulls over at a gate. A dusty footpath lies beyond. We jump off our bikes and push through. One side of the path is fringed by leafy woodland, while on the other the ground falls steeply to the valley below. I take a moment to drink it in. The shade is refreshing and we're the only people around. As I soak up the joyous sound of birdsong, I glance at Danny. He's in his happy place, relaxed but alert. Pulling a small pair of binoculars from his pocket, he scans the trees.

"Look! A hare!"

"Where?" I squint but the hare has gone.

He places a finger to his lips. "It might come back. Let's wait."

We lay our bikes in the bracken and sit quietly. For once, it's peaceful, not awkward. Just me and Danny hanging out. Like we always do – did. The scent of late blossom fills my nostrils, the sunlight slants its fingers through the trees, and every so often Danny points out interesting plants or insects – things I'd never have noticed in a million years.

"You've got eagle eyes, you know that?"

"I just pay attention." His eyes sparkle. "I saw a crested lark the other day when I was cycling home from college. They're rare."

His mention of the lark makes me tense. Is this why he's brought me here? To tell me he's in love with my sister?

"What about wrens?" I say sourly. "Do you ever see those?"

"Of course!" he laughs. "Wrens are common. We'll see them here." He passes me the binoculars and his bare arm brushes my skin. "Have a look." I lift them to my eyes and his mouth quirks. "Other way round."

"I knew that." I turn the binoculars round and squint through the eyepiece.

"You know, *Wren* is a good name for you..." Danny

167

leans back on his elbows, waiting for me to take the bait.

"Oh yeah? Why's that?" I lower the binoculars with a frown, turning to face him. "Because they're boring and common?"

"Er, no." Danny looks bewildered and I feel bad. I don't know why I'm being snippy. "But they are pretty feisty…" He sits up, taking my hands in his, and guiding me to look again in the opposite direction. As he twists the inner ring of the binoculars, the tangle of branches sharpens … and a tiny brown bird comes into focus. "There's one now," he breathes. "Keep your eyes on it. They're small, but they're fast!"

Too late. The wren has gone.

I smile. "Small? Me? Yes. Fast, no way. You saw me just now on a bike."

"Yeah, that's fair." Danny hides a smile. "OK, what else?" He thinks. "Wrens are pretty territorial. They're very aggressive to rivals—"

"That's not like me!"

He opens his mouth then closes it. "I just mean … they're loners. They live a solitary life—"

"Wow, you really know how to pay someone a compliment."

"Well, maybe if you stopped interrupting, I could get to the good part—"

"There's a good part?"

A sound makes me jump; the clanging sound of metal, and a deep rumbling sound coming from somewhere below us. It's close enough to be jarring. Almost threatening. Definitely at odds with this lovely, peaceful place. "What *is* that?" I scramble to my feet.

"That's what I wanted to show you—"

The clanging starts again, drowning Danny out.

We leave our bikes hidden in the bracken and follow the path further up the hill in the direction of the noise. A few minutes later we come to a grassy outcrop bleached by the sun. It looks down on a bowl-shaped valley.

"Down there."

Danny points, but I've already seen. Smack in the middle of the wide, green expanse is an enormous construction site. Metal roads criss-cross the mud, cranes swing slowly round, and trucks reverse with a persistent beep. A couple of excavators are digging what looks like a series of tunnels, while dozens of workers in high-vis vests and hard hats crawl everywhere like ants, rigging scaffolding up to create a domed metal structure. The entire site is encased by tall metal fencing, protecting it from outsiders like a steel shield.

I look at Danny. "Is that…?"

He nods. "The festival site. We're on the other side of the valley."

He passes me his binoculars and I stare. Adam said work was starting soon, and progress has been rapid. Now I can make out the different areas, from the beginnings of the main stage to the backstage enclosures and the huge audience arena, where a tall tower stands in the centre.

"The mixing tower," Danny says. "For the sound and lighting engineers."

At the other end of the site, far away from the main stage, another stage is being built. It's miniscule by comparison and miles from anything, but a thrill rushes through me anyway. I nudge Danny. "That must be the local talent stage. That's where I'll be playing."

But Danny isn't listening. He's peering across the valley towards the rising form of the Wrekin.

"And there's Adam's recording studio." He points at a shape in the distance. Bright sunlight bounces off glass and his eyes narrow, like he's trying to catch a glimpse of Lark.

I bite my lip and look back at the site. The clanging noise has temporarily stopped. "It's so massive. I can't believe it's happening."

"Neither can I," Danny mutters, looking down at me. "That's what I wanted to talk to you about. Why *is* it happening, Wren? An enormous festival in a tiny town like Hamlington? Why here? Why now?" He stares at the studio again and his eyes grow dark and serious. "I've been doing some research. Into Adam."

Oh god. Here we go again…

"That photo you sent me. How closely did you actually look at it? Did you see what was written on those discs?"

I frown. "What?"

He sinks down on to the parched grass, so I do the same. "They were awarded to Piper Productions."

"O-kay…" I wait for him to get to the point.

"Well, I googled Piper Productions. It's a US music studio – or it was. The director was a guy called Adam Piper. I think Adam Webb is Adam Piper. They're the same guy."

"Why would he use a different name?"

"Good question," Danny replies, though he doesn't answer it. He pulls out his phone instead. "I ran an image search on Adam Piper. Look."

I squint at the picture he shows me. Sunlight glances off the glass and there's a crack across Danny's screen so it's difficult to see in detail. It's a candid photo, not very clear, taken facing into the sun. I make out a handsome man leaning against a wall. He's dressed casually in jeans with shirt sleeves rolled up and gazing slightly off camera, a superior expression on his face. I zoom in. It *could* be Adam, I suppose – but without the long hair, the beard, the robes, it's impossible to tell.

I shrug and pass the phone back.

Danny ploughs on. "I found out some other things too. Piper Productions was big. Massively successful. It was based in Albuquerque."

Albuquerque. The name rings a bell.

"Loads of famous artists recorded records there. But then…" Danny stops.

"Then what?"

"In March 2023, totally out of the blue, the studio closed. And Adam Piper disappeared from the music scene for good."

"He stopped working?"

"No, he completely disappeared. Literally overnight. The studio shut down; the staff lost their jobs. He hasn't been seen since."

"Huh." I don't know what to say or think. It's a dramatic story and Danny's clearly fired up, so I humour him. "What happened to him?"

"No one knows for sure," he says darkly. "But there are rumours. Conflicting reports. Some people think Piper was disillusioned with the music business and gave it up on a whim. But that doesn't explain why he'd disappear. Other people think he must be dead – that he took his own life or had some kind of accident. He used to go hiking alone in the desert. He could have been injured, or attacked by wild animals…" Danny pauses – "Except they searched his home, the surrounding countryside. They never found a body."

"I see…"

Danny takes a breath. "There's another theory." His chestnut eyes glimmer. "Adam Piper might have been running away from something. But nobody knows what." He sighs. "But all the reports agreed on one thing: Piper was eccentric. He had some strange beliefs. The word they used was… 'fanatical'."

"'*Fanatical*'?" I screw up my nose. "But that means passionate, right? Passionate about what – music? What's wrong with that? I don't understand what you're saying."

Danny stares again at the timber-clad studio in the hills.

"All I'm saying is, if Adam Webb is Adam Piper, then he obviously didn't die. And he isn't done with music, or he wouldn't be planning Enrapture. Why change your name and start from scratch when you're already a successful producer? So the last theory, the one that says he's on the run from something … that starts to look quite interesting, don't you think?"

I don't have an answer. We gaze at the huge festival site below us, a hive of bustling activity, each of us lost in our own thoughts.

15

We push our bikes back to the main road.

I can tell Danny's annoyed by the stiffness in his shoulders and the quickness of his pace. I have to jog, hot and thirsty, to catch up. It's obvious he thinks he's uncovered something shifty about Adam and he wants me to agree with him, but the problem is – I don't know that I do. It sounds so far-fetched, and it's not like Danny has any solid proof. He's been sceptical about Enrapture from the beginning and I'm sure he's letting it affect his judgement. It suits him to believe that something dodgy is going on, because it gives him an excuse to prise Lark and Spinner apart.

I think about the festival site and all the construction work – from the enormous arena and the monumental main stage, right down to the small local talent stage… A shiver of excitement ripples through me. Money and opportunity have come to boring, rural Hamlington. In two weeks' time, our tiny town will finally be on the map. For once, every teenager for miles around has something to look forward to. Especially me. I'm facing a once-in-a-lifetime opportunity that could finally set my dreams in motion. Does it matter who's behind it?

Why spoil things by asking questions?

I try to put this into words, but Danny won't engage, and by the time we make it back to the estate, I'm feeling bruised, and not just from cycling.

"Let's wait till Lark gets home," I say gently, hoping it will placate him. "See what she says. She's with Adam almost every day. If something is off, she would notice."

Danny raises an eyebrow. "Would she?" he shoots back.

There's another problem.

Lark doesn't come home.

By nine in the evening, she still hasn't appeared, although a message from Mum and Dad has popped up in our family chat. Their plane has landed safely and they've checked into their hotel.

I know Lark has seen it, because she's replied with a thumbs up, and a message:

Lark

Have fun! Boring here. Just been revising with Aisha x

I wonder whether to expose her lie. My stomach twists, thinking of the anxiety in Mum's voice as she left and my promise to look out for my sister.

No. I bite my lip. I can't rat on her when our parents have only just touched down. A moment later, I add a thumbs up and message of my own.

Wren

All fine. Hanging out together at home x

It's humid in the house and guilt makes me restless. I wander into the study and open the itinerary that Dad left on the computer. Three nights in Bergen followed by a string of tiny B&Bs in increasingly remote locations further north. I picture ice and mountains and fjords. I'm used to my parents being here at home whenever I need them. Now there's more than a thousand miles between us.

A news channel notification pops up in the corner of the screen.

It stops me in my tracks.

BREAKING: Following autopsy reports, police rule out drowning and substance abuse, confirming death of Shropshire teenager Mia Hall is being treated as suspicious.

The stark words turn me cold. Mia's friend was right. They didn't find drugs in her system. But she didn't drown either. Which means something else caused Mia to end up in the reservoir.

I gaze out of the window. It's dusky, starting to get dark. Lark really should be home by now. I send her a message.

> Where are you?

> If you expect me to lie to Mum and Dad, at least tell me when you're coming home.

No reply, but a message comes in from Danny:

> You talk to Lark yet? x

I ignore it, pulling up a playlist in the hope it will busy my brain. It doesn't work. Danny's in my head now, niggling at me. He's not usually cynical or suspicious. In fact he's the opposite. He tends to think the best of people, not the worst. It's one of the things I love most about him; how he thinks for himself, weighing things up rationally and balancing the facts.

I decide to do some digging of my own.

Pulling up a chair to the computer, I do a search for "Adam Piper", but the name is too common to produce any useful results. Next, I try "Adam Piper/Adam Webb", but there's nothing to connect the two. I try a third time, typing in "Adam Piper, Piper Productions". Finally, a smattering of articles appears.

OK.

I switch to images, and a grid of photographs fills the monitor. They're sharper and clearer than the picture on Danny's phone.

I pick an image at random and enlarge it.

On a big screen, the resemblance to Adam is... Is it stronger, maybe? But it's hard to be certain, without the ponytail and beard. A glance at the date tells me the image is more than five years old, and this man is certainly younger – tanned and muscular in shorts and a T-shirt, a far cry from Adam's long, multicoloured robes. He does share the same upright posture and intelligent expression, but that's about as far as the similarities go.

I switch back to the articles. The first link leads to a Wikipedia page about Piper Productions, with information about the studio: lists of artists, albums recorded, awards won. I read it twice, impressed. So many of the artists are household names. According to a quote from a magazine, the studio even had a trademark style.

> Love it or hate it, Piper Productions have discovered the secret formula for churning out the kind of catchy, hooky earworm that loves to pollute your brain.

A tingle of excitement zips through me. If Adam really is Adam Piper, he's even more successful than I thought. And he auditioned *me*. He chose *me* to play!

I lean back in my chair, mulling things over.

Say Danny is right, say Adam did decide to leave his old life, move to England and start again… What's wrong with that? Mum did it. People move. They change their names. For reasons that are totally legitimate. Why should Danny think otherwise?

At the bottom of the page, I see a section titled '*The Closing of Piper Productions*' with a link to a newspaper article.

I click on it.

Albuquerque Journal, April 14th, 2023

NO NEW CLUES IN SEARCH FOR
MISSING MUSIC PRODUCER ADAM PIPER

Albuquerque Police Department report no new clues in the hunt for notoriously private music producer Adam Piper, now missing for nearly three weeks. According to reports, Piper was last seen leaving Piper Production Studios, his place of work, on Saturday 25th March. Piper got into his jeep without his cell phone and drove in the direction of Rinconada Canyon, an area popular with hikers. He failed to turn up at work the next day. A controversial figure, though respected in the industry, the eccentric Piper lived alone on a luxury ranch outside

Albuquerque. Born in New Mexico and raised in a small community outside the city of Truth or Consequences, he was a musical prodigy in his youth and majored in music and psychology at Columbia University before returning to New Mexico to set up his own studio. Dogged by rumors of arrogant behavior and contentious beliefs, Piper nevertheless had a reputation as a successful if somewhat formulaic hitmaker. In recent months, however, he had focused his attention on discovering new talent, his last known signing being 18-year-old singer Fernanda Alvarez. Deputy Chief John Velasquez, leading the search for Piper, told this newspaper that police believe a tragic accident or suicide to be the most likely explanation for Piper's disappearance. However, with no body yet recovered, all other avenues of enquiry remain open and anyone with information to share is asked to come forward.

I read the article again. That's why Albuquerque rang a bell. It's a city in New Mexico, the same state where Mum grew up. I pull up a map. The state is enormous, bordering Colorado to the north, Texas to the east, Arizona to the west and Mexico to the south. Whatever, the connection is irrelevant. Closing the map, I return to the article, pondering the writer's choice of words. *Controversial … arrogant … contentious…* It's a pretty harsh description; there's no way it can be Adam. That's nothing like the warm, kind, charismatic man I've met.

The front door slams and I breathe a sigh of relief. Lark is home.

"I thought I told you not to wait up," she says, leaning against the study doorway. An engine roars and a car streaks down the street.

"Did Spinner bring you back?"

"Evan? Yes." Her eyes are misty, a little unfocused. "He's a gentleman."

I snort, and she scowls. "He *is*. He has some pretty old-fashioned values."

"Like telling you what to wear?"

I bite my tongue. I need to talk to Lark, not wind her up.

"He only wants me to look my best," she replies, but the way she says it sounds odd – like she's reciting from a book. "It's all confirmed. I'm performing on stage with Evan at Enrapture."

"Wow," I manage. There's something strange about her. Maybe it's the heat, maybe it's tiredness, but she sounds so … bland. I would have thought she'd be more hyped.

"Adam wants to create a persona for me. A kind of brand. A femme fatale figure – silent, mysterious. 'Never complain, never explain.'"

"Never *complain*?" I can't quite believe what I'm hearing. It's so passive, so totally unlike my sister. She's never been one to hang back.

"I trust Adam," Lark intones. "And Evan too. They

know the business. They know what's best for me." Her voice lacks colour.

"Are you *sure* you should trust them?" I say, treading carefully. "Danny has a theory. He did some research. He thinks Adam isn't Adam Webb. That he's using a different name…"

"Danny's so funny," Lark sighs. She drifts out of the room and down the hallway.

"Wait!" I run after her. "Where are you going? Can we talk?"

"I need to sleep. I have an exam in the morning."

She does look exhausted, her eyes all glossy. Still, I promised Danny I'd have this conversation, and he'll give me hell if I don't. I catch Lark by the arm.

"Please just listen. It might be important."

I start to tell her about Adam Piper and his mysterious disappearance. As I do, she leans against the wall, her eyes glazed. I can see her switching off and shutting down. "At least have a look at the articles," I urge.

"Articles?" Her head snaps up. "Evan mentioned those. They're written by jealous women. Spreading lies to undermine successful men."

"*What?*" I'm lost for words. "No, I'm talking about—"

"I know what you're trying to do, Wren."

"Trying to do?" I blink. "I'm not trying to do anything."

She peers at me with vacant eyes. "You're another one. You're jealous too. You've always been jealous of me."

"That's not true!" I protest, but my face gives me away.

182

"Evan said this would happen." Her voice is flat. "He says I'm far too trusting. I shouldn't trust other people, other women. They're not my friends." She turns away.

"What the hell are you on about?" I almost laugh. This conversation is taking a seriously bizarre turn.

"We're all in competition," Lark mutters. "Every woman, every girl." She pushes opens her bedroom door.

"Rubbish." Bile rises in my throat. "Who told you that?"

"Evan." She smiles. "He cares about me. He tells the truth."

I don't know what to say. "I think you need to be careful," I manage, finally. But Lark has already disappeared into her room, shutting the door behind her.

I slide into bed, uneasy. My phone is full of notifications – Mum and Dad spamming the family chat. There's a photo of the band looking windswept on top of a hill. Behind them is a watery city peppered with colourful weatherboarded houses. It looks like something straight out of Arendelle. I half expect to see Anna and Elsa in the background.

Mum

Bergen this afternoon. SO beautiful! And thankfully cool! ❄️

Dad

So expensive you mean! Two beers for 270 kroner!

Dad

That's twenty quid!!!

Mum

Stop stressing, Mac, and enjoy yourself.

(Get me, girls. Soooo relaxed LOL)

Dad

First gig tomorrow. Did I mention it's SOLD OUT?

Mum

Only once or twice! Guess who got asked for their autograph in the Strandgaten?!

Dad

Was it my beautiful wife? 😄

Mum

😳😳

Mum

Girls: just a heads up. After Bergen, we're heading to Trondheim, then on to Bodø and Tromsø for the next few gigs. Travelling overland to save the budget = very long hours on the road but at least we'll see the sights! ☺ Slight problem, data not working and signal poor so we might be out of range. Email if you need us, we'll pick up messages at our lodgings 😳

Dad

Good luck tomorrow, Skylark. Smash that exam.

Mum

Good luck! Love you both xx

I smile at their flirting on the chat, and look again at the photo. Seb must have taken it, because Rob and Alys are pulling funny faces and Dad's got his arm round Mum. They're laughing into the lens, their faces flushed. It's been ages since I've seen them looking so happy and relaxed. No way can I burst that bubble.

I tap out a reply.

Wren

All good here. Lark is in bed.

Enjoy the gig! Enjoy your road trips!

Don't worry about us xx

16

Lark leaves for her exam early the next morning, so there's no chance to continue our talk. As Aisha's dad's car pulls into our drive, I shout good luck from the window, but she doesn't turn round. Perhaps she didn't hear.

Ruby has a dentist's appointment, so I ride the bus to college by myself, left alone with my thoughts. A sick feeling swirls in my stomach. My sister has never been a pushover. Yes, she's annoying, but she's sparky and assertive, she always has opinions. And yet the way she was talking last night sounded more like she was quoting from a book, or parroting someone else's words.

That someone being Spinner.

I sigh. It's probably just exam stress, getting to her. And the heat. It's getting to me, too. I shove in my earbuds, hoping music will transport me out of my head, but it doesn't work. I give up and turn it off.

Whispers reach me. The gossip on the bus is still about Mia – grisly rumours about serial killers, thrown around like candy. They set my teeth on edge. And if that wasn't enough, someone keeps humming, the same low riff, over and over and over. I try to see who's doing it but I'm greeted by blank stares. The annoying thing is, now I'm humming it too. Somehow the riff has hooked itself into my brain.

A girl with a high, slicked-back ponytail leans over the seat in front of me, her eyes still early-morning hazy.

"Is it true that your sister's dating Spinner?"

Around me, the air goes still. The humming and chatter stops.

"She knows him," I say carefully. "Why?"

"Told you." The girl nudges her friend. "Have you met him then?" She directs this back to me.

I keep my voice even. "Once or twice."

"For real?" The second girl turns round.

"Oh my god, if I met Spinner I would be, like … screaming, crying, throwing up!" The two girls giggle and clutch one other. They beckon to a boy with short bleached blonde hair, who crosses the aisle to join them.

"She knows Spinner."

"Truth." The boy twists his hand in a salute, and waits. I think I'm supposed to do it back.

"What do you like about Spinner?" I ask instead. It's a simple enough question, but the three of them stare at me, like I've grown another head.

"He's *Spinner*," the boy says finally, as the bus pulls into the school driveway.

As the doors open, a blast of hot air hits me. The humming starts up again.

First period is cancelled to make way for an emergency assembly.

"I bet it's about Mia," someone stage-whispers as we trudge solemnly out of our sticky tutor rooms. It's not much cooler in the main hall. The entire sixth form is here, bar the students in the sports hall like Lark, sitting their exams. We sit in restless lines, eyes fixed to the front to where our headteacher Mrs Woods is sitting alongside a ruddy-faced female police officer. The officer watches us with beady eyes. Someone's phone chimes and a dozen people jerk.

"Phones should be off." Mrs Woods shoots dagger stares at everyone. There's a radio transmitter sitting on a table in front of her, and my eyes stray to Danny, a few rows ahead of me, wearing the receiver like he does in class. Turning in his seat, he smiles a tight smile at me.

A hush falls over the room as the police officer stands up to speak. Fanning herself pointlessly with a piece of paper, she confirms last night's news story in terse, detached words. Yes, Mia's death is being treated as suspicious. Yes, anyone with information should come forward. Yes, we should walk home in pairs, socialize in groups, and make sure an adult knows our whereabouts at all times.

In the stifling hall, I suddenly feel cold.

A hand shoots up. "Is it true that Anna Walker's death is being reinvestigated?"

The officer looks uncomfortable. Mrs Woods steps up quickly to shut things down. Gravely, she addresses the room.

"I understand the temptation to engage in speculation. I would remind you all, however, that doing so, either face to face or online, is not helpful in the slightest and could potentially hamper the police investigation."

People squirm, chastened. I make a mental note to leave that horrible chat.

Assembly dismissed, I head to second period, guilt twisting in my gut. I told Mum I'd look out for Lark. We made a promise to have each other's backs. And while Lark hasn't exactly been keeping to her side of the bargain, I know I could try harder.

I'll find her as soon as her exam is finished and try to talk to her again. Make her listen to what I have to say.

At twelve, I fly to the exam hall and hover outside on the grass, watching the last remaining students file out.

Lark isn't among them.

"Wren?" Ms Mayer, Lark's English teacher, spots me

189

and hurries over. "Do you have any idea where your sister is? Is she unwell?"

"I thought she was here."

Ms Mayer flaps the folder in her hand. "She was. I mean, she went into the exam hall this morning, I saw her go in myself. But one of the invigilators told me that she barely wrote a word. She got up and walked out early."

I don't like the sound of this.

Ms Mayer looks distraught. "It's not like Lark. I've tried her phone but she's not answering. I assume she panicked. It happens. This weather doesn't help. Perhaps I'll call your parents."

"Don't call them," I say, quickly. "I'll speak to Lark. I'm sure there's a simple explanation."

I hurry away before Ms Mayer can say anything more. The moment I'm round the corner, I try Lark's phone. It rings out.

I blast a barrage of texts.

> You WALKED OUT of an exam?
> What were you thinking?

> Lark, is everything OK?

> Don't ask me to cover for
> you to Mum and Dad.

> Are you at home? Ms Mayer is upset.

I'm not expecting a reply, so when one comes through I'm surprised. But I'm even more surprised by what Lark says.

> I'm fine. A levels are a waste of time.
> Evan picked me up.
>
> Adam says I need to focus on my career.

> What the hell? You're joking!
> Your exams are important.
> What would Adam know about it?

> He knows what he's talking about. It's
> not my job to question him.
>
> My job is to receive his teaching.

I stare at her last message.

Receive his teaching? What the hell is she talking about?

Last period passes in a daze. I'm going through the motions like a zombie. Luckily, there's a young student teacher covering and she doesn't seem to notice. She's too busy trying to control the class. Nobody can muster the energy to do any work. A group of boys keeps humming while she's talking, and roughly every thirty seconds a telltale chord chimes, broadcasting the fact that someone is blatantly looking at the Enrapture app. Each time it sounds, my body seems to twitch.

The minute the last bell rings, I hunt down Danny.

"Lark walked out of her English exam."

"What?" His face flipcharts through emotions: shock, horror, concern...

"She spent the day with Spinner."

...Anger, dismay, disgust. "Are you sure?"

I nod, waiting while he gets his bike. I can't think. My shirt is sticking to me, and nearby someone is humming; a year nine boy with a shaved head, unlocking a scooter. It's that same riff; low, urgent, over and over and over. I'm not even sure he knows he's doing it. I want to tell him to be quiet, to let me have a minute's peace, but at the same time I'm tempted to join in. There's something about that riff. It sticks like Velcro to my brain.

Danny and I walk the road way home, and I start by filling him in on my one-sided conversation with Lark the night before. His eyes narrow as I tell him how she spoke to me so strangely, how she totally refused to listen. When I reach the part about her performing at Enrapture and Adam's plan to create a "persona" for her, his jaw clenches.

"There's nothing wrong with Lark's image. She looks great as she is."

His words sting, but I push the feeling down.

"Tell that to Spinner," I say, getting out my phone and pulling up his Instagram account.

Ruby showed me during history. She got a notification early this afternoon. Clearly, no time has been wasted in creating Lark's new image. The picture Spinner has posted mainly features himself, one muscled arm slung carelessly round my sister's shoulders. Lark is secondary to the picture, more like an accessory, only partly visible to one side. Behind her is the shop window of Harvey Nichols in Birmingham and in her arms are numerous shopping bags.

The caption reads: *A woman should dress for her man. #SpinningTheTruth.*

It already has four thousand likes.

"I don't get it," Danny spits. "That's not Lark. Lark would never let some guy tell her what to do."

I don't argue, because he's right. Lark's had a few rubbish boyfriends in the past but she's always seen the light and binned them quickly. This feels different. Somehow Spinner's pulled the wool over her eyes.

"Do your parents know what he's like?" Danny asks.

"I don't think so," I say, showing him our family chat, updated only a few hours earlier.

Dad

How did the exam go, Skylark?

Mum

Only one more to go! Drink lots of water. Keep cool!

Lark

It went fine thanks. It was a breeze :)

193

"She lied to them," Danny murmurs. "Lark's not a liar."

"She never used to be." I think of Mum's whisper, *I'm worried about Lark.* "I don't know what to do," I say truthfully. "If I tell them, they might not believe me. Or else I'll worry them. They only just arrived in Norway yesterday, and they're living their best lives. Mum would insist on coming home. This tour could turn things round for them…" I trail away.

"But this is serious, Wren." Danny shakes his head. "Something's off. They need to know."

We trudge on in silence, the guilt eating away at me. Danny's right, something does feel off, and I hate how disappointed he is in me for not acting on it. But if I contact my parents and ruin their tour – maybe for no good reason – then I'll never forgive myself. And Lark will be livid with me too, for interfering in her life. And then there's Enrapture…

The festival … my big chance…

We've reached our estate. I turn to Danny.

"You're right. Spinner is a dick. But Lark's love life is her business." I keep going before he can object: "As for Adam being this shady Piper guy … we don't know that for sure. Even if we did, it's not necessarily sinister that he's rocked up now in Hamlington. We can't go pointing fingers without proof."

"Then let's get proof," Danny says. "We could speak to someone. Someone who worked with Piper in the States. Someone who could identify him."

"He worked with huge stars…" I shake my head.

"Not always." Danny's eyes flash. "I read about a girl…"

"Me too. Fernanda something?" I dredge my memory. "Fernanda Alvarez? She was mentioned in an article."

He nods. "I saw it. She was unknown when Piper signed her. We could contact her, reach out. I could come round later, if you're free?" His expression is so hopeful, I don't need to think for long.

"Sure. Of course."

"Thanks." Danny looks shyly at me.

I'm sitting next to him on my bed, waiting for my laptop to fire up. The window is open but the air is close. Danny's so near I can feel the heat radiating from his body and, where our thighs are touching, my skin feels like it could burn a hole through the fabric of my skirt. I don't move away. Instead, I try to ignore it.

"Thanks for what?" I ask.

"For taking this seriously." He shoots me a smile that makes my heart sing and my stomach squirm. Yes, I'm worried about Lark, and my dislike of Spinner is growing by the minute, but, when it comes to Adam … I honestly don't know. I still think that Danny, for reasons of his own, is determined to see danger where there's none and make connections between things that aren't connected. But if this is what it takes to put his doubts to bed, then fine. When he realizes he's got the wrong end of the stick about Adam and Enrapture, perhaps he'll finally change his mind about playing.

I sigh as the search results appear. "This won't work. There are literally hundreds of girls called Fernanda Alvarez. It's not an unusual name. We need to be specific."

"Add 'musician', or search by location," Danny suggests. "Put in 'New Mexico', or 'Albuquerque'. That might narrow things down. She's bound to have social media. Or a SoundCloud."

He's right. It makes a difference. The field narrows drastically to a group of six women.

"It can't be that one." Danny points. "She's a cellist, not a singer. And this Fernanda plays the drums." He clicks methodically on each link in turn. "This Fernanda Alvarez teaches Spanish guitar in elementary school. The other three are singers, but of those, only this girl looks young enough."

We're staring at a picture of a fresh-faced girl with curly brown hair and olive skin; she's holding a microphone. "I suppose it could be her," I say. "She was eighteen when she worked with Piper last year. She'd be nineteen now."

We land on a social account. There's a bio beneath the header photo:

> Fernanda Alvarez Ruiz, 18. Singer. Music is my life
> ♥ La música es mi vida!
> For more info, email: sofia@hermanamúsica.com

"It has to be her," I say, scrolling down the account. Then I frown. "That's annoying though. The most recent post is from February 2023. She's not active on here any more."

"Click there." Danny points at the pinned post at the top. It's simply captioned *UPDATE*.

We're taken to a blog. Dozens of photographs of the same girl are peppered throughout. Fernanda as a toddler singing into a plastic spoon; Fernanda as a schoolgirl in plaits, performing on stage. There are close-ups of an older Fernanda standing front and centre in the school choir, and an image of her wearing a headset and an elaborate feathered bird costume, dancing on a festival float. The last one links to a YouTube video, and I press play.

Oh. Goosebumps pepper my arms. Danny's nose wrinkles; I don't know how much he can hear. Amid the noise of the festival, Fernanda's voice is exceptional. Uncannily sweet and pure.

She sounds exactly like Lark.

I keep the thought to myself as I scroll down to the comments section.

Bendecida con la voz de un ángel ♥

"'Blessed with the voice of an angel'," Danny translates smoothly. I'd forgotten he did GCSE Spanish.

"'*Qué rango vocal tan increíble*.'" He moves on to the next comment. "They're saying she has an incredible vocal range."

"What about that one?"

¡ Ay, la estrella de Fernanda estaba en ascenso !

"'Fernanda's star was rising'." Danny blinks.

The warm room feels suddenly chilly. "Why is it written like that?" I look at him. "Why the past tense?"

"I don't know." Danny checks something on his phone. Then he frowns.

"What's the matter?"

"There's no mention of Fernanda Alvarez in the Piper Productions' discography. She never released a record."

I let this sink in. "What does that say?" I ask, pointing to a longer comment, further down:

> Mi querida hermana Fernanda fue al cielo antes de
> que el mundo descubriera sus dones. Canta con
> los ángeles, mi amor.

We paste the text into a translator. The results make us catch our breath.

> My dear sister Fernanda went to heaven before the
> world could discover her gifts. Sing with the angels,
> my love.

The shock on Danny's face mirrors my own.

I say what we're both thinking. "She's dead."

17

With a heavy heart, I start another, more morbid search: *Fernanda Alvaraz Ruiz. Singer. Death.*

A few articles appear, mostly in Spanish, but one is in English — a short obituary in the *Alamogordo Daily News.*

Fernanda Alvaraz Ruiz, 18, born January 14th, 2005, in Alamogordo, New Mexico, passed away March 11th, 2023, from complications caused by an undiagnosed heart condition.

   Fernanda was a talented singer who loved performing from an early age. A memorial will be held at Immaculate Conception Catholic Church on April 4th, 2023, at

11.00 a.m. and will be for family members only. She is survived by her mother Anita, her father Carlos, and her sister Sofia.

"A heart condition," Danny murmurs. "That's sad."

"Yeah. She was talented."

I swallow, thinking again of the video of Fernanda singing on the carnival float. The similarity between her voice and Lark's feels uncanny. "Well, I guess that's that," I say with a shrug. "Obviously, we can't make contact."

"We could try her manager," Danny says. "They would have met Piper. There was an email address on Fernanda's socials. If we word the message carefully, they might reply."

We decide the email should come from me.

From: wrenmackenzie@gcloud.com
To: sofia@hermanamúsica.com
Subject: Adam Piper

Dear Sofia,

My name is Wren Mackenzie. I'm a 17-year-old musician from Hamlington in England. I hope you don't mind me contacting you. I believe you represented the singer Fernanda Alvarez Ruiz.

I was sorry to learn of her death.

This is a long shot, but I'm contacting you for information about a man called Adam Piper. I understand that Fernanda was the last artist to work with Adam Piper before his disappearance. Three months ago, a music producer named Adam Webb moved to our town from America. He is organizing a festival here. This might sound unbelievable, but my friend Danny thinks that Adam Webb could be Adam Piper, living here under a new name. I was wondering if there was anything you could tell us about Piper that would help us resolve the matter.

Kind regards,

Wren

"Did you have to make me sound completely irrational?" Danny shakes his head. Then he smiles. "I'm kidding. I hope she replies." He stands up, and my heart sinks.

"You don't have to go. You could stay longer…" For some reason, I don't want to be alone. The house feels too quiet. And if Lark isn't avoiding me, it could be hours before she shows her face. "I could make us dinner…"

Danny quirks an eyebrow. "Oh yeah? And what would you cook?"

"Um … toast?" I flash a winning smile. "I make excellent toast!"

He smothers a grin. "Toast does sound delicious. And I would love to take you up on that offer another time, but…" He shrugs, apologetically. "I've got a biology assignment due. I really do need to get back. I'm sorry."

The door closes behind him, leaving me bereft.

*

I'm at Enrapture – not on stage, but in the audience – packed tight in the middle of the crowd. Panic seeps into my veins. It's too hot. I can't move. I can't see Danny. Where is he? I thought he'd be here. I look around but there's no sign of him. Everyone is dressed the same. They're all wearing long, multicoloured robes. I shout Danny's name and the people near me turn to stare.

Instead of a face, they only have an eye.

The arena lights grow dim. The stage gives off an eerie glow. Suddenly the lights go up and a figure in a hooded cloak steps out. The crowd is going wild! It must be Spinner!

But no. The hood drops and my mouth falls open. The figure is a boy. The boy is…

… Danny?

Danny straps on his guitar and my heart lifts. He's going to play!

A girl runs on to the stage. She's wearing a beautiful feathered bird costume and she's holding a golden microphone in her hand. I recognize her immediately. It can't be… But it is.

Fernanda.

"We are The Silenced." Fernanda speaks into the mic. Then Danny strikes a chord, and she opens her mouth to sing…

I wake in the middle of the night, covered in sweat. Slowly, I come round. I've fallen asleep in my clothes, my laptop still open on my bed.

The time glows on my bedside clock: 2.34 a.m.

I shudder, remembering my weird, creepy dream. Danny was in it, performing on stage – but not with me.

202

With Fernanda. A dead girl. I shake my head, trying to delete the memory from my brain, and accidentally knock my laptop with my arm. The screen illuminates, bathing me in a ghostly blue light. I catch my breath.

An email has come in.

From: sofia@hermanamúsica.com
To: wrenmackenzie@gcloud.com
Subject: Re: Adam Piper

Dear Wren,
I receive your message. Sorry my English is not good. My name is Sofia. Fernanda Alvarez Ruiz was my sister.
It is difficult to answer your question. The media report that Adam Piper is dead, but my family do not believe. There is one way to tell if the man you know is Piper: on his neck is a tattoo of a bird.
Wren, I advise you to be careful. If this man is Piper, do not go to this festival. Do not give him a platform. Do not trust him.
Your friend,
Sofia Alvarez Ruiz

I shake the sleep from my eyes and read the email again. *On his neck is a tattoo of a bird.*

Goosebumps prickle my skin. Adam *is* Piper.

Danny was right.

I do a quick calculation. If it's early morning here, it must be evening in New Mexico. If I reply quickly, Sofia might still be online.

> Sofia,
> Thanks for writing back. I'm so sorry about your sister.
> Please help – I don't understand. Why can't Adam be trusted?
> Wren

An email pings straight back.

> I am sorry. I cannot discuss this further. Goodbye.

My mind explodes with questions.

> Sofia, please. My sister Lark is a singer like Fernanda. Adam discovered her. He has been acting as her mentor. Should I be worried? I don't know what to do.

No reply.

I wait, but either Sofia has gone offline or she's sticking to her guns. I chew my nails to the quick. Why is she being so cagey? What can she not discuss? I only wanted her help to identify Adam as Piper. Her sister was the last person to have worked with him. Obviously, it's tragic that Fernanda died, but – surely I'm imagining it – she can't be implying there's a link?

My thoughts are tangled in knots. Still, I stop short of messaging Danny. He'll be asleep, and if he's not he'll jump on this and make a mountain out of a molehill. He'll tell me to pull out of Enrapture, then he'll go rushing off to warn Lark so he can be her knight in shining armour.

No.

I need time to process this. It's no good jumping to conclusions. I once read somewhere that, at night, the logical side of our brain goes to sleep, leaving our irrational, emotional side awake.

I am being very irrational right now.

I tiptoe down the hall to get some water. That's when I notice.

Lark's bedroom door is open. Her bed is still made.

She didn't come home last night.

18

It's nearly 3am. Where the hell are you?

Radio silence.

My mind is doing mental gymnastics. This isn't good. Either Lark is out somewhere in Hamlington, with a potential killer on the loose, or she's with her control freak of a boyfriend—

At Adam *Piper*'s house.

Perhaps I should wake up Debs ... or call the police? Even as I think it, I know it's ridiculous. Lark is eighteen, a legal adult. What are they going to do? And yet...

Danny is worried. He thinks Lark could be in trouble,

and what if he's right? He was right about Adam's real identity. Lark *is* different. Lark *has* changed. She's been so distant lately, so submissive – almost unrecognizable as the feisty sister I know. Mum must have spotted it too. Ever since that day in the cavern, Lark has been more like Spinner's puppet than a person in her own right. And maybe it's the heat, maybe it's just stress, maybe it's infatuation, stopping her from thinking clearly, except … what if it's not? What if *Adam* is behind it? Eccentric Adam Piper, known for his "arrogant behavior and contentious beliefs"?

What if *he's* been pulling the strings?

No. I shake my head. It can't be. I don't want it to be. The Adam I know is nothing like the man Sofia and the article describe. Warm, softspoken Adam, who chose me to play at Enrapture, the benevolent champion of young musicians who's giving me a chance to fulfil my dream.

Unless I'm ignoring "red flags", like Danny warned me?

Believing what I want to believe?

Throwing on some shoes, I tiptoe down the inky path to the cavern. I don't know what to think or who to trust. But I do know there's no more sleep for me tonight – and when I'm feeling this unsettled only one type of medicine can help.

I unlock the side door and flip on the light. The cavern seems bare without Dad's gear. I reach for my Fender, propped against the wall.

Hello, friend.

My guitar is cool to the touch, the smooth wood silky and soothing. As I give it a tune, the buzzing in my brain begins to dim. No amp this time – don't want to wake the neighbours. I pick up my plectrum. My hand hesitates.

What to play?

I could comfort myself with any number of well-known songs, lose myself in other people's lyrics. I could go through the motions until tiredness descends. It's the easy option, and it's tempting. But then my eyes fall on my lyric notebook, sitting on a shelf.

What if I don't choose the easy option?

What if I let myself feel?

Dad told me not to overthink things – to trust my instincts instead, and play from the heart. He said that if I let my emotions rise to the surface and say what's on mind, then everything will fall into place.

I need everything to fall into place.

I play without thinking – whatever comes into my head – letting my left hand find chord shapes, my fingers dancing around the frets. My right hand keeps rhythm, strumming softly or picking patterns, whatever feels right.

I start to explore different keys, seeking something that mirrors my mood. The chord progression comes easily – instinctively – simple, yet powerful, building on the work I did with Danny. Everything feels natural, nothing is forced.

The seeds of a melody appear next, glimmering like magic in my head. I hum it over the harmonies, tweaking and adjusting as it comes along. Goosebumps bloom on my forearms; a sign that I'm getting it right.

This. Actually. Works…

Suddenly I have the outline of a verse. Adrenaline rockets through my veins. I pull out my phone, recording my seeds of sound before they disappear. The chords aren't complicated and the melody is simple, but I can feel it in my bones…

These seeds could grow.

What if I add lyrics?

My eyes flick again to my notebook, but for now, I leave it where it is. Instead, I call up my melody and my confusing, mixed-up feelings.

And then I let the words come spilling out.

Everything is changing. Nothing is the same.
I don't know who to trust or to believe.
I'm scared of what I know, afraid of what I don't.
I'm losing any faith I had in me.

I let out a breath. It's simple, but Dad said it could be simple. So I tell myself not to worry, not to stop and analyse the lyrics, or try to change them. I can tweak things later on. I need to keep on going. Give voice to the stuff I need to say.

Immediately, I think of Lark.

He's going to break your heart. He's forcing us apart.
He fills you up with hateful twisted lies.

He moulds you to his whim, denies your inner fire.
He'll crush your spirit so that he can rise.

As the words jump into my mouth, I suddenly realize.

I miss her.

My infuriating, annoying, special sister – I actually miss her. She's letting Spinner dilute and control her, when she's the one holding all the cards, with her vivid personality and her stunning voice.

I just wish she could see.

And like that, a chorus appears in my head.

You need to wake up.
I wish you'd wake up.
Why don't you wake up and see?
You're sleepwalking through life,
And you've wandered from your path.
Don't listen to him. Hear me.

I stop, my hands shaking. Putting aside my guitar, I grab my notebook and write down everything: the chords, the basic melody and the lyrics, while it's all still fresh and fizzing in my head. The song isn't finished – it needs another verse, maybe even two, a bridge and an ending...

But I've made a start.

I let my fear and confusion inspire me – and while I still don't have any answers, somehow, it felt like fighting back.

19

I crawl into bed around four and wake a few hours later, groggy but buzzing, my song still playing in my ears. Adrenaline fizzes through my veins. Last night in the cavern everything came together. A perfect alchemy of words and music, melody and harmony.

It's never happened before.

Part of me is scared I must have dreamed it, but as I play back my recordings and check my notebook my heart beats fast. It's real. I've finally caught a butterfly in my net.

My first instinct is to tell Danny. I know he'll understand. It's the same thrill he gets whenever he spots some rare creature or natural phenomenon, like that murmur-thing he mentioned at Charlie's party.

I smile. I have the bones of a song – a great song – and I can flesh them out, building up the layers until I've got something really special. Just in time for Enrapture.

But Enrapture is Adam Piper.

The thought sobers me up.

I switch on my laptop and read Sofia's emails again, scouring them for hidden meaning. *Why does she hate Adam? Could he really be behind Fernanda's death?* In the cold light of day, my logical mind quickly lands on a more mundane interpretation: Adam divides opinion, Fernanda was unlucky. Sofia, grieving the loss of her sister, is looking for someone to blame.

I can believe it, but will Danny?

Sofia replied.

His reply comes in seconds.

On my way x

I message Lark next.

I assume you're with Spinner?
Text me back ASAP!!!

Danny arrives in less than ten minutes, hair wet from the shower and cheeks still striped with pillow creases. It's cute, but I stamp down the urge to reach out and touch. Instead, I push my laptop across the kitchen table towards him.

He reads Sofia's emails with a stony face, leaving the coffee I make him untouched.

"Adam *is* Piper. I knew it." His fist bangs the table, making me jump. "Where's Lark? Has she seen these?"

I pause. "She didn't come home last night."

"She's with Spinner." It's not a question. Danny's eyes turn flinty and his lip curls. I feel it in my gut, an actual stab of pain, seeing how it affects him; the confirmation that Lark spent all night with another guy. "Do you know where he lives?"

"Spinner?" I blink. *Oh god, I never told him.* "Um, yeah… He lives with Adam."

Danny's eyes pop. "Lark is at Adam Piper's place? Right now?" He pushes back his chair. Coffee droplets splatter the table like gunshot.

"Where are you going?"

"You mean, where are *we* going?" Danny shoots back. "We need to warn Lark—"

"Warn her about what, exactly?"

Danny studies me. "Sofia told you not to trust Adam. Why would she make that up?"

"Because she's upset?" I try to sound reasonable. "Her

sister died. That doesn't mean Adam had anything to do with it."

Danny looks unconvinced.

"Danny, come on. Sofia didn't say—"

"Maybe she *couldn't*," he interrupts me. "Maybe she's scared." He gestures at my laptop. "Wren, do the maths. Fernanda died in March 2023. The same month Piper disappeared."

I take this in. He's right, but…

"It's a coincidence," I say, gently. "Fernanda had a heart condition…" Then I stop.

So did Anna Walker.

Anna went missing in March *this* year. Just after Adam arrived in Hamlington.

Danny is looking at me, waiting. "Lark is your sister," he says softly. "Could you honestly live with yourself if something happened to her?"

I remember my promise to Mum.

Then I get to my feet.

I never skip college. But until yesterday, neither did Lark.

I pump the pedals hard, trying to keep up with Danny. "I can't believe you made me cycle, *again*," I shout.

He streaks up the incline, muscles popping in his shins, not even breaking a sweat.

The narrow road hugs the Wrekin and continues to climb. I get off my bike to push, muttering to myself. Somehow I'm here, in the middle of a heatwave for god's sake, helping the boy *I* like, rescue the girl *he* likes, when she might not need rescuing, and doesn't even like him back. Well, there we go. *Welcome to the latest edition of* The Lark Show*!* I could be in the cavern right now, working on my song. I could be playing it to Danny, teaching him the chords, trying to convince him to play it with me at Enrapture. *Except...*

Danny is right. Something feels off. It has for a while.

I find him waiting for me round the corner. Behind him are the two tall stone gateposts standing sentry to the black wrought-iron gates. "We're here," he says, grim-faced.

Unsurprisingly, the gates are closed. I go to press the buzzer on the gatepost, but Danny catches my hand.

"No. You'll activate the camera." He points at a discreet black box fitted to a tree. "We don't want to announce our arrival. We need to speak to Lark alone, without Adam or Spinner breathing down our necks."

"You're saying we break in?" I gaze up at the gates. They must be ten feet tall.

"Not *break* in." Danny's eyes track the wall. "Find another way over. Come on."

There's a ditch on the other side of the road, safely out of view of the camera, and we bury our bikes there under long fronds of bracken. Danny grabs my hand and drags me along. Leaving the imposing entrance gates behind, we skirt the tall stone wall that circles Adam's estate.

"There."

He points. A short distance further down, a section

215

of wall is starting to crumble. The capstones have fallen into the undergrowth, dislodging some of the stones underneath. The top here is a good three feet lower than elsewhere, and there are some decent footholds.

"Could you get over?" he asks.

I inspect the wall. "I think so. You?"

He pulls face. "Maybe. My balance isn't always great. I'm OK on a bike, but heights…" He looks around. "Any traffic coming?"

I shake my head.

"OK. You first. I'll give you a boost."

Before I can say anything, his hands are on my waist, pulling me towards him. His fingers brush the skin beneath my shirt, sending an electric shock shuddering through me. He locks his hands and nods.

I place my foot in his palms, flustered by the fire in my cheeks. "You sure you can take my weight?"

He chuckles. "You're joking, right? You're as light as feather, little Wren."

My heart is thumping madly, I don't know why. Maybe because someone might spot us, although the road is quiet and I can't see any more cameras in the trees. It's hard to ignore how close I am to Danny, or the musky sweet scent of his skin warmed by the bike ride. I clear my throat. "OK. Let's go."

"One … two…" His warm breath caresses my ear. "Three!" And then I don't have time to notice anything else because suddenly I'm catapulted halfway up the wall, gripping on for dear life. Danny boosts me again, pushing the seat of my jeans. I cringe, embarrassed, but it works. Somehow, I'm sitting astride the wall.

"It's higher than it looks!" I grimace at an evil clump of nettles on the other side.

"Can you drop?"

"Do I have a choice?"

Danny takes a run up at the wall. At the same time, I plummet, landing heavily and pitching straight into the nettles. A crop of stinging welts is my reward.

He lands lightly beside me and lifts my arm to inspect my wrist. "Ouch. You're gonna need a dock leaf."

"A dock *what*?"

He pounces on some weed-like plant. "Come here." The next thing I know, he's dabbing it gently on my nettle stings. Coils of dark hair fall into his eyes. He looks up. "How does that feel? Any better?"

"Actually, yes." My skin may be soothed but my face is in flames. "Cool trick, Nature Nerd."

"*Nature Nerd*?"

"You know it suits you." I smile.

"I'll take it." He smiles back. *That dimple…* He drops my wrist with a cough. "We'd better get going."

We head through dappled woodland in the direction of Adam's house, following the main driveway but staying undercover. I have no idea how Adam would react if he found us on his property. He seems so mild-mannered that it's hard to imagine him getting upset about anything. But

217

unlike last time, we don't have an invitation, which means we're basically trespassing. We need to keep out of sight.

We reach the edge of the woodland. I can see the large curved drive with the fountain in the middle. The water isn't running today, but two cars are parked outside the main house: Spinner's BMW and a silver space-age-looking Tesla.

The one from the market square.

"They're at home," I mouth to Danny.

"Where?" he mouths back. There's no sign of life anywhere. A glance at my phone confirms there's still no message from Lark, although the signal here is almost non-existent.

I hesitate.

The distant hum of activity from the construction site in the valley reaches my ears. A spontaneous shiver ripples down my spine, like it always does whenever I think of Enrapture. Part of me itches to disappear into the woods and see how the festival site is progressing. But I'm here with Danny, on a mission to find Lark, so I stamp down the urge. My eyes fall on Adam's recording studio instead.

A light is on somewhere in the building.

I nudge Danny, but he's already seen it.

"Time to break cover." He grabs my hand and winks. "Watch out for peacocks."

The sun blasts us like a spotlight as we dash across the drive towards the recording studio, gravel crunching noisily beneath our feet. Swerving the front entrance, we duck down the side and lean against the timber-clad wall to catch our breath.

"What next?" I mouth. My forehead is soaked with sweat.

"Window," Danny mouths back. "See inside."

The first window we come to looks on to the reception lobby. I risk a peep. A light is on but the space is devoid of life. Or not quite. Beneath the velvet sofa, a metallic shimmer catches my eye. Lark's sandals. I nod at Danny.

"I can see her shoes. She's definitely in there."

We follow the length of the building, heading down towards the recording studio itself. I know the walls are soundproofed, but I walk on tiptoes anyway, praying that Adam's outside grounds staff aren't on the prowl. I can't hear a thing from inside.

We come to a stop at the end. It's too risky to turn the corner and peer in through the huge glass doors. If Lark is in there with Adam or Spinner, they'll have a clear view of us.

On a whim, I glance up. Where the roof overhangs the wall, a shallow window runs parallel with the eaves. *Yes!* If I had something to stand on, I could see inside.

Danny reads my mind. He points towards a small wooden outbuilding under some nearby trees: a sort of toolshed. By the door stands a large green plastic rainwater butt. We dart over. Luckily, with the weather so dry, the butt is almost empty. Together, we tip it on its side. The sound of the remaining water sloshing out sounds colossal in my ears, but nobody comes, and once it's empty the plastic butt is light and easy to roll into place alongside the studio building.

"I'll hold it steady," Danny whispers. "You climb up."

He grips my ankles firmly, using his weight to anchor the barrel. Even when I'm balanced on the water butt, the window is higher than my line of sight. I stand precariously on tiptoe and peer over the sill.

I freeze.

Lark is standing in the middle of the recording studio, a microphone in front of her on a stand. Adam is sitting at the grand piano with his notebook placed open on the lid. Fortunately, he has his back to me. There's no sign of Spinner, but I can't see the control room from this angle, so I hazard a guess he's in there.

I turn to Danny. "I can see her."

"How does she seem?"

"She seems fine." I turn back round.

Lark is nodding at something Adam's saying, her golden head bobbing up and down. He starts to play something on the piano, a melody in the right hand. I can't see any music because his body is blocking my view, but Lark blinks slowly, listening, her brow creased in concentration. Adam lifts his left hand to cue her, then she opens her mouth to sing.

Even though I can't hear a note, I can tell my sister sounds incredible by the way that Adam reacts. He leans forward, tense, every fibre of his body alert and tuned in to her sound. As he reaches for his notebook, I stop watching him. My attention has returned to Lark.

Yes, she's singing. But there's no sparkle to her performance; none of her usual charisma. Nothing like her karaoke turn at Charlie's party, or the show she put on when we busked in The Square.

She looks tired and pale, her expression vacant, her mouth moving mechanically.

"What's happening?" Danny whispers.

I turn back to him. "I'm not sure."

I look back through the window and my body goes cold. Lark has stopped singing. She's leaning over the piano with her fingertips outstretched, clutching at the glossy veneer. Her eyelids flutter for a second.

Suddenly she crumples in a heap.

20

I stifle a cry.

"What is it?" Danny hisses.

I stare at my sister's body lying motionless on the floor. "*Wren!* What *is* it?"

I rip my eyes away and turn to face him. "She was singing. But then she just ... collapsed!"

Danny's eyes widen. "Is someone getting help?"

I look back. Adam is standing over Lark, looking down. Spinner has joined him. The two men are deep in conversation. Neither looks at all concerned. I shake my head. "No one's doing anything!"

Anger courses through my body. Why aren't they

acting? That's my sister! Don't they care?

I raise my fist ready to hammer on the glass, but the next moment Adam bends down to Lark. Brushing the hair from her face, he whispers something in her ear. She stirs briefly. Then he and Spinner lift her up and carry her over to a green chaise longue. Her small body sinks into the cushions.

Spinner produces a blanket and Adam lays it over Lark's body. Then he picks up his notebook and sweeps out of the room, Spinner following him.

"They left her." I scramble down. Seconds tick by, then I hear the sound of a car engine. "They're driving away." I grab Danny's arm. "Quick! Something's not right. I think Lark's sick. Come on."

Panic pools in my belly as we race round to the large glass doors of the recording studio. I try the handle.

"It's locked. Lark!" I lift my fist again to bang on the glass, but Danny stops me.

"Wren, wait. We don't know she's alone."

"Then how—"

"It's OK, look."

Inside the studio Lark is stirring.

"Lark!" I hiss. We wave and jump, trying to attract her attention.

She sits up gingerly, glancing around, as though she's forgotten where she is. When she spots Danny and me, she blinks.

"Open the door!" I gesture.

Casting the blanket aside, Lark struggles to her feet. She manages to lift the lever to unlock the door but doesn't have the strength to slide it. Danny and I heave it open and stumble into the room.

"What the…?" Her voice is flat. She drops back on to the chaise longue and stares at us, dead-eyed. "Why are you here?"

"We came to find you!" I whisper. "You didn't come home. You haven't replied to my messages. Lark, you collapsed! Did you take something? What happened?"

"Nothing happened," she murmurs. Her voice is thin and weak. "I don't know what you're talking about."

Danny moves closer. "What did she say?"

"She reckons there's nothing wrong," I tell him. I turn back to my sister. "You don't look well," I say, taking in her pale skin, the dark shadows beneath her eyes. "Are you eating? Drinking? Have you even slept?"

"We were worried about you," Danny adds.

"Why?" Her question lacks intonation. She doesn't seem to care.

"We'll explain later," I hiss. "Come on, you have to get up." Adam and Spinner could be back at any moment, and I'm not sure Lark is taking much in. She keeps gazing out into the distance. I shoot a panicked look at Danny. He's moved over to Adam's piano.

I wave to get his attention. "How do we get her home? It's so hot. We've only got our bikes."

Danny frowns. "We could flag down a car…"

"Come on," I tell Lark. "You need to stand."

"But Evan…" she begins. Her voice trails away.

"What about him?" I snap. I see him again in my mind's eye, standing calmly over Lark's prone body, as though she was nothing but a piece of furniture. "He's not worth a second of your time."

Her eyes harden. "We're soulmates. He loves me."

I glance at Danny, but he doesn't flinch.

"Of course Evan loves you," he says softly, coming over and squatting down in front of her. "We all do. Come home for now. You'll see Evan later. You need to rest."

His words have an effect. She gives a tiny nod and, when Danny offers her his arm, she takes it, rising from the sofa with all the energy of an eighty-year-old.

"What the hell is going on?"

I spin round. Spinner is standing in the studio doorway.

"What are you two doing here?" Without waiting for a reply, he strides across the room and yanks Lark away from Danny. "Get your hands off her." He turns to Lark. "Where do you think you're going, Aurora?"

Aurora?

Spinner's presence triggers something in Lark. "Nowhere," she says, jerking upright. She moves towards him. "I'm staying with you."

"Good girl." He drapes an arm round her shoulder and she melts into his side.

The hairs on my arms rise. "Evan, my sister isn't well. She needs to be at home."

"It's *Spinner* to you." His eyes glitter. "And she needs to be here. There's nothing wrong with Aurora, is there, baby?"

Lark shakes her head. It's the second time he's called her that, and she doesn't correct him.

"She collapsed," I say. "She needs a doctor."

"She's fine. It's hot. She's just been working hard." Spinner locks eyes with me, unblinking. "We were rehearsing all night. The festival's in ten days. Adam needs her perfect. No mistakes. That's what it takes, yeah? If you want to make it in this industry. You need commitment to be a star, isn't that right, baby?"

"That's right," Lark echoes, eyes glassy.

Spinner nods approvingly. He turns back to me and Danny. "You see? Everything's fine. Time for you to leave. I wouldn't want to have to call Adam."

"Adam *Piper*?" Danny challenges.

But his words fall flat. Spinner just blinks, like Danny's speaking French.

"I told you before," he says, "Adam's a private man. He doesn't like people interfering." He smirks. "He might change his mind, know what I mean? About *your* performance at Enrapture."

My body goes cold.

Spinner pulls Lark closer. "Better be on your way, little sister."

"Lark?" I try again. "Are you *sure* this is what you want?

Just come home tonight, take some time to think things throu—"

"I'm sure." She cuts me off abruptly, her voice colourless but clear. "I want to be here. I need to rehearse. Adam chose me and I won't let him down. I'm the songbird that heralds the new dawn. And I'm not Lark. I'm the Aurora."

21

We leave the studio in silence, Danny striding fast, his brow furrowed in thought, while I jog beside him, too baffled to speak. An argument is raging in my head:

Something is wrong with my sister. Why else would she collapse?

Because of the heat. Because she was rehearsing all night. She's totally exhausted.

Right. That explains her strange, disorientated state. But then…

"I'm not Lark. I'm the Aurora."

What was that about? What's with the total personality transplant, the ominous new name?

"Adam chose me and I won't let him down."

I shiver in the scorching sun. Perhaps this is what it's like being the protégée of some big music guru. They work you and work you until they break you, until you've conformed to their vision, reduced to a shell of your former self. Adam chose Lark, and there's nothing I can do about it – not if it's what she truly wants.

Not if she's chosen him too.

Questions fly like crossfire. *What will happen now? What will Spinner tell Adam?* There was an empty space on the drive where the silver Tesla stood. Perhaps Adam went to check on progress at the festival site. If so, he's bound to be back soon.

My heart quickens, despite everything. The thought of being stripped of my performance slot smothers me in fear. But what could Spinner say? We came to visit Lark – she is my sister, after all. We never got a chance to tell her about Fernanda, and Spinner seemed oblivious when Danny mentioned Piper's name.

Is Adam deceiving Spinner too?

The gates open eerily at our approach – another camera is watching us from a tree. As we haul our bikes out of the undergrowth, Danny turns to me.

"Wren, can we go to the cavern?"

"Now?" I frown. "Sure, but … why?"

A flash of something in those warm brown eyes. "Just something I noticed in the studio. A theory I want to check out."

Whatever Danny's theory is, it's clearly urgent because as soon as we get back, he tosses his bike against the hedge in the front garden without bothering to lock it up. I'm parched, desperate for a drink, but I follow his lead and do the same.

"Quick. Let's get in and close the door."

I look at him quizzically but I do as he says. As soon as I shut the cavern door, he waves his phone in my face.

"I took a photo."

"A photo of what?" I squint at the black-and-white image on his screen.

"The music on Adam's piano."

So that's what he was doing by the Steinway. I wait for him to explain.

"Zoom in." Danny taps his foot impatiently. "It's the music from the audition, right?"

I peer at the handwritten lines. "Maybe? But the paper was folded. I only saw the first two lines."

Danny nods at the screen. "There are creases in the paper, see? I think this is the whole thing."

I pinch out, enlarging the image. It's not a great shot – crooked and blurry – but it's distinct enough that I can make out eight clear staves, an intricate pattern of grey, fuzzy notes…

And a title.

"'Lullaby'," I read.

"'Lullaby'," Danny echoes. His eyes meet mine. "Wren, you sang two lines of this at the audition, then you got a headache. Lark sang the same two lines and felt faint. Was she singing this just now?"

I nod slowly, his implication dawning on me. *Was Lark singing this when she collapsed?*

"Adam played something on the piano," I murmur. "She sang it back like a zombie. Like she wasn't all there."

Danny nods slowly, grimly. He waits.

"No." I stop him. "That can't be…" I shake my head. "Danny, no. Lark is exhausted. Dehydrated. Adam is pushing her way too hard. That's why she collapsed. The *music* had nothing to do with it."

Danny shuffles. "You sure? We could test it out."

"You mean play it?" I start to laugh. *Now* I know why he wanted to come to the cavern. But what he's suggesting is ridiculous.

Isn't it?

Danny isn't laughing.

"OK, why not?" I say, handing the phone back to him. "I mean… it can't hurt. Airdrop the picture to me and I'll see if I can print it."

I move over to Dad's workstation in the corner, where his ancient Mac keeps company with an elderly printer. I fire them both up.

"Done," Danny says, and a minute later, the image is blown up on the monitor. In five more minutes, I'm holding a fuzzy hard copy in my hand.

"OK…" The air in the cavern is heavy, still. We look at one another, oddly on edge.

"I'll play it." Danny takes the music from me. "It's safer. You should wait outside."

I take the music back. "Don't be silly. She's my sister. It ought to be me." I prop the music on the keyboard stand and hesitate. "Sing or play?"

Danny bites his lip. "Maybe… play? For accuracy."

I giggle, suddenly nervous. "You'll stay with me, right?" My pulse is racing. *Stop it, Wren. You're being ridiculous.*

"Of course I'll stay." Danny pulls a stool up next to mine. "But I'll take out my hearing aids, just in case."

He does, placing them carefully on top of the keyboard. Then he turns down the volume as low as it can go, while I arrange my fingers on the keys.

I can't believe we're doing this.

"I'm right here," Danny whispers. "You can stop at any time."

"I'm fine." I laugh, smiling up at him. "Honest. It's going to be fine." I squint at the music in front of me. It looks so simple. So innocuous. *What on earth are we thinking?*

I take a deep breath and start to play.

Right from the very first line, my memories of the audition come flooding back – the sweet sadness of the melody, its beautiful refrain. It's eerie, yet soothing, and strangely irresistible, with hidden claws that seem to snag my brain.

"Still here," Danny murmurs next to me. "Nod if you're OK."

I nod, lazily. I'm OK. *More than OK.* A smile tugs the

corners of my mouth. I play the third line and the fourth, and the melody grows more complex, more compelling, difficult to describe – ancient yet modern, old yet new, playful like a folk-tune and as solemn as a hymn.

"Wren?" Danny whispers. "Can you hear me?"

I don't answer. Time is slowing down. My fingers keep on playing; the fifth line and the sixth, moving almost of their own accord. I feel the tension leave my body and my worries smooth away.

From far in the distance, Danny mumbles something, but I don't pay attention. It's not important… I play the seventh line, then the eighth. I'm nearing the end now, and my fingers start to slow. My mind feels loose, unmoored; starting to unravel. My thoughts are dissolving … draining away. My head feels heavy, hollow. Vacant. *Ready to receive.*

"Wren!"

A sharp sting makes my eyes water. I clasp a hand to my burning cheek. "What the hell?"

"Sorry, I'm sorry." Danny replaces his hearing aids with shaking hands. "I didn't mean to hurt you." He looks upset.

"It's fine," I murmur, groggy. "I was fine. I just zoned out for a second."

"Zoned out?" He blinks. "You're kidding, right?"

"No, I…" I stop. The expression on his face shuts me up. "Why, what happened?"

He looks at me. "You don't remember?"

"No." I remember feeling good. Content. *Amazing…* "Just tell me."

233

Gravely, he nods. "You started playing. I kept track, following your hand. You seemed OK at first, but then … I don't know. You were kind of … overwhelmed."

"The melody is really beautiful," I tell him. I can just about hear it, dancing in my head. I open my mouth to try to sing, but Danny puts a finger to my lips. "Don't!"

His tone takes me aback. "OK." I try to put my thoughts in order. "It's sort of … sad and sweet and intense, but in a good way," I say. "What's that word – *cathartic*? When you let all your feelings out?" I frown then, remembering. "Only… It's just that, afterwards, there was nothing left. And I felt sort of … empty."

Danny is listening intently, focused on my lips. "You fell forwards, do you remember that part?" He demonstrates. "It was scary."

I shake my head, not quite believing.

"I didn't finish playing," I say pointing to the music. "You interrupted me. You see this notation? The final lines are meant to repeat, an octave above. I couldn't have sung that. You'd need an incredible range to sing that high—"

Like Lark. Like Fernanda.

I don't say this out loud, but I wonder if Danny's thinking the same thing.

"There was something else," I say, sitting up. The memory pierces like a skyscraper through the fog still clouding my head. "It was more like an understanding really. When my mind was empty, I had the weirdest feeling. That I was 'ready to receive'."

Danny is watching my mouth. "Say that again."

I say it clearly, carefully. "My mind. It was 'ready to receive'."

The stifling air in the cavern suddenly seems to drop several degrees. Danny is sitting very still.

I look at him. "Receive what?"

22

"*Ready to receive*," I repeat the words again, shaking my head. "No. It doesn't make any sense. I must have imagined it."

"Did you, though?" Danny grows thoughtful. "Music is powerful. Sound is powerful, right? You don't need perfect hearing to know that. The effects can be profound – on your mood, your body, your brain." He stares into space, and his face takes on the sweetly serious look it always does when he's about to deep-dive into something scientific. "It's why people think that playing classical music to babies stimulates their development, or that gong baths have healing vibrations..." He pauses. "But what if somebody used the power of music for a more ... let's say, *unethical* purpose?"

He's losing me. "You mean like, subliminal messages, or backwards lyrics?" I giggle at the ridiculousness of it. "But 'Lullaby' is just a melody. It doesn't have any words."

"That doesn't mean it isn't powerful." He scowls at the thin piece of paper sitting innocently between us. "What if the music is a trigger? What if it prepares you for a message by making you more receptive?"

A realization dawns on me.

"This melody…" I look at Danny. "I've heard it before. And I don't mean at the audition, although come to think of it, it *was* kind of familiar, even then." I take a breath. "At Charlie's party. Spinner played this amazing track. There was a sample on it, just a phrase. I think it was *this* melody: it was 'Lullaby'. The first line. It was playing when Charlie fell."

A photo gallery flickers through my head: a sea of joyful faces, cascading neon feathers, Charlie's body lying in a heap.

Danny absorbs this information. "Do you remember what Spinner did next?"

I scrape the corners of my memory. "No, not really. It's all a blur."

"He took the mic." Danny frowns. "Do you know what he said?"

"No, do you?"

Danny scowls and shakes his head. "I'd taken my hearing aids out, remember? And I couldn't lip-read either – it was dark, I was too far away. Then Charlie fell and it was chaos." He looks me in the eye. "What if Spinner delivered a message?"

"A message? What kind of message?"

"About Enrapture." As soon as Danny says the word, I shiver. "Think about what happened next," he goes on. "Everyone became obsessed with the festival. You did. So did everyone we know. Everyone bought tickets. The festival sold out." He gets to his feet, pacing the cavern floor. "And who's the only person immune to all the hype? The only person who doesn't want to go?"

I look at him. "You."

"Right." Danny stops pacing. "Because I didn't hear Spinner. I didn't hear him or the music."

I'm silent. Hot, confused.

"You're saying we were, what, hypnotized?"

"Or brainwashed," Danny corrects.

I want to laugh, but I don't dare. His eyes are flints.

"What if Charlie's party was an experiment?" He starts pacing again. "Adam made Spinner play 'Lullaby' – a sample of it – to see if it had an effect." A pause. "And it did."

Something Spinner said comes back to me. *We were trying something out.*

Danny glares at the flimsy sheet of music. "The question is, now that Adam knows it works, what else is he planning to do with it?"

"Wait." I blink. My head is still fuzzy. "Slow down…"

"This music is dangerous, Wren." Danny turns to

look at me. "It puts people in a trance. And when they're entranced, they're empty vessels, 'ready to receive'. Ready to believe what Adam wants them to believe."

I stare. "You're not serious, Danny? Come on…"

Danny's eyes flash with inspiration. "Sofia said something about a platform…" He snatches up the music and brandishes it at me. "Wren, this is a tool. A weapon. A melody that controls behaviour. Adam Piper was a prodigy, remember? He studied music and psychology. If anyone could write this, he could. And now he's teaching it to Lark!"

Lark.

Of course. That's why Danny's so worked up.

"God, you're obsessed with her," I mutter.

"What? You're mumbling." Danny looks annoyed.

I look up at him. The cavern feels small and stuffy. Claustrophobic. "It's just a song, Danny!" I snap. "You're getting carried away."

"'*Lullaby*'!" He barks the word at me. "Wake up, Wren! The title says it all. It's so blatant! Adam wants Lark to sing this at the festival, when she performs as the Aurora with that prick Spinner on the main stage, and when she does, the audience will fall into a trance."

I wait for him to laugh, to tell me he's joking, but he doesn't. He doesn't even blink.

"OK…" I say, warily. "And then what?"

"And then he'll brainwash everyone!" Danny fires back. "With a message."

239

"But *what* message?"

His shoulders sag and he deflates. "I don't know."

Silence.

Part of me wants to put my arms round Danny and comfort him, but I'm hot and thirsty and irritable, and there's another, bigger part of me that's had enough. Danny's theory is *wild*. It can't be right. His obsession with Lark is ruining everything – our friendship, Enrapture, my big chance. Someone needs to put things in perspective.

"I don't want to argue," I say coolly, "but let's think this through. Say the music is … powerful." I choose my words with care. "Why isn't Adam affected by it? Why isn't Spinner? Adam could release 'Lullaby' as a record. Why put on a festival and get Lark to sing?"

"I don't know that either." Danny sinks into a chair. "Maybe Adam is immune. And Spinner. Both of them." He bites his lip thoughtfully. "Perhaps the music is more potent when it's live." His eyes narrow. "But as for why Adam needs Lark? That's easy. It's her voice. The melody is already powerful, but Lark's voice is something else. Put the two together and…" His hands imitate an explosion. "She's just … special."

Special. Of course she is.

Unlike me.

A door slams shut in my heart.

Danny stands. "We have to tell someone. We need to get Enrapture shut down."

Shut down? It echoes round my head. I find myself rising to my feet too.

"No." The word comes out calm and clear. I reach for my guitar; it gives me strength. "You've got this wrong, Danny. Enrapture is just a festival, that's all." Ignoring his glare, I battle on. "Lark is going to sing at it, I'm going to play at it, and if you don't want to come then that's your choice…"

"We need to tell someone." Danny's voice is shaking.

I grip my guitar like a shield.

"Do we? Who would we tell? What would we say?" I laugh, wildly in his face. "It's a crazy theory, Danny! Nobody's going to listen. Think of the businesses who've invested in the festival. Think of the work that's gone into the planning and the site. Hamlington *needs* Enrapture. *We* need Enrapture! We're bored and lost and broken, with nothing to look forward to. This could turn our lives around!"

Danny takes a step back. His huge brown eyes are wary.

I take a deep breath. I need to slow down, my heart's beating too fast. "Enrapture could change my life. I may not get another chance like this."

"Is that all that matters to you?" Danny growls. "You care about that, more than *your own sister*?"

"No, of course not. I—"

I reach for his arm but he shakes me off, moving towards the door.

Panic grips me. "Where are you going?"

241

He turns, his face filled with disdain.

"Oh, don't worry, Wren. I'm not running off to cancel Enrapture, if that's what you're afraid of." He laughs bitterly. "I wouldn't get very far by myself." His eyes shimmer, but there's a coldness within. "Think about it. There's only one thing more 'crazy' than this so-called 'theory' of mine. And that's the totally batshit idea that a deaf kid could know *anything* about music."

The cavern door slams shut.

I sink into the swivel chair, legs pulled up into my chest. Salty tears slide down my cheeks.

I love Danny, but he's not thinking clearly about this. He doesn't understand what this opportunity means to me. Enrapture is my chance to emerge from my sister's shadow. To be seen in a different light.

Everything's always about Lark.

Why can't it – for once – be about me?

I pick up my guitar and my hands move without thinking, finding chord shapes with my left, picking patterns with my right. There are a million things I'd like to say to Danny, but he's gone – so I throw my hurt and anger and confusion into the music instead.

Harmonies intertwine with melody as my song becomes more and more layered. Soon another verse begins to surface.

She's the special shining star who captivates your heart.
Everything she does makes people stare.

I'm singing in the shadows, desperate to shine,
Wishing you could see how much I care.

You need to wake up.
I wish you'd wake up.
Why don't you wake up and see?
You've been sleepwalking so long.
You don't notice me at all.
Don't be blinded by her light. See me.

23

I'm in the audience at Enrapture. Lark is on stage, dancing on a platform high above the ecstatic crowd. She's wearing a white dress and a flower crown, her body moving hypnotically to the creeping bass. Spinner is on another platform, huddled over his control deck.

The music starts to build. When Spinner salutes the crowd thousands of hands reach up into the air. The audience is going wild. People are crying with joy.

Lark lifts the microphone in front of her. She opens her mouth to sing.

But something isn't right.

From the shadows at the back of the stage, a ghostly girl group emerges. Fernanda is among them; I recognize her feathered costume. But who are the other two? One is wearing school uniform; the other is dressed in black. They sway to the music and I stare.

Fernanda. Anna Walker. Mia Hall.

But now something else is happening. Their movements are starting to change. They're jerking and twitching, becoming robotic. Staggering towards the front of the stage. One by one they slump, dropping to their knees.

Up on her platform Lark staggers too, perilously close to the edge.

"Lark!" I scream, but she doesn't hear me. I scream again.

Slowly her body keels forward and she falls—

I jerk awake, drenched in sweat. What the hell is going on? It's the bloody heat; my dreams are getting worse. And my head is so messed up, everything is merging into one.

I smash out some messages.

> Lark, it's me. Please don't ignore this. Are you feeling better? Have you had some rest? I know it's your last exam this week. I'll see you at college? Please tell me you'll be there x

> Mum, Dad: I think you might be on the road. Can you call me when you get this message? Nothing to worry about. Wren x

Danny, are you there? I know
you're reading this. Please reply.
I just want to talk. W x

No reply. I'm shouting into the void.

Danny's silent treatment hurts the most. Every message I send he leaves on read, and for the rest of the week at college all I seem to see is the back of him, slipping out of stale, muggy rooms the moment I enter them. In English, the only class we share, he keeps his eyes firmly fixed forward, never once turning round to catch my eye. The moment class is dismissed, he vanishes. Sometimes, at break or lunchtime, I see him chatting briefly to Jiv or Alex or the rest of the gang, but the minute he sees me approaching, he walks away.

"What's the matter with Danny?" Ruby asks, distantly.

We're walking to the library, or just barely. The heat makes it hideous to move. Meena is flagging a few steps behind us, humming distractedly under her breath. The tune snags my ears and I recognize it; it's that riff, the one I keep on hearing.

Ruby looks at me with empty eyes. "He's acting strange. Did you have a fight?"

"More a ... disagreement." I bite my lip to stop it wobbling.

"A lovers' tiff?" Meena finally tunes in. I start to correct her but she only smiles vaguely. "Like Ruby."

"What? Did something happen with Isaac?" I peer more

246

closely at Ruby. Her eyes are red-rimmed.

"Isaac kissed Isla," Meena says. "Yesterday, in the canteen. In front of everyone." She says it carelessly, digging in her bag, fingers groping for her phone.

"Oh, Rubes," I murmur. "I'm sorry."

"It was my own fault," Ruby intones, staring into the distance. "I haven't been making enough effort."

"*What?*" I'm about to say more, but a chord chimes, distracting me. I turn to see Meena gazing at her phone screen and catch a flash of rainbow colour.

"What happened with Danny?" Ruby asks again, though I'm not sure she's really interested. Her eyes keep darting back to Meena. Meena has completely stopped and is staring blankly at her screen. Ruby slows to a halt too.

"We had an argument," I say. "About Enrapture."

"Enrapture?" They both twitch and look at me, alert.

I hesitate. There's so much on my mind. I need to talk to someone, but I haven't a clue how to begin. I make it simple. "Danny doesn't want to go."

Just then the library door opens and Ms Mayer comes out, her arm round the student teacher, the young woman who took my history class the other day. It's obvious she's been crying. I shoot a look at my friends.

"Year nine boys," Meena shrugs, casually. "They put her in her place."

I blink. "What do you mean, *her place*?"

"Oh, you know. Boys will be boys," Ruby says, vaguely. We find a shady corner in the library. I'm about to challenge Ruby's comment when she murmurs, "Danny won't go to Enrapture?" Her brow is furrowed, like she's still processing the conversation from two minutes ago.

Meena stares. "He has to go. We all do."

Ruby nods. "He'll be the only person in Hamlington not there."

"Danny doesn't care about that," I say, taking a breath. "He thinks there's something … sinister about it."

"Sinister?" Meena echoes. Ruby giggles as she pulls her phone out. Giggling is so not Ruby. She opens the app with well-practised fingers. Around us, heads turn as the chime sounds and the beat kicks in. My own heart flips and my ears prick up.

"Phones away!" The librarian looks in our direction.

Reluctantly, Ruby mutes the sound. She recites from the app in a whisper. "Briar Stage, local talent stage, mindfulness, meditation, spiritual guidance… Sounds very sinister to me!" She giggles again.

When she puts it like that…

"I guess Danny's not a big fan of Spinner," I whisper. "I mean, it's understandable, right? You've seen the stuff he posts?"

I expect them to agree, so it's jarring how vacantly they stare back.

"Spinner is inspiring," Meena says. "He's overcome oppression to define his own success."

"He's controversial," Ruby adds. "But that's deliberate. He wants to provoke debate."

"He spins the truth," Meena adds, and they both nod sagely.

I open my mouth but no sound comes out. I don't know what to say to them. These girls are my friends. We've known each other for ever. They're smart and assertive and perceptive, yet they're defending Spinner unquestioningly, reciting verbatim from his socials.

"Is it true he's dating Lark?" Meena whispers. "Ava Martin said his car was parked outside school last week."

A girl close to us turns round. "Are you talking about Lark and Spinner?"

"Was that Lark on Spinner's Insta the other day?" her friend chips in. "Are they really together?"

More heads turn, rubbernecking. Strange, blank eyes all staring at me.

I push back my chair, uncomfortable under their gaze. "Sorry, I have to go."

I can't get out of there fast enough.

I pass a miserable weekend, feeling lonely and conflicted. The house feels huge without my family here to fill it, the rooms oppressively hot and silent. I miss a call from Mum on the Saturday, but when I try to return it I'm cut off, and there are no more updates on the group chat. According to Dad's itinerary, my parents are trundling in a tour bus somewhere on their way to Tromsø, about as far north as it's possible to go. All I can do is be patient and wait until they're back within signal or range.

I'd give anything for an argument with Lark, but I don't hear a peep from her either. I can't say I'm surprised. There's less than a week until the festival, and no doubt she's spending every spare minute preparing to be the Aurora, doting on Spinner and worshipping Adam's every word.

It's like she's forgotten I exist.

With Danny, there's no ambiguity. He's definitely still ignoring me, and it feels like a punch to the stomach. I spend all my time in the baking heat of the cavern, playing my guitar and trying not to think about him, my amp turned up as loud as it will go. With every rehearsal my song has improved until now I couldn't be more ready to perform. And yet… I can't find any satisfaction in it. Danny is angry with me. Our argument has hurt him.

He thinks I'm in the wrong.

Somehow I make it through to Monday. As the week of the festival dawns, incredibly the temperature rockets higher, and school is next-level intense. With Enrapture scheduled for Friday night, Mrs Woods calls another assembly, supposedly about the dangers of heatstroke but with a barely concealed subtext about the consequences of skipping school to get to the festival early. Nobody is listening, nobody can concentrate; phones chime constantly and people hum, even as she's speaking. I slump wretchedly in my chair at the back, torn between running out and joining in. Only one thought can calm my inner turmoil: My parents come home on Thursday.

They'll help me work out what to do.

It's Tuesday night when Mum calls.

I pounce on the phone. I've spent the evening motionless on the sofa, watching mindless TV to stop me brooding and pushing cereal around in a bowl. My appetite is non-existent.

The line is terrible. I can barely hear Mum over the crackling static. There's a delay that makes it difficult to talk naturally, and huge chunks of her conversation keep cutting out. As she tries to tell me about Runaway Summer's recent gigs, the distance between us feels enormous. A lump forms in my throat. There are so many things I'd wanted to talk to her about – Adam and Enrapture, Lark and Spinner, Mia's investigation, my friends being weird – but now I have the chance, I don't know where to start. Plus, there's something in her voice that stops me, something that translates clearly across the hundreds of miles, despite the terrible line. Something I haven't heard in years.

Joy.

How can I spoil that?

"... missing you so much ... incredible gigs ... everyone dancing and singing ... fans of the TV show ... brand new audience ... forgotten how much I love it ... Dad is in his element ... a beautiful country ... exploring every day ... so good for us—"

I push down my problems and swallow back my tears.

"... everything fine back home?"

I mutter something bland and hope she can't tell that I'm struggling to form words.

The subject turns to Lark.

"… exams going well? … very sparse messages … suppose she's revising … quick word? … if she's there…?"

I falter. *Do I tell the truth?*

I choose a version of it. "Lark's, um, busy. She's not said much about her exams. She's been … spending a lot of time with Evan, that DJ guy, remember? They're getting pretty serious."

A long delay. The line fades in and out.

"… intense relationship … when I was her age … unhealthy … be careful…"

I get the gist and squirm with guilt. Mum changes the subject.

"… Danny … rehearsals…?"

"Danny's… It's all good." I sniff back tears. "I wrote a song."

"… hear it … proud of you, sweetheart … get ready for tonight's gig! … put Dad on … wants to ask you something…"

"Wait! Mum—"

I'm not ready for her to go. But there's a buzzing sound and suddenly Dad is on the other end. He must have found a better signal, because the line is slightly clearer.

"Wren, love! It's so nice to hear your voice… Listen, just quickly, there's something we need to ask you … leave Tromsø early tomorrow … meant to be heading back to

252

Bergen but Seb's had an offer ... chance to extend the trip ... just a couple more nights ... drive to Oslo instead ... there's a big venue ... gap in their schedule ... it's a massive opportunity..."

"Right." My phone feels heavy in my hand.

"... very long drive ... and we'd be home a tiny bit later, on Saturday ... miss your festival ... we won't agree, if you're not happy..."

A pause. I know he's waiting, but I can't find the words.

"Wren? ... hello? ... hello? No, I think I've lost her..." There's a static hiss, like wind blowing, then the line goes dead.

Anxiety twists in my stomach. My parents won't be home on Thursday, after all. They're driving to Oslo for a gig and extending their tour. They're having the time of their lives – this is the breakthrough they've been waiting for. *But they're going to miss Enrapture!* They won't be back *before* the festival, unless I give them cause for concern.

Could I do that to them? I can't.

But what about Lark...?

I pull up my email. It's pointless calling back when they've got no signal, but they'll pick this up at their next hotel.

From: wrenmackenzie@gcloud.com
To: macandpaloma@themackenzies.net
Subject: Oslo

Hey Dad, Hey Mum.

So good to hear from you, although that phone line was terrible! Glad the tour is going well. Oslo sounds amazing, but it's a shame you'll miss Enrapture. I've written a new song, and Lark is performing on the main stage with Evan. She even has a stage name, "the Aurora". It was Adam's idea. Turns out he used to have a big recording studio in Albuquerque where he went by the name Adam Piper. Danny won't play at the festival with me. He's not too keen on Adam.

I miss you.

Love, Wren xx

I press send and sink on to my bed. It's the right thing to do, making out that everything is fine. Everything *will* be fine. I'm just tired, hot, emotional. And missing Danny. Although it's better he's not here with me right now, planting more doubts in my mind and messing with my head.

My laptop chirps, making me look up. A new email has dropped into my inbox, but it's not from Mum and Dad. The sender isn't in my contacts.

Their pseudonym makes me shiver.

From: A. Sister
Subject: Important: please read.

I click.

There's no message, only a file attached. I know it could be spam, junk, a virus – but something tells me I have to open it.

A photo fills my screen. It's a scan of a clipping from a newspaper, all in Spanish, but at the top left is a picture of a girl, a photo that looks like it's been taken from a high school yearbook. I recognize her immediately.

Fernanda.

The date on the newspaper is *13 de Marzo 2023*, and beneath the photo is a small box of text. I paste it into a translator and read it quickly.

Local girl Fernanda Alvaraz Ruiz died on Saturday 11 March, after collapsing three days earlier. According to a witness who asked not to be named, Fernanda was working on her new song "Canción de Cuna" at the renowned Piper Productions Studio in Albuquerque when she suddenly became ill. By the time paramedics arrived she was unconscious. Fernanda was transferred to Presbyterian Hospital, Albuquerque, where she remained in a comatose state for 72 hours. After doctors failed to detect any brain activity, her family took the difficult decision to terminate her life support. A close friend of Fernanda said the singer had been in good health, but that her behaviour had been erratic in the weeks preceding her death. Fernanda's family were unavailable for comment.

The blood drains from my body. I read the article again. I know Sofia has sent this to me. She's used an anonymous account to avoid detection. She did it because I told her about Lark. Clearly, there are things she wants me to know.

That Fernanda fell ill *during* a session with Piper.

That she was otherwise in good health.

That her recent behaviour had been strange.

Fernanda was just like Lark.

I swallow. Sofia wasn't being difficult, refusing to engage with me. She was *scared*. She wanted to help me, but she couldn't talk freely – and there must be a reason why. Could her family have been threatened? Has their silence been bought?

Canción de cuna...

I type the words with leaden fingers. My language skills aren't up to much, but I'm pretty sure I know how the song title will translate.

Cradle Song.

I read it again, slowly.

Cradle Song. Or in other words: "Lullaby".

24

I'm in a large, white place that smells of disinfectant. There are curtains and machines, and people moving purposefully, with cold, serious faces.

Lark is lying silently in a bed. Her eyes are closed and her beautiful white dress has been replaced by a thin blue gown. Her body is hooked up to one of the machines. It's the only thing keeping her alive.

But hers is not the only bed here. Four more beds, four more people lying in this room. Five girls in a coma. Slowly, I count them.

Fernanda. Anna. Mia. Charlie. Lark.

The digital pulse of their heartbeats fills the room, beating

together in sync. Someone – I don't know who – starts humming.
It seeps into my brain, fogging my thoughts. I try to shut my ears
and block it out.

And now, the pulse becomes a drone as the displays on the
machines all flatline as one. Doctors swarm, confused. Mum
is here, and Dad too, crying and shouting. And now Danny
has appeared. He's waving a red flag and pointing a finger in
my face.

"This is your fault, Wren. I tried to tell you. There were so
many signs, but you refused to see."

No.

I lie there frozen, paralysed with understanding.

Fernanda died, learning to sing "Lullaby". And now
my sleeping brain has done what my waking brain refused
to do earlier, and untangled another mystery that's been
staring me in the face.

My sister is not the only singer Adam has recruited since
he arrived in Hamlington.

Anna Walker sang soprano in a choir.

Mia Hall sang vocals in a band.

I dredge up the toxic group chat, and the cold blue
screen confirms my fears.

Mia – amazing bass player, awesome vocalist 😁

Both Anna and Mia were found within a few miles of
Adam's studio, without a mark on their bodies, or any sign

of violence or substance abuse. *Because the music killed them.* The thought turns my flesh clammy.

"Lullaby" entrances listeners, but the singers never wake up.

I think of Charlie dancing on the PA. Not a singer maybe, but close enough. Like a singer, she was an instrument for the music, the vibrations rushing through her body.

I shiver.

If one short, recorded sample was strong enough to put Charlie in a coma, how powerful will the melody be when the perfect voice performs it, live? Suddenly I'm horribly certain.

The entire audience will be enraptured…

And my sister won't survive.

I sit up, blood roaring in my ears. I don't need to check Lark's bedroom to know that it's empty. She hasn't come home. She might never come home again. With trembling fingers, I pick up my phone and add another message to my pleading line of texts.

> LARK
> Call me! It's *URGENT*!
> You're in danger.
> Please. You have to trust me.

No answer.

What the hell do I do? There's no point forwarding the newspaper report. Lark wouldn't understand it, and I can't compromise Sofia's family's safety. I'll bet anything that Adam is checking Lark's phone. I can't even report her missing. She's an adult, staying at her boyfriend's place — what would the police do? I have no real proof that her life is in danger, and nothing to connect Adam with Anna and Mia. Only an anonymous email about a random girl from Albuquerque. My parents are in deepest Norway, totally out of reach, and last night I told them to extend their stay.

As for Enrapture, stopping it feels impossible. I'd be the most hated person in Hamlington. Festival fever is out of control.

I bury my head in my hands.

I need to speak to my sister. I need to stop her from singing.

Enrapture is three days away.

First thing in the morning, I make a beeline for the sixth form social hub. I need to find Danny, but Lark is my priority; I have to put her first. And if she won't answer my messages, perhaps her friends can help.

As soon as I walk into the room, the heat hits me and my eardrums are assaulted. Tiny chimes, going off like fireworks. That heartbeat pulse. The jagged riff. My thoughts start to fog and my purpose dims…

But not for long. I'm ready for it.

Jamming my earbuds in my ears, the sound muffles and my focus returns. If Adam helped Spinner to create that riff, I know enough to steer well clear.

"Looking for Danny?" Isaac is idling in the doorway and he steps into my path, blocking my way. His glassy eyes slide all over my body. "I heard that Lark is dating Spinner to get famous. Are all the Mackenzie women sluts, or just your sister?"

"Get out of my way, creep." I push past him, feeling sick. Sweet, shy Isaac has become a total Spinner clone. He throws an insult after me but I ignore him, my eyes scanning the room. *There.*

On a sofa in the corner, nursing a cup of coffee, is Charlie. She looks up in surprise as I approach.

"Wren."

"Charlie. How are you?" It's quieter in the corner. Cautiously, I take my earbuds out.

"I've been better." Charlie stares blankly at her hands. "I have to repeat the year. My recovery's been slower than they thought it would be."

"I'm sorry," I say, and I mean it. "I … um … I need to speak to Lark. I was wondering if you'd seen her?"

Charlie shakes her head. Aisha wanders over, followed by Jasmine. They eye me warily, perching on the arms of the sofa either side of Charlie, like guards.

"I need to speak to my sister," I try again. "She's not answering messages and she … she's not been home."

The girls exchange slow, impassive glances. "We don't see Lark any more," Aisha states, coolly. "We're not in touch." Her stare goes right through me.

"You mean she's dropped you?" I can't believe what I'm

hearing. These girls have been Lark's friends since primary.

"Lark has dropped everything," Charlie says, flatly. "None of us have spoken to her. We've tried but she doesn't reply. Maybe she has a new phone." Her voice lacks emotion. She doesn't seem to care.

"We don't blame her," Jasmine adds, blandly.

"That's right. We understand."

"Things are different now she's the Aurora."

The room feels suddenly chilly. "You know about the Aurora?" I say.

"Everyone knows," Aisha says, dreamily. "She's everywhere."

"Her and Spinner." Jasmine's face is wistful. "I can't wait to hear her sing."

"See you at Enrapture," they chorus, getting up to go.

"Wait." I block their way. "Hold on a minute. You're still going to the festival?" I blink, surprised. "Lark dropped you, but you still want to hear her sing?"

"Of course." Aisha shrugs.

"She's the songbird," Jasmine adds. "She heralds the new dawn."

"Everyone will gather." Charlie's eyes take on a glossy sheen. "It's Enrapture. Everyone must go."

They leave and I stare after them, horrified. They're acting like they don't have a choice, and, until recently, I felt the same. But the scales are falling rapidly from my eyes. Spinner's music has indoctrinated all of us.

And they all know Lark's new name.

I pull out my phone, foreboding fluttering in my belly. I rarely look at Lark's social media – I couldn't care less about her shopping hauls, her parties, her new acrylic nails. But now I open Instagram and search for her account.

It's gone.

The account has been deleted. All Lark's posts – photos of her trip to Barcelona in the summer, last year's school production and the lower sixth form prom, all the house party shots and karaoke clips, all the selfies she loves to take.

Vanished. The whole lot.

With dread in my heart, I search for "the Aurora".

My breath catches. *There she is.*

Except it isn't Lark at all. It's someone else. A version of Lark I've never seen. Someone oozing glamour, charisma, poise. Her profile picture looks utterly unreal, as though it's been generated by AI or thrown through an "international superstar" filter. It's a close-up shot of Lark staring into the camera, her expression blank and inscrutable. Bare shoulders hint at out-of-shot nakedness; her skin is flawless; her make-up impeccable; her ice-blonde hair tinted subtly with feathery rainbow strands.

She looks how she sounds – like an angel.

Underneath her profile picture are three words:

HEARING IS BELIEVING

Beneath the text is a video link. An uneasy feeling washes over me. Even so, I know I need to watch it. Turning the volume down low, I hold my breath and click.

That chord. That pulsing heartbeat. That snaking bassline. That hooky riff.

And now a film starts to play, a series of images flickering on the screen; snatched pieces of footage, handheld and shaky, like a nostalgic, old-fashioned home movie. A girl in a white dress is running through a wood. Her hair streams behind her in the colours of the rainbow. The same girl, a crown of flowers on her rainbow hair, looks over a sun-baked valley. Here she is again, reclining gracefully on a grand piano. And here, peacefully asleep, with her crown cast carelessly aside, her rainbow hair splayed on her pillow.

I shiver. It's Lark, of course, at Adam's studio or in his grounds and in his house; Lark – looking like a film star, a vision. I can't take my eyes off her. The images are hypnotic; I feel like I could watch them for ever. And all the while, the music is mesmeric, even at this muted volume. I know deep down I shouldn't listen to it, that I should block it out, but my finger hovers over the controls, itching to turn the sound up.

Lark stretches, rising from her slumber, and the camera zooms in on her face. I catch a quick glimpse of cold, empty eyes – but then she opens her perfect red mouth, and a high, pure sound comes forth.

The first line of "Lullaby".

I swoon, almost dropping my phone. Just as suddenly,

the video fades, the sound cuts completely, and I jerk upright, blinking as a caption appears on the screen.

LULLABY

The stunning new single from Spinner,

featuring the Aurora

Hear it **LIVE** at Enrapture

June 21

PLAY VIDEO AGAIN

My hand creeps towards the play button—

NO.

I need to resist; I *force* myself to resist.

I sink on to the sofa, shaken. The clip was barely thirty seconds long, and I had the sound turned right down, but the effect it had was immense. And now that riff is stuck in my head again, an insidious earworm, impossible to ignore.

And I'm not the only one affected.

I don't know how long this account and video have been live, but already the Aurora has tens of thousands of followers – hundreds and hundreds of comments from people all raving about her beauty, her talent … and "Lullaby".

Her profile picture glows with a rainbow shimmer to indicate that a new story has appeared. I click, and an announcement fills the screen.

Excited to reveal that we are **HEADLINING**
at Enrapture!
So grateful for this opportunity ♥
COUNTDOWN TO THE NEW DAWN
See you at sunset on the Briar Stage.

My head starts spinning. My pulse is racing fast.

Lark isn't simply playing at Enrapture – she's *headlining* the main stage. Spinner and the Aurora are the festival's closing act. My sister – my annoying big sister – has been plucked from obscurity, catapulted to fame, and given an extraordinary opportunity to perform. Once, I would have been jealous, maybe – but not now. Not anymore. Because this isn't an opportunity, it's a catastrophe.

Lark has a deadly job to do for Adam.

And she clearly hasn't the faintest idea.

25

I'm sitting on the wall between Danny's house and mine, the sun beating on my head and my legs bouncing nervously.

Where is he? I need to talk to him. I need his help. I couldn't find him after school, and he's still not replying to my texts.

I open my lyric notebook, making tiny tweaks to my song in an effort to distract myself. It has a name now, "Song for a Sleepwalker", not that it matters any more. I jot a few words down, my writing jittery.

Come on, Danny! When will you be home?

The second the car pulls into the drive, I jump down

from the baking hot wall. I must look a mess because Debs shoots me an odd look, but mercifully she says nothing. Danny silently helps his mum get the shopping bags from the boot, stubbornly refusing to acknowledge me or even look in my direction – but as he doesn't tell me to go away either, I follow them both into the house and meekly help to put the groceries away. Debs frowns and withdraws, leaving us to it.

I stand in the middle of the kitchen, waiting. Danny's jaw is locked and his shoulders are stiff. He's deliberately not looking at me so that we don't have to talk. But I'm not leaving until we do.

I dip into his eyeline.

Danny scowls. "What do you want, Wren?"

"I came to say sorry. You were right."

A raised eyebrow. A tiny nod.

"There's some stuff I need to show you. I, um, finally figured some stuff out. And it's… Well, it's not good."

Danny stands, studying me for a long time. Finally, he jerks his chin towards the ceiling. I follow him upstairs.

Danny's room is small and cool and smells of Danny. I stand for a moment, breathing it in. It feels like the first real breath I've drawn all week. It's comforting being here, surrounded by all his familiar things – his battered guitar case and second-hand amp; his bookshelf crammed with science books; the beautiful print of a barn owl hanging above the bed; his faded beanbag, where his ancient cat Darwin is stretched out blissfully in sleep.

I have so many things to tell him, but suddenly I'm overwhelmed, and something else slips out of my mouth.

"I missed you."

I crouch down to stroke Darwin, blinking back tears.

Danny squats down beside me. Reaching out, he gently lifts my chin to see my lips.

He didn't hear. I open my mouth with an excuse—

"I missed you too." His thumb softly traces my cheek.

We look at each other without speaking.

"So…" Danny stands up abruptly, his long fingers running nervously through his hair. "You said you had something to show me?"

"Yeah." I blink, thrown. "That's right." I pat my pocket, but my phone isn't there. Flustered, I tip out my bag on his duvet … pens, papers, textbooks, lyric notebook … there it is. Quickly, I find the email then I hand Danny my phone and watch as he reads the report about Fernanda.

"Sofia sent this?" He sinks on to the bed.

"From an anonymous account. I think you're right: she's scared to speak."

He's too kind to say, *I told you so.*

"But that's not all." I sit down next to him and tell him everything – including my theory about Anna and Mia. "I think Adam's been searching for the perfect singer."

Slowly, Danny takes this in. "And he'd already found Spinner." He nods. "A good-looking guy with a ready-made following and a truckload of anger and ambition.

269

All he needed was the voice."

I shudder. "Have a look at this." I pull up the Aurora account on Instagram and play the film, carefully muting the sound.

"There's a riff at the beginning of the video," I explain, as the screen fades to black. "It's on Spinner's socials and the Enrapture app too. Everyone is humming it. I think it was also part of the track that Spinner played at Charlie's party. He called it a 'work in progress'." I pause, giving Danny time to process. "I don't know when Adam wrote the melody for "Lullaby", but I think he's been testing it, perfecting it, for a while. First on Fernanda. Then on Anna. Then on Mia. And he's been working with Spinner on the arrangement, making it as powerful as possible. The lead-up to "Lullaby" – the opening bars before the vocals come in – it kind of … gets inside your body and hooks itself inside your brain."

Danny nods slowly, his forehead a criss-cross of lines.

I go on. "When you hear it, it … *intensifies* your feelings about whatever you're looking at: Spinner, the Aurora, Enrapture. It heightens your obsession and turns you into a fanatic." I look Danny in the eyes. "But the melody is the most dangerous part of all. You were right. Adam's been training Lark. He needs her to be perfect. At Enrapture, all the elements will finally come together, live, in a massive arena. Spinner's music and Lark's voice. Nobody will be able to resist." I swallow. "Lark's going to mesmerize the crowd, even if it kills her."

Danny's eyes flash. "*The Aurora*," he murmurs. "Of

270

course. It means the Dawn." He shakes his head. "Lark is just a puppet and Adam's the puppeteer. He's using her. He only needs one performance; he doesn't care what it does to her." He scowls. "The part I don't get is *why*. Why is he doing it?"

"I don't know." I shrug, miserably. "He wants what Spinner wants, I suppose. Fame, money, adoration…"

"No." Danny shakes his head. "He already has money. And he had fame…" He falls silent, thinking. "Sofia said he wants a *platform*…"

"It doesn't really matter what he wants," I say. "It's how he's going to do it. We have to stop Lark from performing."

It sounded simple in my head.

"Enrapture opens on Friday," I say, forging onward. "We have to go, it's the only way. The festival is the one place we know that Lark will be, the one place we can reach her. We're meant to be playing, so we'll have passes, right? Backstage access."

Danny says nothing. We both know I'm running on assumptions.

I carry on, regardless. "We get there. We find Lark, and we show her this –" I point at Sofia's clipping – "make her understand the danger she's in if she sings. And then we get her out of there."

Fear flits across Danny's face. "But Wren, you've been just as obsessed with Enrapture as anyone. You're not immune to the music. It won't be safe."

I falter for a second, taken aback. *I thought his priority was Lark?* Then I pull my earbuds from my pocket. "Active noise-cancelling?" I smile, nervously. "You should bring some too. They're not foolproof, they won't block absolutely everything, but they'll help. After that, we'll just have to be careful."

Danny nods. Then his eyes narrow. "Wait a minute. Are you sure this isn't some elaborate scheme just to make sure you get to perform?"

I swallow.

He doesn't know about my song. My poor, redundant song.

"What's wrong? Is there something you're not telling me?"

"Of course not. I'm fine." I pull myself together. *This is not about me. Not today.* "Danny Akintola, you can trust me." I place my hand on my heart. "I'm a reformed character and a true believer. I've seen the error of my ways." I look him directly in the eye. "I still want to go to Enrapture. But all I want to do is save my sister."

26

The twenty-first of June, the day of Enrapture.

My nerves jangle as I stare out of my bedroom window, across the garden to Danny's. His curtains are still drawn. Surely he can't be asleep?

I smile softly, remembering all the times we've signalled to each other with torches, or left secret symbols on our windowsills; private messages for the other to decode. My stomach twists. Danny's my best friend and today, he'll win my sister's heart. If everything goes to plan, by sunset tonight he'll be the handsome prince on the trusty steed, hacking back the thorns to free the princess.

How could Lark not fall for him after that?

I sweep the thought aside. It doesn't matter. The only thing that matters is getting her back.

The heat scorches me through the glass. It's not even eight, but already the sun has burned off the mist that shrouds the summit of the Wrekin and is climbing high in the sky. By this afternoon, Hamlington will be blazing.

In time for the start of Enrapture.

That familiar thrill zips through me, but I summon the strength to ignore it, like an addict trying to dry out. The way I'm feeling isn't real. It's a product of Adam's programming – his music and his messaging – working on my brain for months. Even so, as I dress, I can't help feeling that I'm standing on the cusp of something. Something *life changing.*

After all, that's what Enrapture promised us.

At one, I meet Danny and we leave for the bus. The sun is blistering and my shoulders are tight with tension. To distract myself, I dig out my phone and find the email that came through last night. It was sent by someone called Jim, the stage manager for the local talent stage, and – just as I'd hoped – he attached two QR codes as a substitute for official festival tickets. No mention of backstage access, but at least we'll be able to get in.

The bus swings into the road and when it reaches our stop, I blink at how busy it is. It's only a public bus, not some official festival transport, but it's already crammed with teenagers from all the local schools. Clearly everyone has decided to ignore their teachers' warnings and take the afternoon off. We squeeze down the aisle, the crowded space hotter than a sauna, and I catch sight of Danny's expression; a tight grimace directed at the din. The noise is intense, way beyond regular excitement, a clamouring that borders on the hysterical, with people shrieking, whooping and drumming on their seats. My hand slides into the pocket of my cut-offs, checking yet again that I've got my earbuds with me, fully charged and already enabled. I need my wits about me today.

"It's five miles to the main car park," Danny says, as miraculously we grab the last two seats.

I nod in reply and re-read Jim's email, butterflies darting in my belly. There's no special treatment for the lowly local musicians. From the main car park, it's a walk to the main entrance. The gates open to the public at two, and our artist wristbands will be waiting for us. After that, we're supposed to head to the local talent stage to sign in.

Not that we'll be doing that.

I smile a rueful smile. Jim has included the line-up order and the sight of our names on the list makes my heart ache. *Wren Mackenzie and Daniel Akintola.* We're scheduled to play at six, right after a band called Cosmic Kittens, and just before Jiv and Alex.

"You would have killed it," Danny murmurs, reading over my shoulder.

"It doesn't matter." I stamp my disappointment out. Lark is my priority, like she should have been from the beginning. Plus, it's clear how insignificant the local talent

275

stage is in the grand scheme of things. When I check the Enrapture app – the sound safely on mute – it doesn't even warrant a mention.

That's odd. I frown. There's still so little information. The only stage mentioned is the Briar Stage, and the only artists listed are the headline act: Spinner and the Aurora.

Danny is gazing out of the window, but I can feel him getting antsy and tense. The bus keeps stopping – five, six, seven times – to let more people cram on, and, every time it does, he tuts and jiggles his leg impatiently. Soon, it's standing room only on board, with dozens of teens clinging to the poles and overhead straps, a restless army in festival clothes. Lots of girls are dressed in white – thin, skimpy nighties to offset the heat. I glance down at my red T-shirt and cut-offs.

Guess I missed the memo.

Suddenly the bus jerks and comes to a creaking halt. Everyone groans.

"What's going on?" Danny mutters. "Why aren't we moving? We should be there now. It shouldn't take this long." He stands up, craning his neck over the crowds to see. "Oh shit. Wren, look!"

His panicked tone pulls me to my feet. The bus has stopped at the top of an incline and I look down at the single winding road ahead. It's jam-packed with hundreds of cars, bumper to bumper, as far as the eye can see. Everyone is heading in the same direction, towards the bowl-shaped valley of Devil's Dale. More cars are trying to join the road at every junction, countless shiny tin boxes, blocking the narrow country lanes. Horns blare angrily as drivers lose their tempers. Not a single vehicle is moving.

"This is gonna take hours," Danny wails. "We haven't got time!"

"I know."

I press my nose to the window, my mouth open in dismay. Cars are pulling over on to the verges now. One by one, engines cut out around us and car doors slam, as drivers give up and start traipsing the remaining distance on foot. Hordes of teenagers are funnelling towards the valley, like rats scampering down a drain.

Danny turns to me. "We'll have to walk too."

"How far are the main gates?"

He shrugs. "Dunno. Miles probably. But we've got no choice."

The other passengers have the same idea. We're caught in a virtual stampede as kids hammer on the driver's cabin, demanding to be let off. Finally, the doors hiss open and we all stumble out.

Unsurprisingly, the road is crammed with people. Heat rises up from the tarmac making the air shimmer, as I stand for a moment, just staring. I knew Enrapture was sold out, but I never knew how many tickets had been sold. This is more than just the population of Hamlington. The whole county could be here, maybe more. And there's something else surprising, too – everyone is around our age.

I shiver as a thought occurs to me.

It's no coincidence. It's deliberate. Adam's music hooks the teenage brain.

Danny and I merge into the crowd, slowly swimming downstream with single-minded determination. The mood is strange, the hyper energy of the bus morphed into something much more twitchy and intense. I see more girls dressed in white, plodding along automatically, like semi-vacant brides. One girl next to me is dressed in a long white gown with a crown of paper flowers in her hair. With a start, I recognize it as a home-made version of the one Lark was wearing in the video clip. Another girl is wearing a long blonde wig and she's tinted the tips with rainbow-coloured pens. Now that I'm alert to it, I see dozens of them, hundreds even. Aurora superfans – fans of my sister – totally, utterly obsessed.

I know Danny's noticed because his eyes are wide, but now I'm picking up something else, something he's probably not aware of – the conversation running through the crowd. Like a fly buzzing at a window, the same words keep hitting my eardrums, over and over and over: *Spinner. The Aurora. Spinner. The Aurora.*

They're all anyone can talk about.

The girl in the flower crown starts humming under her breath, and people around her join in. Before I can react, the "Lullaby" riff seeps in and a heady rush of euphoria engulfs me. Quickly, my thoughts begin to cloud. With a massive effort, I dig out my earbuds from my pocket and plug them in my ears.

"That was close." I link arms with Danny as the noise dims. We edge a safe distance away.

The crowd moves at a snail's pace. After more than an hour, everyone is hot, frustrated, sunburnt, and we've only just passed the main car park. Two o'clock has been and gone, so I'm guessing that the gates must have opened, but there's still no sign of the main entrance. The sun beats down relentlessly as the road curls ahead, thousands of festivalgoers still in front of us. I spot Alex, Jiv, loads of people from college, and Ruby, trailing after Isaac, with Meena trudging by her side.

"This is impossible," I mutter, the tension mounting inside me. *We're not going to have enough time!*

Danny is silent next to me, his jaw locked tight. I know he's thinking the same thing. It's claustrophobic, pressed in tight against so many bodies, and I can sense tempers fraying. People are rattled, getting impatient. It's a scary feeling; not quite safe.

But then—

"Look!" Danny points.

I look. We've turned a corner. At the bottom of the hill, the road widens and comes to an end.

I stifle a gasp.

Stern-faced marshals in high-vis vests stand as stiff as soldiers in front of a bank of silver turnstiles. But the thing that takes my breath away is the beautiful carved wooden sign, arching dramatically above them.

YOU ARE NOW ENTERING
A STATE OF ENRAPTURE

I give in to the rush of adrenaline.

27

Danny is unmoved. "Creepy," he mouths as we edge forward, closer to the turnstiles.

The crowd turns rowdy and excitable again, everyone shouting and pushing as they get closer. I hear the noise like a muffled roar. Danny already looks shattered. Today is going to be hard for him. I find his arm and squeeze.

Finally, finally, we reach the front. I pull out my earbuds and slide them back into my pocket as a dead-eyed marshal with a shaved head scans our QR codes. He eyes us with suspicion.

"This says you're 'artists'. Where's your gear?"

"It went ahead in a van," I improvise, holding my

breath. *What if they don't let us in?* "Jim said to collect our wristbands at the gate." My heart flaps wildly in my chest. "He said—"

"Hand," the marshal interrupts. I hold mine out and he snaps a brightly woven band round my wrist. Instantly, my heart rate calms. The band reads ARTIST: GENERAL ACCESS.

"Turn," the marshal says, flipping over my wrist. He stamps the top of my hand. "You'll need this for the Briar Arena."

I peer at the murky print. *Yuck.* It's an eye.

"Which stage?" the marshal asks Danny, but he mumbles the words and Danny misses them.

"Local Talent," I answer for us both. The marshal shoves a map into my hand and points vaguely beyond the turnstiles. "Follow the path, then bear right." He waves us through.

I exhale.

We made it.

We're at Enrapture.

I stand for a moment, taking in the scene. Straight ahead is a wooded area with a sweeping tunnel of trees through the centre. Twisting thorns entwine like fingers, and fairy-light tears weep from the upper branches. A wide path beneath climbs steadily up a gentle incline. Dotted among the trees, I spy bizarre, illuminated sculptures: a hare, a goat, a lion, a deer, a figure – half man–half beast…

"Wren! Come *on*!"

Danny doesn't have to tell me twice. As we head towards the tunnel, I fight the urge to turn cartwheels. We're here. We're inside Enrapture! We're actually made it! And though I feel like a traitor for thinking it...

... it's everything I dreamed it would be.

Like Narnia or Wonderland, right here in boring Hamlington, it's more vast and fantastical than I ever expected. I think back to when I first looked down on the festival site from Adam's studio, back when it was a quiet green valley, and then the second time I saw it, teeming with the chaos of construction. In only a matter of weeks, the site has been completely transformed until now it's virtually unrecognizable.

Like a brand-new world.

Beyond the trees, nestled in small sunlit glades, I see stalls being set up; vintage clothing rails and food stands, with smoke plumes curling from their ovens. The smell of roasting meat drifts towards my nostrils, making my stomach rumble. Colourful marquees pop like flowers in other leafy dells, their bright flags fluttering in the breeze. Connecting everything are dozens of snake-like paths, illuminated by small burning torches.

My mouth has fallen open. My eyes are darting everywhere.

The tree tunnel opens on to a dry, grassy clearing peppered with screens mounted on tall posts. Above the screens are speakers. Black-and-white static is playing on the screens like an eerie plague of locusts, while the speakers crackle and hiss. Danny adjusts his hearing aids, scowling at the sound. The jangle of funfair music reaches my own ears, and I turn to see the golden flash of a carousel and the distant silvery outline of a big wheel.

"Come on!" Danny yanks my arm. "Stop staring. We need to find the Briar Stage." He plucks the map from my fingers and frowns at it. "This way."

Bearing left, we push past crowds wandering aimlessly, as wide-eyed and bewildered as me, until we find ourselves in a glade surrounded by a circle of trees. On every tree trunk, there's a burnished gilt frame, and inside each frame are signs, bearing cryptic messages.

THE WORLD OUTSIDE IS BROKEN

YOU NEED SOMETHING TO BELIEVE IN

LET ENRAPTURE HEAL YOU

WHEN THE TIME COMES, LET YOUR SELF GO

Goosebumps break out on my arms. It's eerie and enticing; a visual overload. My brain is buzzing and my senses are stirring. I want to absorb every tiny detail, lie down in the parched grass and soak up every sound and smell and sensation. We're in a cut-off world of no rules and no adults, where anything could happen – where our worries could dissolve and our problems disappear...

"Wren!" Danny is on to me. "Stay focused," he hisses in my ear. "Don't fall for it, don't read the signs! We need to find the Briar Arena. Remember Lark!"

Begrudgingly, I nod.

We keep on walking, through more small copses and more glades. Soon we reach a place where the dusty paths all intersect. Standing in the middle is a signpost like something out of a fairy tale, with arrows pointing in dozens of different directions.

I read the destinations out loud: "'Reflection Pool'; 'Mending Monument'; 'Psychic Field'... Hmm..." I frown. "'Nostalgic Adjustment'; 'Spiritual Realignment'...? What do they all mean?"

"Nothing. It's all rubbish." Danny rolls his eyes. "Wren, come on. Stay on track."

"'Nourishment and Refreshment'..." My stomach rumbles. "Well, that's food and drink. Oh, look!" I point. "'Local Talent Stage'. It's in the East Field."

Wistfully, I turn to see a long path leading to a distant field in a far-flung corner of the site. If I squint, I can just about make out a dull brown marquee covering a modest platform. Someone has strewn a few hay bales in front of it. There's a sad string of faded bunting. Clearly, no one's expecting much of an audience.

"It's not exactly Wembley, is it?"

I turn, but Danny isn't looking. He's heading through the trees in the opposite direction, focused on something in the distance. "Wren!" he shouts, without looking back.

I jog to catch him up. Then I follow his gaze.

The breath catches in my throat.

28

At the opposite end of the site, right on the other side of the valley, a huge structure looms.

"The Briar Stage," I murmur.

"Yup." Danny pulls his binoculars from his pocket and passes them to me.

Wordlessly, I stare. The stage is an enormous black dome, framed by powerful PA systems and screens mounted on criss-cross metal scaffolding. An equally imposing sound tower sits opposite the stage, within the audience arena. The arena itself is massive – stadium size – but by far the most striking detail is the lattice-like framework that coils all round its perimeter and up and over the roof of the stage.

The effect is of a thorny, sculptural inverted nest. I shiver. It reminds me of the tangled rose bushes that suffocated Sleeping Beauty's castle, beautiful yet deadly, the poor unknowing courtiers trapped inside, frozen in time. Even now, with the stage basking in full summer sunlight, the entire arena gives off a dark, otherworldly vibe.

"Let's go." Danny strides ahead, weaving forcefully through the growing crowds towards the spiky outline of the Briar Arena, like a dark-haired knight on a quest.

I follow with slightly less conviction. Seeing the arena has brought the enormity of our mission home to me. Persuading Lark to shun the limelight was never going to be easy, but we're up against something far stronger than my sister's stubbornness.

Adam Piper.

This is *his* world that we're in.

The closer we get to the Briar Arena, the busier it gets, and now thousands of people are swarming, spilling in from all directions and making it harder to make progress. Anticipation hangs heavy in the dry air, punctuated by piercing screams from the fairground, the rumbling sounds of distant sound systems, and the persistent static crackling from the speaker screens.

"Hurry up, Wren!" Danny shouts over his shoulder, in tunnel-vision mode. My hair is already plastered to my forehead but I force my legs into action, trying to keep pace with his rapid strides and not lose sight of his green T-shirt and dark head before the swelling crowds swallow him up.

We come across more girls, dressed in white – they seem to be everywhere I turn. As they drift between the trees, I briefly wonder what Lark would say if she could see them. Perhaps she *can* see them from backstage. She probably doesn't care. It's not the first time she's had copycats. Back in year eleven, Iris Clark bleached her black hair blonde and made a homemade version of Lark's favourite green jacket. Lark found it funny at the time.

This does not feel funny.

The closer we get to the Briar Arena, the more Aurora clones we see – and now I'm spotting Spinners too. Soon I've lost count of how many eyebrow piercings, mirror sunglasses and bleached, close-shaven heads I've seen. And that eye symbol – it's everywhere: on jewellery and T-shirts, and all over the boards at the temporary tattoo stands where long lines of people are queuing up to have it embellished on their arms and shoulders and legs.

I catch up with Danny. "It's like a massive super-fan convention," I point, panting for breath. "Everyone's dressed like them."

He shakes his head. "I know."

A sudden sharp crackle makes me jump. High above me, a screen splutters into life. A low hum breaks into a thunderous chord. I jerk reflexively, and people around me do the same. Everyone stops what they're doing to look up.

A beating drum pulses from the speakers, regular like a heartbeat. It throbs deep within my body, echoing round the valley. Heads begin to nod in time.

Danny looks at me in alarm. He can obviously hear – or at least feel – the beat. "Earbuds!" he manages, gesturing wildly.

I find them quickly and jam them in. The beat softens to a dull thud.

Up on the screen, grey locusts morph into black-and-white shapes. With a flash of rainbow light, the picture sharpens and a video begins to play. Lark is sitting at a dressing table in nothing but her underwear, her rainbow hair cascading down her back like a silken waterfall. She looks so incredibly beautiful a girl next to me claps her hand to her mouth. The camera moves closer until my sister's face fills the frame. She stares at her own reflection, passive and blank. Suddenly the camera swings round. The screen fills with the shit-eating grin of Spinner. A caption appears on the screen. He's streaming live from his social account.

> Check out the Aurora in her dressing room!
> Join us at sunset. Bring on the New Dawn.
> #Spinner #TheAurora #CommunityofTruth

I feel the thudding stop and know it's safe to remove my earbuds. The screen flickers and goes dead.

Danny speaks first. "What kind of sicko films his girlfriend getting changed and broadcasts it to thousands of people?"

"You're right." His anger fires me up. "But at least we know she's backstage."

"Let's go. We're wasting time." Danny grabs my hand, picking up the pace. "The quicker we get there, the better. Just be ready for those speakers."

Heads down, we zig-zag through more bustling fields, down more winding paths, past fake streams and stone circles and monuments, dodging people chanting and swaying. Eventually we reach the arena. We double over, breathing heavily. Up close, the effect is totally intimidating. The thorny, tangled fence encircling the arena is at least ten feet tall, and the three entry points are guarded by headset-wearing marshals. They lean against the barriers with their arms crossed, gazing stonily out at the crowd.

"Is it closed?" I ask.

Danny kicks the grass. "Damn! How will we get backstage if we can't even get inside the arena?"

"Let me talk to someone," I say.

Tentatively, I approach a marshal.

"Entry to the enclosure is at seven," he recites, before I've even spoken.

"No entry until *seven*?" I echo, turning round for Danny's benefit.

The marshal nods. He's a young guy, barely twenty, with a pinched face and a close-cropped head. "You can start queueing now if you want." He nods at a number of teenagers corralled in a large pen. Eighty per cent of them are dressed like clones.

"Wait." I frown. "Aren't there other bands playing here this afternoon?"

"Not on this stage," the marshal replies.

Danny is at my side. "We need to get backstage," he tells the marshal bluntly. "We have to speak to someone in the band." He offers up his wristband. "We're artists. We have access all areas."

The marshal snorts. "No one goes backstage at Briar. Promoter's orders."

My heart sinks.

"But this is her sister!" Danny pushes me forward.

"Whose sister?" The marshal yawns, bored. He turns away.

A screen right above us flickers into life. This time I'm prepared. The moment the crashing chord sounds I'm ready with my earbuds, cramming them in my ears. The Spinner-Aurora clones waiting in the pen lift their heads like sunflowers. As the beat pounds inside my body, I focus on staying alert.

Playing up on the screen is another handheld video clip. Lark is lying on a bed with her hands clasped across her chest. Her body is still and her eyes are closed. For a second, my heart stutters.

Is she…?

The camera flips to Spinner, and another caption appears.

They're even more beautiful asleep, am I right?
#Spinner #TheAurora #CommunityofTruth

Anger rises inside me as the screen cuts back to static. I rip my earbuds out.

"That was her!" I yell at the marshal. "That was my sister!" I point to the screen. "Her name is Lark Mackenzie."

"That was the Aurora," the marshal says reverently. His eyes have a strange, glazed sheen.

"We need to get a message to her," Danny insists, struggling to replace his hearing aids. "It's important."

The marshal blinks. "Nobody may see the Aurora except for her mentor. She is resting, preparing for her role." His voice is staccato like a robot.

"But she's in danger!" I say, helplessly.

The marshal snorts. "The Aurora has full security. Come back at seven, like everyone else."

Danny catches the marshal's last words and steps forward, his hands balled into fists. "Listen, mate. We're not trying to get in early. Wren's not a fan, she's *family*. You need to let her see her sister."

The marshal takes in Danny's six-foot frame. "I'm warning you. Don't get aggressive with me. Come any closer and I'll call security. I know your type."

My mouth drops open.

"Excuse me? My *type*?" Danny chokes. "What the hell is my *type*?"

"Danny, be careful—" I touch his arm, but he shakes me off.

"Wren, do you hear this asshole? He's nothing but a racist Spinner clone!"

"Who are you calling an asshole?" The marshal's face is red.

Danny barks with laughter. "*That's* the part you deny?"

"Please!" I turn to the marshal, desperate to de-escalate the situation. Plenty of people are staring, but no one seems willing to help. "Please, I just need to speak to my sister. Five minutes, that's all I'm asking. It really is important…"

"It could be life or death!" Danny finishes.

The marshal's eyes narrow. "Did you just threaten me? Stand back." He speaks into his headset, palm outstretched.

"Let's go," Danny mutters, but already three burly security guys are heading our way. There's no time to run.

"This man threatened me," the Spinner-marshal shouts over Danny's protests. "Search him, then remove him from the site."

"Sir, please come with us. Don't make a fuss."

Unfortunately, Danny is facing the marshal so he doesn't hear the guard, and when he doesn't respond, the other guards leap into action, grabbing him roughly and dragging him away. He struggles against them, shocked.

"Stop resisting! We told you to come with us."

"He didn't hear you!" I shout. Tears spring to my eyes and fury bursts like fireworks in my chest. "He's deaf! He didn't hear! Leave him alone, you're hurting him! He didn't threaten anyone. He didn't do anything!"

"Stay out of this, darling," the Spinner-marshal smirks.

"Don't call me 'darling'!" I'm shrieking now, spitting with rage.

I stumble after Danny. He twists against the guards' grip as they manhandle him away, trying desperately to turn round.

"Leave it, Wren!" he shouts. "Don't make a scene. They'll throw you out too. Find Lark. Tell her what we know. And if you can't do that, tell other people. Tell them 'Lullaby' is dangerous. Tell them to boycott the show…"

There's no time to reply. An ominous black security van approaches, a golden eye emblazoned on the side. Moments later, the guards bundle Danny inside and the doors slam shut.

I don't even get the chance to say goodbye.

The van moves off and, within seconds, it's swallowed by the crowds. I stand there, numb and motionless, in a field outside the Briar Arena. I'm surrounded by thousands of people, but I've never felt more alone.

29

I have no idea what to do. I've been so reliant on Danny's help – for his ideas and his certainty, as well as his immunity to Enrapture's lure; and now I'm on my own.

It's up to me to somehow save Lark.

I pull out my phone, but either there's no signal in the valley or there are too many people here, overloading the networks. In any case, there's no one I can call. Lark won't respond, and there's too much of a risk that Spinner or Adam would see my message. Mum and Dad are miles away in another country. And if the security guards search Danny, like the marshal threatened, they might confiscate his phone.

I try anyway.

> Danny, don't leave the valley.
> I'll find a way to get you back in.

> *Sending*
> *Text Message Not Delivered*

Blinking back tears, I wrack my brains for a plan. I can't make another attempt to get backstage through the arena. The marshals will recognize me and evict me straight away. But if I can't reach Lark, perhaps Danny's idea isn't terrible. If I can warn enough people and we all spread the word, we could deny Spinner and the Aurora an audience.

Without an audience, Lark wouldn't have to sing.

It's a long shot, but I open the group chat.

> **Wren**
> Hey, everyone, I'm at the festival.
> DON'T go to Spinner's set tonight.
> It's not safe. Please trust me on this.
> Tell EVERYONE you know.

No reply. Messages aren't going through. The last one was sent by Ruby at ten this morning. I read it twice.

> **Ruby**
> Hey gang! In case we get separated later, pin a note
> on the forum on the Enrapture app!! Truth xx

Her sign-off chills me, but my heart lifts. *The app! The app is working.* I mute my phone and check … Ruby's right! I don't know how Adam is doing it – maybe with signal blockers and special mobile cell towers. Whatever, there's a message board in the app's menu, and the feed is constantly updating.

Hi to my squad at Enrapture! Liv xx

Megs and Ro, meet Annie at the Stone Circle 3pm

JEZ! I've saved you a place in the Briar line, Lou X

Enrapture = TRUTH 🖤

Emmy and Sasha say bring on the New Dawn!

Sunila marked her location: BRIAR ARENA MEETING POINT

Kaya + Owen pledge allegiance to #CommunityofTruth

MARRY ME, AURORA!!

SP, George says get chips!!!!

Meena + Ruby pledge allegiance to #CommunityofTruth

My fingers falter. What the hell is the Community of Truth, and why are Meena and Ruby pledging allegiance to it? But there's no time to ask questions. Quickly I log into my profile and smash out a post.

> DANGER! PLEASE READ!
> <u>DO NOT</u> GO TO THE BRIAR ARENA AT SUNSET
> <u>DO NOT</u> WATCH SPINNER + THE AURORA
> GO HOME. <u>YOU ARE NOT SAFE</u>

The backlash is vicious and instant.

> Who the hell is this?

> STFU Troll

> Fake news!

> Find and destroy Little Brown Bird

> Kill LIES Protect TRUTH

> Little Brown Bird REPORTED

Three minutes later, an anonymous moderator has blocked my post. I shut the app, trembling. I'm going to have to persuade people another way. I'll have to talk to them face to face.

Coming towards me is a couple, yet another pair of Spinner–Aurora clones. The boy swaggers confidently, in loose jeans and a baggy shirt unbuttoned to reveal the eye-shaped pendant round his neck. The girl staggers a few paces behind him in ill-advised heels. Her thin white dress is bordering on transparent, the hem trailing in the dust. I frown at how naked she is, and how blank her expression, as she totters after her boyfriend like a second thought. Her costume isn't the only reason she makes me think of Lark.

"Hey!" I put an arm out to stop her. "Can I talk to you a minute? What's your name?"

The girl jumps as if I've startled her. "Oh! Um … it's Clara."

"You're a fan of the Aurora, am I right?"

Clara nods eagerly. "Yeah, of course."

"Why?"

The question stumps her. "I just … am." She goes to walk on but I block her way.

"How long have you been a fan?"

"Er … Luke?" She calls to her boyfriend and he turns round. Seeing he's lost his shadow, he sidles back.

"I've followed Spinner since the beginning," he says proudly. "I'm an original Truth-seeker."

"And I loved the Aurora the minute I heard her sing," Clara adds.

I bite my tongue. "But what is it you like about them?"

Luke starts to recite. "Spinner's the definition of a man. The world was against him, but he overcame."

"The Aurora is so pretty and perfect," Clara adds. "She deserves Spinner. They're couple goals, y'know?" She glances shyly at Luke, who ignores her. "Their music speaks to me… I can't explain."

The day is boiling, but my body feels cold. "Try," I urge.

Clara screws up her face. Thinking seems to be taking all her effort. "It just … makes me feel better…" She shakes her head. "No, what I mean is … it stops me feeling anything at all."

Hairs rise on the back of my neck. I recognize the reaction she's describing.

"Do you have a favourite track?" I ask, although I think I know the answer.

Clara brightens, but Luke answers for her. "'Lullaby'. The new track. Spinner's been teasing it for weeks, and it finally drops today."

"Listen," I say, taking Clara's hand. "'Lullaby' is dangerous." Her eyes grow wide and confused. "Please, Clara. You have to believe me. Don't watch the set tonight. Don't go to the Briar Arena. Something bad is going to happen. Tell your friends to stay away."

"Why would you say that?" Clara snatches her hand back.

"Because it's the truth!"

"Spinner speaks the truth." Luke's face is stony. "Stop spreading lies." He spins round, his voice loud. "She's trash-talking Spinner and the Aurora! She's saying we should boycott the show!"

301

My heart pounds as dozens of pairs of eyes lock, magnet-like, on me.

"It's her!" someone shouts. "She's the troll. She's Little Brown Bird!"

"No!" I take a step backwards, sensing the threat of violence in the air. It's scary how fast the Spinner–Aurora zombies find the energy to defend their heroes.

"You're Little Brown Bird!" A torrent of jeers and insults fly my way.

I turn and run, slamming through the crowds. I don't waste a second looking back round. I duck and jump and swerve between stalls and food stands, under bunting, over blankets and behind generators, not stopping until I'm totally sure I've lost them.

I slip into a tent to catch my breath.

Wow.

It's a merchandise stall, but every single item is branded for Spinner and the Aurora. Badges, posters, necklaces, notebooks, T-shirts, hoodies, hats. If they're not covered in images of Lark, they feature Spinner and his strange salute. The eye logo is everywhere too. But one slogan stops me in my tracks:

I BELONG TO
THE COMMUNITY OF TRUTH

A huge line of people snakes through the marquee, all desperate to buy. Foreboding grabs me by the throat. The air in the tent smells stale and thin. Suddenly I'm finding it hard to breathe.

I lurch outside, gulping in fresh air.

"That's her. She's the one causing trouble."

Two thickset men step into my line of vision. Not marshals; these two are wearing stiff black suits. A third, behind me, is dressed the same. They're completely out of place against the vibrant backdrop of Enrapture, more like mafiosi than festivalgoers. Definitely killjoys.

Not that I was filled with joy.

"You need to come with us." Hands clamp down on my shoulders.

"Get off me! I haven't done anything!" I make myself go floppy, trying to wriggle free, but the claw-grip on my shoulders tightens, steering me away.

"It's come to our attention that you've been harassing guests," one of the suits says. "Asking questions and attempting to cause panic."

"Asking questions isn't a crime!" I struggle again. A crowd is forming around us. I spot Luke's smirking face among the onlookers, filming on his phone. Catching my eye, he mouths, "Truth."

"Get in."

I'm pushed towards a small black golf buggy with a golden eye logo, like the one on the van that took Danny away. It's pointless to resist. I slump onto a burning leather seat and the men get in too. One is driving, while the other two flank me at the back, presumably to stop me jumping out.

"Where are we going?"

"You'll see," the driver answers gruffly. "Someone wants a word."

My pulse quickens as the buggy judders over the dusty field, motoring in the direction of the Briar Arena. "Is it my sister? Has she been asking for me?"

No answer.

We're approaching the thorny barricade enclosing the arena, but instead of driving up to one of the entrance gates, the buggy turns sharp left, following the perimeter fencing round to the left. In a short while we reach a closed-off area full of shipping containers, hidden from the main site behind hoardings. We slip between them, passing more dead-eyed marshals on the way. The buggy pulls up outside a heavy metal gate.

The first suit jumps down and speaks into a radio. "We're outside."

A buzz-click and the gate opens. The other two suits motion for me to go through. Silently, I obey. They're courteous enough, but at no point do I think I have any choice. The gate slams shut behind us.

I take in my surroundings. I'm standing in a compound full of small metal buildings on stilts; a miniature village of trailers nestled in the spiky shadow of the Briar Stage.

Each trailer has blacked-out windows, making it impossible for me to see inside. The compound is unnervingly quiet, a world away from the chaos of the festival in full swing a stone's throw away.

"What is this place?" I ask. "Are we backstage?"

"This way." The suits lead me to the biggest trailer and deposit me at the door.

"Lark!" I call. "Lark, are you in there? It's me, Wren!"

As the door opens, my body floods with relief at the thought of seeing my sister.

But it's not Lark behind the door.

30

"Wren Mackenzie."

A tall, upright figure is standing on the threshold dressed in heavy, multicoloured robes. His long dark hair is tied in a knot on top of his head. I tense, but there's a kind expression on his face.

"Welcome." Adam holds out his hands. "I'm very happy to see you again. I do hope you're enjoying Enrapture. I'd be honoured if you would come in."

His voice is tranquil, warm, melodious. Still, I hesitate.

"I understand you have… Let's call them 'misgivings'." Adam winces, as though hurt. "I would sincerely like the chance to allay your fears. It will only take a minute of your time. You must be keen to return to the emerging artists' stage in time for your own performance."

My performance. I'd forgotten about it... I brush it off.

"Where's my sister? Where's Lark?"

Adam smiles fondly. "*The Aurora*, as she prefers, is absolutely fine. She's simply busy, preparing for her appearance." His lilting accent is soft and reassuring. "Your sisterly concern is commendable, Wren, but there really is no need to worry. If you don't believe me, let me show you." He beckons.

Tentatively, I step into the trailer.

"You can go," Adam tells the suited men. He smiles at me. "We'll leave the door open, shall we? You're my guest, not a prisoner. You're free to leave at any time."

The men withdraw.

I let out a breath and look about me. Inside the cool, air-conditioned trailer is the most luxurious office I have ever seen. Two soft, leathery sofas, piled high with velvet cushions, sit either side of a small, walnut coffee table. Adam's notebook rests on top. There's a bar and kitchen area to one side, with crystal glasses on display and a glass-fronted fridge filled with bottles of champagne. The end of the trailer nearest to me has been converted into a modest recording studio with video and audio equipment, while at the opposite end a huge bank of monitors covers the wall above a desk. The black-and-white images change frequently, showing an array of different angles on the festival. I shiver as I realize: the tall screens outside aren't just *broadcasting* sound and image; they're closed–circuit TV cameras, *recording* footage too.

From this cosy hidden office, Adam can see every corner of Enrapture.

"Look. Here's your sister, right as rain." He moves towards the wall of monitors and taps a button. Lark's image fills the largest, central screen. It's a close-up shot, with only her head and shoulders visible in the frame. She's smiling and laughing, looking chilled and relaxed, but without any context, I can't trust what I'm seeing.

"Is that footage live? Where is she? Is she in one of the other trailers?"

"She's…" Adam consults a tablet. "Right now, she's in wardrobe, getting dressed."

I frown. "And you're filming in there?"

He bows his head. "Before you judge me harshly, let me reassure you that everything has been done with your sister's full consent."

I blink. "Can I see her?"

"No." Adam's voice snaps from warm to cold, like day to night. He recovers quickly. "No, I'm afraid that's impossible. We must not interrupt her process, her routine. Everything is designed to help the Aurora achieve the right mindset. She must perform perfectly, at her very best." He smiles again; friendly, benevolent Adam is back. "You may see your sister after tonight's show. It will be a time of great rejoicing, with much to celebrate."

"Like what?" I ask, dubiously.

He moves to the sofa, motioning for me to join him. Reluctantly, I sink on to the seat opposite.

"Wren, my dear, let's talk. I know you've been asking questions. Voicing a few … concerns." His face falls. "I'm a little disappointed to hear this, after all the opportunities I've given you. I thought we trusted one another, you and me."

"How can I trust you?" I summon all my courage, my heart thumping violently. "You're not who you say you are. Your name is Adam *Piper*, not Adam Webb."

I wait for his reaction; his face gives nothing away.

"You've been searching for a singer," I plough on. "The perfect singer with the perfect voice. And you chose my sister. But the song you want her to sing, the melody to 'Lullaby'…" I falter.

"What about it?" Adam asks. His eyes bore into mine, daring me to go on.

"It's dangerous," I murmur, weakly.

"Dangerous?" He raises an amused eyebrow. "What on earth do you mean?"

"You know what I mean." I pull myself up taller. "When someone listens to it, something strange happens. First, they feel good – euphoric – like they haven't a care in the world, but then…"

I hesitate. Adam's blank expression is unnerving. I can't tell what he's thinking. Danny has been thrown out of the festival and apart from Adam's weird suited henchmen nobody knows where I am. If I say the wrong thing now,

I could make him angry. And then what might he do?

"But then…?" he prompts, gently.

I take a breath. I mustn't be intimidated. I have to be brave, for Lark.

"Then they fall into a trance. They don't care about anything at all—"

"Oh, but young people today have far too many cares and problems, don't you think?" Adam muses, interrupting me. He gazes into the distance. "The world is a challenging place. I should think it would be nice to have those cares taken away."

"But music is supposed to make you feel things!" I cry. "'Lullaby' just leaves you empty…"

"Ready to receive," he murmurs.

His words chill me. "Yes." I stare at him. "But receive *what*?"

"What an excellent question!" Adam's grey eyes flash as they lock on mine. "You're a clever girl. Why don't *you* tell *me*?"

My heart is in my throat. I can see I've ruffled his composure.

"Some kind of message," I say, carefully. "I don't know what the message is, exactly."

But I'm starting to get an idea.

I swallow. "All I know is, 'Lullaby' is dangerous. And not just for listeners; for the singer, too. Whatever you're doing with Enrapture, you've been planning it for a while. You started experimenting in America, with Fernanda

Alvarez. Then you carried on here in England, with Anna Walker and Mia Hall. You singled them out for their voices, but when they sang for you, they died."

"That is quite an accusation, Miss Mackenzie." Adam's voice is a whisper. Still, I notice he doesn't deny it.

I'm making him angry.

I take a careful breath. "You found Spinner and Lark, and brought them together. You mentored Spinner and the Aurora, and created Enrapture so they could play. You want every teenager in Hamlington to listen to 'Lullaby' tonight, and there's nothing I can do to stop you." I hold out my hands, to demonstrate how utterly powerless I am. "So, *you* tell *me* the reason why. Why are you doing this? What's going to happen next?"

The silence stretches out. Adam stares at the coffee table – at his notebook sitting between us – like he's considering his reply. I wait, expecting nothing. Someone as powerful as Adam doesn't need to explain himself to anyone, let alone me, a random teenage girl.

But no. It turns out Sofia was right. Adam loves a platform.

"What's going to happen?" He sits up taller, unfolding himself to his full height. "Tonight I am going to open people's minds. You see, the world is broken, Wren. Young people today are so misguided. You've taken wrong turn after wrong turn, travelling fast down a terrible path."

I stiffen in my seat. I know he's going to tell me where

he thinks we've gone so wrong, and I'm not sure I want to hear it.

"We need a New Dawn," he continues, hatred and zeal suddenly stamped across his face. Gentle Adam has disappeared, and in his place is a bitter, bigoted man. "We need to return to a simpler time, a *better* time – when lines were not blurred, divisions were clear, and everyone knew their place. Especially young women like you," he spits.

I gape, but Adam doesn't seem to notice. He simply ploughs on, spewing out his toxic opinions. "Your generation needs a wake-up call, and it's my mission to deliver it. Call it a consciousness crusade."

I shrink into the sofa, cringing. How loathsome can one guy be?

"I have a gift, a very rare talent. I've committed my life to experiments and research." Adam's eyes flick to his notebook again. "And now I'm ready. I've refined my arrangement, perfected my composition, and found the perfect *instrument* to deliver the performance."

"She's not an instrument. She's my sister!" My hands form fists of anger.

"Ah, yes, that's true." Adam looks at me with pity. "But don't be downhearted. The Aurora bears no grudge. In fact, she accepts her role willingly. Great work always demands a sacrifice." He affects a reverent expression. "Your sister knows the risk involved, and she knows it's for a greater good. Tonight's initiation will be quick and painless. Our followers come of their own accord."

Icy fingers walk my spine.

"It's very simple," Adam declares, bathing me in a smile. "Tonight, they gather. The children come to Enrapture seeking a life-changing experience, and I intend to give it to them. To deliver an effective sermon, I need a receptive audience. Before you can wake to the truth, you must be empty of all lies."

"Wait…" I'm battling to take it all in. I focus on my sister. "Lark *knows* everything you've just told me? She agrees? She knows the risk?" I can't believe it for a second, but I try to keep an even tone. I'm dealing with a fanatic and I do not want to get him riled up.

"Oh, she does!" Adam smiles. "She truly believes. Your sister is trusting, Wren. Tractable. She embraces her status as figurehead. Like my first disciple, she's attracted many new recruits."

His first disciple. He means Spinner, or rather – Evan. Does Spinner hold the same twisted ideas as Adam? I don't need to ask. He does, I've seen his socials. Adam has groomed him, and he's been grooming Lark *through* Spinner, ever since she pricked her finger on his turntable needle.

"With her beauty and her exceptional voice, your sister is the perfect songbird to herald the New Dawn, the birth of our beautiful new world."

"Except she won't get to see it, will she?"

At my outburst, Adam tenses. The room goes quiet and still.

"I knew someone once," he murmurs. "Someone

insolent like you, with no regard for duty. Someone who didn't know her place." He gazes into the distance. "She thought to make a fool of me, but I will have the final say. When you and your sister walked into my studio, I knew this was fate."

I fall silent. I don't know who or what Adam is referring to, but I sense that any wrong word from me could tip him over the edge.

"It's my destiny to lead," he continues, grandly. "The Community of Truth will be born tonight in Hamlington, but soon my pulpit will be global."

Global? It finally slaps me in the face.

He's talking about a cult. A cult, with Adam at the helm and a following of impressionable teenagers. For months, he's been preying on our insecurities, pushing his message that we're powerless and lost and broken, that the reason we're suffering is because the world has gone 'wrong'. He's spread the word that Enrapture will fix everything, give us somewhere to belong.

I shudder.

Enrapture is only the beginning. Tonight Adam will deliver his "sermon", founding his so-called Community, not on truth at all, but on lies and prejudice and hate. And with donations and subscriptions from a lied-to, brainwashed congregation, it won't be long before his despicable values have a worldwide reach.

Suddenly I'm *very* keen to leave.

"I think I understand now," I say carefully, getting to

my feet. "Thank you for explaining. I should really go. It must be almost time for my set."

"Of course." Adam nods knowingly. "That was the Aurora's wish."

I freeze. "Her wish?"

He waves a careless hand. "As a condition of my mentorship, she insisted that you must perform too. She strikes a hard bargain, your sister."

I blink. Have I got this right? Lark *insisted* that Danny I got the gig on the local talent stage? My selfish sister, who only thinks about herself ... she brokered a deal, for me? Lark knew how much I wanted to play at Enrapture. Did she gamble her own opportunity, so that I could have mine?

Another thought jumps into my head: *If it's true, it means I'm no good.*

Adam didn't choose me. He didn't spot my potential. He only agreed to get Lark.

I sway on the spot, a thousand feelings rushing through me.

"Please don't be upset, Wren. I can guess what you're thinking, but you're wrong. Your sister didn't need to convince me. You deserve to be here. You deserve to play."

I try to shut out Adam's words, but my ego is weak.

"You're a talented musician. I'd expect nothing less from a Mackenzie."

Whatever that means. I let it go.

"Your performance is scheduled for six." Adam's eyes

dart to a clock on the wall. "I think we can do better than that. Let me make a quick call to the stage manager. I'm sure he'll be happy to move an exciting young artist like yourself to the final slot of the evening." He looks me in the eye. "Wouldn't you like to be the closing act, Wren? The one that everyone remembers?"

I'm never the one people remember.

"You're special," Adam croons softly. "Your sister's voice is beautiful, yes – but you… You're different. A true original."

I stand, soaking up his words.

"Not only that…" Adam smiles. "You have ambition, drive – that's something I admire. Your sister is docile, weak. But you think for yourself." He pauses. "Someone like you could bring the house down."

His pale grey eyes meet mine.

"I'll radio the stage right now." Adam walks towards the desk beneath the monitors. "The audience prize would be as good as yours. What do you say?"

My sister is not "weak".

I give a tiny nod.

"Excellent!" Adam turns his back and speaks into the radio. "Gentlemen, there's been a change of plan… If you could return and escort Miss Mackenzie to the local talent stage … tell Jim to put her on at nine. Yes, nine, exactly. Keep an eye on her … give her everything she needs—"

I'm out the door before I hear any more.

31

I run, darting between the trailers as fast as I can.

Who the hell does Adam think I am? Does he really think I can be bought off – bribed – by the promise of a prize and a better slot on his tiny local talent stage? My sister's life is at stake. I need to get out of here; I need to warn everyone that Enrapture is fake, that we've all been manipulated by some smarmy guy with a God complex.

He even has a man-bun, for goodness' sake.

I want to hammer on the other trailers, screaming Lark's name, but I know it will do more harm than good. Adam implied that she's being guarded, and his heavies will be looking for me too, as soon as he raises the alert. I swerve away from the main gate and head instead for the perimeter fence, desperately scanning for another way out of the enclosure.

There.

An industrial-sized wheelie bin is pushed against the wall and I launch myself at it, heaving myself up on top. From here it's another six feet to clear a corrugated metal wall.

Where's Danny when I need a boost?

Using all my strength, I spring up and grab the rim of the wall, hauling myself up until I can swing my leg over. The muscles in my arms scream with pain. Then, closing my eyes and hoping for the best, I plummet down to the other side.

Ouch! That really hurts.

I've landed on hard dirt in a field of navy-blue Portaloos, all lined up in rows like a Tardis army. As I hobble to my feet, checking myself for injuries, a boy with a shaved head applauds.

"Bloody hell! That's even higher than the fence I came over. Respect. You made it in. Saved yourself a hundred quid. You need the eye stamp now. I can do you one in Sharpie for a tenner."

"Wait." I look up. "What did you say? You got into the festival over a wall?"

He grins. "Yup. Far end of East Field." He points way back, even further than the local talent stage. "Some bright spark brought a ladder. Security haven't sussed it yet; they're focused on the main gates."

"Thank you!" I grin at the boy and start to limp away.

"Hey, come back!" he shouts. "What about the eye stamp?"

It's a long way to East Field, about as far from the Briar Arena as it's possible to get, and, now I'm back out in the sweltering festival, I've never felt so vulnerable. Adam is no fool. He'll know I've done a runner. His eyes are everywhere and he'll be combing the place for me.

"Someone like you could bring the house down."

I shake my head, angrily. It's his *own* house he's worried about – his Community of Truth, his horrible cult. That's why he wants me out of the way, on the other side of the festival, at nine o'clock tonight. As far from Lark and the Briar Arena as can be.

But what's he afraid of, exactly?

What could "someone like me" do?

I lose myself in the seething mass of bodies, trying my best to blend in. I mustn't run. Running looks weird here – it's too hot, no one else is rushing. I keep my head well down, especially when I pass the tall posts with their mounted screens. If I'm caught on camera, it's game over.

Finally, I see a sign for East Field, and I turn into it, my eyes peeled for a blind spot, a place where no camera lenses can pick me up. At last I find one; a funny little no man's land tucked behind two food stands, about fifty feet from the steel fencing that marks the edge of the festival site. A willow tree stands in the middle, its branches trailing to the ground. I duck beneath the fronds and catch my breath in the cool, green bubble of the space. I'm a very long way from Adam's trailer, and safely out of sight.

The first thing I need to do is message Danny, somehow.

I log in to the Enrapture app, changing my username for safety. If I'm going to risk posting on the forum, it'll have to be in code.

Nature Nerd. Get to East Field for a boost. Dock Leaf

I pray he sees it and gets my meaning.

Next, I reach into my pocket. As my hand closes round my prize, my pulse starts racing once again. I may be safe for the moment, but Adam will definitely be looking for me.

Especially when he realizes what I've got.

His notebook.

Repository of his fantasies. Keeper of his secrets. I don't think I've ever seen him without it.

I turn it over in my hand, my fingers trembling as I touch the battered leather cover and the soft, time-stained edges. Adam's mask has slipped. Whether he meant to or not, he's shown me the extent of his ambition, the nature of his ugly, regressive ideas. I know what he wants, and what he's going to do.

But I still don't know how the music works.

Adam has spent his life perfecting "Lullaby", and I'm

willing to bet that this small, unassuming book contains that journey – his theories refined, his process honed. If there's any way to stop him, could the answer lie inside?

Out beyond the willow tree, the sun is sliding down the sky. The afternoon is fading fast. We're moving into that strange, shifting time somewhere between day and dusk. It won't be long before the gates of the Briar Arena will open and the crowds will assemble, ready for Spinner's set. A captive audience of thousands, primed and ready to be indoctrinated. I swallow. The Enrapture train left the station long ago, but maybe – just maybe – I can stop the crash. I'm not a scientist like Danny, but I am a musician. I understand the power music holds.

I open the notebook.

Scratchings and scribblings, dense and overwhelming. Diagrams and illustrations, relating to the mind, the memory, the brain. I squint, desperate to make sense of Adam's tiny, looping handwriting. As words like *plasticity* and *malleable* and *irreversible* jump out, any hope I had instantly dies. I don't understand everything, but the gist is chillingly clear: the younger the mind, the easier it is to mould. To warp and change … for ever.

I make myself read on. Some pages are full of music, spidery notes scuttling up and down the stave. Annotations litter the margins – references to pitch and timbre, rhythm and dynamics, melody, harmony and beat. Decades of composing and experimenting, of analysing melodies – picking them apart and assembling them again; of tweaking and adjusting the recipe like a chef.

Slowly, I shake my head. In some ways we're not so different, Adam and me. We've both been looking for the same thing: that perfect alchemy, that elusive song. The song that, once you've heard it, you'll never be the same again.

I made a breakthrough. But so did he.

Even though I know it's coming, it turns me cold, seeing the first notations for "Lullaby" on the page. And I grow colder still as I turn to the next page, and the pages after that. Buried in Adam's research, in his endless tests and experiments, initials begin to appear:

F.A.R.
A.W.
M.H.

I catch my breath.

It's all here: confirmation of my suspicions. Proof that Adam is behind the deaths of three innocent young girls. Proof that Lark's voice plus Spinner's music is the culmination of his deadly research – a recipe for "Lullaby" in the most potent form of all.

And proof that nothing can stop him.

But not all the pages are scientific. Some read more like extracts from a diary; long, convoluted ramblings offering a portal into Adam's messed-up mind. One page in particular catches my eye. I pore over it – a declaration of devotion that spirals suddenly into bitter ranting. It's directed at one person.

A person Adam calls his "dove".

I close the notebook, shaking. I know everything, now. And if I ever get out of here, I've got all the evidence against Adam that I need. But there's one discovery I never could have dreamed. The secret grievance pushing him along.

Adam came to Hamlington deliberately. He always intended to target this town. Because a woman who now lives here rejected him years ago, and he's never been able to forgive her. His Community is his revenge, a sign of his supremacy, and he'll sacrifice her daughter as a punishment.

The daughter is Lark.

The woman is my mother.

Paloma is the Spanish word for dove.

32

I cover my face with my hands.

Everything is a terrible mess and it's my fault it's got so far. I promised Mum I'd look out for my sister, but I failed, and now there's a very real chance Lark will die.

Guilt twists my stomach into knots.

I've made a million mistakes. I was so obsessed with going to Enrapture I ignored every red flag along the way. I should have asked questions; I should have raised the alarm. But I followed the crowd, fell for the hype, believed what I wanted to believe.

My head sinks lower.

And I believed what I wanted to believe about Lark.

My sister isn't my rival. She's never been against me; she's only ever tried to help – right from the time we went busking, through to negotiating with Adam on my behalf. I created our rivalry. I've repeatedly pushed her away. All because I was jealous.

My face burns with shame.

It's not Lark's fault that her voice is amazing – and it's not her fault Adam chose her to sing. Lark is special, but that doesn't mean she isn't vulnerable. She's been lost and confused, trying to find her path. And Adam saw that and took advantage.

Could she have resisted him – if I'd had her back?

I get to my feet, pushing the willow fronds aside. I have to put this right. I've been sleepwalking for way too long, oblivious to the truth.

This is my wake-up call.

"*Nature Nerd?*"

I spin round and my battered heart explodes.

There, coming towards me from the direction of the East Field wall, is Danny. A smile tugs the corners of his mouth. Fifty feet behind him, two shaven-headed boys swing their legs over the steel fencing and drop heavily on to the grass, high-five each other and run away.

"Oh my god, it worked!" I run to Danny and he throws his arms round me.

"*Dock Leaf*," he mumbles into my ear.

I pull back a little so he can see my face. The words come tumbling out: "Adam is founding a cult. It's called

325

the Community of Truth, and he's going to indoctrinate everyone tonight. Listening to 'Lullaby' will alter their brains, for ever. But Lark … Lark…" I start to choke.

"Slow down." Danny is still holding me.

I take a juddering breath. "I think when Lark sings 'Lullaby' to the end, it will kill her. And Adam doesn't care. He thinks it's a fitting sacrifice. He's doing this for the platform, but he's also doing it for revenge."

I tell him everything, all about Mum and the broken engagement. Tears are streaming down my cheeks. "We can't let Lark sing. We have to stop her. I've tried to warn people, like you said, but nobody will listen. So it's on us – on *me*." I swipe at my face. "If something happens to her, I'll never forgive myself. This is all my fault."

Danny holds me while I bawl. "Your fault?" he whispers. "How do you work that out?"

Miserably, I lift my head. "I wouldn't listen, and now it's too late." More shuddering sobs. "I was jealous of Lark. I've always been jealous of her. It stopped me seeing clearly."

"Why would you be jealous of Lark?"

"Isn't it obvious?" I look at him. "She always gets the limelight. I've lived in her shadow all my life. I wanted a chance to shine."

"But you *do* shine, Wren." He pushes the hair from my eyes.

I stare at him, thrown.

"No, I don't. Lark is the special one, she always has

been. You know that, Danny. That's why you—" I bite my tongue and look away.

"That's why I *what*?" He turns my cheek to see my face.

I take a deep breath. "That's why you're in love with her." My skin burns where he's touching it. "I know you are. You don't have to pretend, it's OK. But—"

"Wren, stop." Danny puts his finger to my lips. "I'm not in love with Lark."

Then he kisses me, and for a few unbelievable seconds, the whole world stops.

Crackling static drags me back to reality. A crashing chord fills the air.

I jerk backwards, blinking at Danny, shellshocked. All around, people look up, heads swivelling to look for the nearest screen. I find myself doing the same.

The beat kicks in. That insistent, thudding heartbeat, joined by the slowly creeping bass. My body tenses, starting to react. That addictive riff tunnels into my ears and loops itself round my brain. And now a voice lilts through the speakers– the sound of someone humming softly.

Lark.

I swoon. The melody … it's so beautiful.

There's a screen by the entrance to the East Field and my legs start to carry me towards it.

"Wren! Your earbuds!" Danny blocks my way.

His perfect face wakes something inside me. Clumsily, I fumble in my pockets. As I wedge the earbuds in my

327

ears, the bass dulls and softens, and the treble is drowned out. Gradually, I come to. I can still feel vibrations pulsing through my body, but my head begins to clear.

Danny removes his hearing aids. His lips move: "This is it."

Instinctively, his hand finds mine. And while all I want to do is think about that kiss and what it means, I know there's no time. Leaving the remote East Field behind, together we make our way back into the heart of the festival.

All along the main walkway crowds are gathered round the huge screens, watching, listening, their heads nodding along to the insistent beat. Every screen is filled with Spinner's face.

He starts to speak.

I turn to Danny. "What is he saying?"

Danny's mouth tightens as he concentrates. "He's saying … 'This is … the call.'"

Spinner's face flickers and disappears.

Slowly, purposefully, the crowds around us start to move. As one, they head towards the Briar Arena, a silent, single-minded army. Mouths are still, expressions dazed. Danny grips my hand tighter, partly for reassurance, partly so we don't get swept apart.

"Seven o'clock," I mouth. "The arena must be open. We should go too."

"What if Adam sees us?" Danny mouths back. His eyes scan the distant sky. I look up, following his gaze.

Oh no…

Tiny black specks. They're growing bigger, getting closer, fanning out and circling above us. *Drones!*

I tug Danny's sleeve, an idea forming in my head. "Come on!" Slicing against the current of the crowd, I pull him with me. My heart is pounding. I'm scared of being trampled by the relentless stream of people. Nobody is looking where they're going. All eyes are focused on the dark and thorny outline of the Briar Stage.

Finally, we make it into a pocket of open space and I dive under the canvas canopy of a merch tent. The stall is empty, abandoned now that Spinner has issued his call.

"Grab something!" I gesture at the racks of clothing and costumes. "Anything, quick! We need to blend in."

Danny cottons on fast, swapping his green T-shirt for a white one and grimacing at the irony of the "Community of Truth" slogan. Grabbing a black beanie from a mannequin, he pulls it on and tucks his hair inside. I pull a white oversized T-shirt off a hanger and wriggle into it, pulling it over my cut-offs. A flower crown and an eye necklace complete the look.

We stare at one another.

"Terrifying," Danny mouths, shaking his head.

I nod. But as a disguise it works.

Outside, the throngs are still moving, zombie-like, towards the arena. The light is changing, dying; twilight is on its way. The sun hangs low over the Briar Stage like a warning.

As we near the perimeter of the arena, bottlenecks start to form. Thousands of teenagers are attempting to funnel through three narrow gates, the marshals ushering them in with only a cursory glance at their eye stamps. I look back over my shoulder. We're among the last stragglers and the festival site behind me resembles a desert ghost town; litter strewn on arid paths and flags drooping without a breeze. There are no more snaking queues for the toilets or the bar – and no more bartenders – literally everyone is here, desperate to see Spinner and the Aurora.

The arena must be almost full. People around us start to panic and we're thrust forward in a sudden surge. As a final mass of people rush the gates, the marshals give up trying to keep order. Powerless to stop the tsunami, they stand back to let everyone through.

We're inside.

The vibrations stop suddenly. I guess the music must have temporarily stopped too.

Tentatively, I pull out my earbuds. Something is playing over the PA system, but it's different: a safe, innocuous dance track. I nod at Danny, who replaces his aids.

"Now what?" he asks.

It's a good question. I stare at the vast expanse of the arena. We've come in through the left gate, so we're squished all the way to one side, miles from anywhere. I stand on tiptoes, trying to see over people's heads. The Briar Stage is a dark, foreboding hemisphere, framed by powerful speakers and huge screens. It's set up for a regular band, with drums, guitars and keyboards, but there's a strange rectangular hole in the middle and a walkway at the front that extends out into the crowds. Up on the screens, an abstract film is playing, swirling and hypnotic, keeping the audience distracted. Above us, Adam's drones continue to circle like mosquitos.

I turn to Danny. "We get to the front."

If we're going to stop Lark, we need to be close to her. The problem is, there are thousands of people here, all crammed tightly into the space, all wanting a good view too.

We start to push our way towards the middle, but it's impossible to move anywhere fast. The crowd is dense and unyielding and, the closer we get, the hotter and more tightly packed it becomes.

Pretty soon, we're stuck.

Danny looks at me helplessly. *What now?*

I look about me, desperate for inspiration and daunted by the hopelessness of our task. A sudden motion on the edge of the arena catches my eye. The three thorny gates of the Briar Arena have started moving. One by one, they're slowly swinging shut.

A grinding sound fills the air; the sound of a heavy mechanism, turning.

I look back at Danny in horror. Our problem just got a whole lot bigger.

We're locked inside the Briar Arena.

Trapped.

33

I wait for the protests, the uproar from the crowd. Nothing happens.

"They don't realize we're locked in," I yell to Danny.

"Or they don't care," he yells back.

The crowd around us may be oblivious to their captivity, but they're starting to get restless. They stare up at the stage, the sun setting rapidly behind it. Fiery fingers of orange and red light pierce through the framework of thorny wicker branches. The effect is magical but unsettling, bathing everyone's faces in a deep demonic glow. Goosebumps prickle my arms. In spite of the screens, the PAs and the high-tech sound tower, the main stage looks exactly like the setting for some ancient ritual. I have no doubt that it's intentional. We're immersed in Adam's world. Everything is under his control.

The heat in the arena is intense. I look again at the walkway where the stage projects out into the audience. At the end of the walkway, a few steps lead up to a small raised platform, where a microphone is mounted on a stand. *That's where Lark will be performing*, I think, craning my neck for a better view. A squadron of shaven-headed marshals have been deployed in a pit directly in front of the stage and all along the walkway, with a metal barrier between them and the audience.

I do a double take.

The marshals have riot shields strapped to their chests.

Wow. This crowd is far from rebellious, but Adam clearly isn't taking any chances. Nothing can go wrong tonight; he's seen to that. There'll be no stage invasions, no intruders…

And he doesn't want his performer to escape.

Danny is staring at the sound tower, a huge imposing monolith in the arena. "If we could get inside it, we could cut the sound channels," he shouts. "But I can't see any access." He frowns. "The tower is totally fenced off. Unless there's a tunnel…"

"There *were* tunnels," I say, thinking back to the excavators I saw when the site was under construction.

"But the entrance is probably backstage."

Our mission seems hopeless. Adam has thought of everything.

The sky is getting darker now. It can't be long before Spinner's set begins. I can feel the anticipation rising, the energy crackling in the air. It's the feeling I've always loved, whenever I've gone to a concert – the sense that you're about to witness something magical. That could even change your life.

But if we don't stop it, this one really will.

"What can we do?" Danny scowls in frustration, and I know he's struggling with the noise. "We can't get closer, we can't get out, we're locked inside the arena. We can't set off an alarm. I don't see any emergency exits or any way to get backstage. We can't even warn anyone." He nods at an Aurora clone swaying softly next to us, her eyes closed. "There's no getting through to them. You and me, we're the only sane people in this place. Everyone else is a fanatic. They want to be here, they came willingly, and now they're sitting ducks!"

I place my hand on his arm. "Let's just keep moving forward." I point at the raised platform. "We get to Lark."

As I say it, the lights in the arena dim. A cheer erupts among the crowd. Around us, every face turns expectantly towards the blood-red sunset and the dusky stage.

The screens on the PAs flicker to life. On the left, a digital clock displays the time: 20:59. On the right, the seconds steadily count down towards the hour.

One minute until Spinner's set begins.

At exactly nine o'clock, the arena falls dark.

I plug in my earbuds, issuing a silent prayer for the charge to last. Next to me, Danny removes his hearing aids, this time replacing them with his own protective earbuds. We're ready. *As safe as we can be...*

Around us, everyone is holding their breath. Suddenly spotlights flood the stage and the huge video screens flicker and change. The word **COMMUNITY** flashes on the left one, its hypocritical partner **TRUTH** flashing on the right, in searing letters twenty feet tall.

I hear the reaction of the audience like a dull roar.

A distant sound of synths fills the air. Slowly, a vast podium rises up from the hole in the centre of the stage. I could almost giggle if I wasn't so tense. It's suddenly clear that the instruments – the guitars, the keyboards, the drums – are more like props, placed there purely to be symbolic, because right in the centre of the podium, behind various space-age looking media players and control panels, lording it over everyone, is Spinner.

He throws his hand in the air in his trademark salute.

The audience goes wild. People open their mouths, screaming, while thousands of others raise their hands to salute him back.

For a moment, Spinner's face fills the screens, his chiselled cheekbones lifted in a smirk, smugness emanating from his ice-blue eyes. He's wearing long, multicoloured robes like a mini-Adam. He swaggers to the front of the podium, soaking up the adoration of the crowd for what seems an age. Finally, he settles behind his control deck again; a shaven-headed king on a throne.

I feel the first beat of the first track drop, and instantly the crowd is in a frenzy. As the masses around us jump and dance, Danny and I are caught in the middle of the mayhem. We hang on tightly to each other to avoid getting thrown off our feet. A dazzling visual display illuminates the screens and the back wall of the stage, digital patterns dancing, mesmerizing to watch. The crowd, spellbound, begins to find its rhythm, moving as one. Bodies are swaying, hands are waving, fists are pounding to the pumping beat.

"Come on!" I yell. "We have to try again!"

Danny nods, letting me know he understands, but when we attempt to squeeze a path through the heaving bodies, we get nowhere. They're a solid, writhing mass. Just then, from the front of the stage, two huge crane arms swing out over the crowd. Cameras are mounted on the ends. I freeze as images of the audience are projected up on the screens. Close-up shots of happy, zoned-out faces.

Happy, zoned-out faces … plus Danny and me.

"Dance!" I gesture wildly to make him understand. "Dance, or Adam will see us!"

His lips move. "Hate dancing."

I grab his waist, moving in time with the crowd. If I wasn't so worried about my sister's lethal lullaby, I'd probably enjoy this moment more. Seeing Danny forced to sway to Spinner's bassline almost makes me smile.

But more importantly, it helps. When people sense that we're with them, not against them, the crowd starts to part naturally, allowing us to weave our slow way through.

Several tracks later, we're closer to the front, and Spinner's set is building to a climax. Although I can't hear clearly, I can feel the music intensifying and the beat pumping harder. I can tell that Spinner's feeding off the crowd, playing with expectations, holding back the bass drop until the audience is practically screaming. Across the sea of heads, I catch sight of Ruby hoisting Meena on to her shoulders. Meena throws back her head, lost in ecstasy. She looks like she's undergoing a religious experience.

On the podium, Spinner grins. He's got the crowd in the palm of his hand, worshipping him like a god.

The track comes to an end, and the audience roars. The lights in the arena suddenly dim.

Silence settles.

Faintly, distantly, I hear it through my earbuds: the siren chord.

A small part of me twitches, but the effect on the crowd is a hundred times stronger. Everyone jerks to attention, triggered.

I glance at Danny. He squeezes my hand.

Blinding white lights distort my view. Mist or fog or dry ice is sweeping across the stage, obscuring Spinner on his podium. At the same time, deep vibrations pound my body, and I know that the driving heartbeat of "Lullaby" has begun.

And now, the dry ice thins and a spotlight falls. Every single face stares in the same direction, attention riveted on one thing.

The figure of a girl.

The screens scream a flashing sequence of words.

WELCOME THE AURORA
WELCOME THE NEW DAWN

I can barely breathe, barely move a muscle.

Standing on the Briar Stage is my sister.

34

Lark looks ethereal, like an angel. Like a vision from another world. She's wearing an outfit that is little more than a tiny white bodysuit encrusted in sparkling crystals, with thin chiffon sleeves and a transparent chiffon skirt. It's sexy yet innocent, both revealing and concealing – *the stuff of a million male fantasies*, I think to myself, angrily. There's no way she chose it herself. Her long hair has been made longer still, silky rainbow extensions threaded expertly into her ice-white roots and cascading almost to the floor.

The crane cameras track the performers, projecting their images on the screens. Spinner on the left, Lark on the right. Her face is expressionless – lips slightly parted, glitter-dusted eyelids closed.

Slowly, she opens her eyes.

My stomach clenches. There's nothing there. No life, no spark. I can't see my sister anywhere.

I turn to Danny, distraught.

"Come on," he says, dragging me forward.

The crowd parts easily. Every person is transfixed by Lark, every face glued to her, as she walks slowly across the stage and on to the small walkway in the middle. Fingers stretch up towards her in yearning as she glides above the crowd. Her feet are bare. It makes her seem so young.

Out of nowhere, I remember a time when we were little, playing barefoot on the street, and I stepped on a shard of glass. I screamed and screamed and wouldn't let anyone near me. It was Lark who calmed me down, Lark who made me laugh, Lark who held my hand while Mum went running for the first-aid kit.

Now, she's the vulnerable one. It's Lark who needs *my* help.

But where is Adam?

I scan the stage wings but I can't see any sign of him. I turn and peer at the sound tower. Bent over the mixing desk is a tall, solitary figure, cast in shadow.

Is that him?

Lark carries on down the walkway, moving as though she's in a dream. She reaches the steps up to the little platform and slowly starts to climb.

Gripping Danny's hand, I push closer. Now, we're less than ten metres away.

"Lark!" I scream, but I can't hear my own voice. She doesn't react, and neither does anybody else. Around me, people are starting to dance. I can tell the riff has kicked in because the bodies around me judder, submitting to the rush of their addiction.

"Lark!" I try again.

Still no response. The music is drowning me out. I'm close enough now that I can see the elaborate gold eye design on the microphone cradled in her hand.

Lark lifts the microphone to her lips.

Her chest rises as she draws a breath.

"No!" I scream, but it's no use.

She opens her mouth to sing.

It's surreal. I can barely hear her voice thanks to my earbuds, but I can feel the beat and bassline of "Lullaby" in every fibre of my body, and I can feel its effect on me too, making me sluggish, slowing me down.

But that's nothing to the effect that Lark's pure, unfiltered singing voice is having on the audience. I look around in disbelief. People are enchanted – there's no other word for it – clasping their faces in transports of joy as tears trickle inconsolably down their cheeks.

"Lark!" I scream until I think my lungs might burst. "You have to stop singing!" I look across to Danny. His arms are waving, his mouth is moving; he's shouting wildly too.

Lark doesn't notice a thing. As she throws back her head, I spot the monitors nestled in her ears. She's not listening to the crowd noise, but to her own voice, carefully controlling her sound. Either that, or Adam is communicating with her, giving her instructions.

She stares out towards the sound tower, her face blank, her movements soulless and robotic. It looks like the perfect impression of an aloof, self-possessed superstar, except I know the truth…

The music is affecting her too.

"We have to climb!" I scream at Danny, pointing to the platform.

How? he gestures. We're still not close enough and we're hemmed in on every side.

It doesn't help that the dancing around us has intensified, becoming even more frenzied. Limbs jerk and twitch, just like they did at Charlie's party. Back then, I thought it was the strobe lighting, but there's no strobe now, and the movements are way, *way* more extreme. In the heat of the arena, my blood turns to ice.

It's the power of the melody, sung live.

The fervency isn't sustainable though, and a few moments later the dancers start to slow. In front of me, and projected up on screen, Lark's beautiful blank face yawns. All around, arms stretch, mouths open, heads loll. Even Spinner seems to droop behind his laptop, his headphones slipping from his head.

Then the first person drops.

It's a girl – I recognize her from school. Laura something, from my English class. She slumps on the ground right in front of me, eyes still open, eyeballs rolling in her head. She doesn't seem hurt; in fact, she's calm, her breathing slow and even. She just seems … blank, hollow. Missing.

Like her identity has been erased.

I scream at Danny. "They're going under! We're running out of time!"

Thud. Another person falls. Then another and another and another; little clusters everywhere.

This can't be happening. This is sick—

Everywhere I look, people are tilting forward, sagging sideways, dropping to their knees or sinking to the ground, bringing down their partners and their friends. Some lie stretched out, while others curl in a ball, but it's the blank stares that give me the chills. They're here but they're not; awake yet asleep.

Empty. Ready to receive.

Within seconds, it's only Danny and me and a smattering of others still standing. And Lark, swaying up on the platform. Her eyes are closed now and her mouth is moving mechanically.

"Come on!" I shout, trying not to hurt anyone as I scramble over the fallen bodies and sleeping statues. The entire arena is like a medieval battlefield. Bodies, bodies, everywhere.

I'm nearly at the metal barriers. Even the marshals have succumbed, keeled over in their high-vis vests.

"Lark!" I scream. "Lark, can you hear me? It's me, Wren!"

Her eyelids flutter.

"Lark! Please!"

Her eyes open. She looks through me, past me, unseeing.

"You have to stop!" I plead. I'm crying now, because I know she doesn't understand. She blinks at the bodies in the arena, detached and unaware.

"No!" I watch in horror as she lifts the microphone back to her lips, her arm trembling with the effort. As she raises her chin, her jaw shakes with vibrato. Then I realize. She's nearly finished the song. She's singing the final two lines of "Lullaby", with that incredible octave jump.

"No!" I scream again, as the last remaining teens in the arena crash and fall to the ground.

The camera cranes swing round and down, scanning the unconscious bodies. Slowly, inevitably, they come to rest on Danny and me. My heart jumps into my mouth as I see our stunned faces staring back at us from the screens.

Adam has seen us. He knows we're here.

Danny tugs my arm, dragging my attention back. He points towards the stage. Up on his podium, Spinner is slumped, lifeless, over his control deck.

But that's not what makes me gasp.

On the platform at the end of the walkway, lying in a crumpled heap, is my sister.

35

"Lark!" My voice breaks as I fly towards the stage.

I can't bear to see her lying on the platform, so small and still and alone. Her hair spills over the edge like a rainbow waterfall, while one hand is flung wide, exposing a slim wrist. She looks fragile and broken, and...

Oh god, don't let her be dead.

Tears fog my eyes as I hurl myself into the pit. I'm not thinking about the marshals waking up, or Adam appearing, or even the comatose teenagers scattered like dominoes all around. All I want to do is reach my sister. She's the only thing that matters now.

Roughly, I push aside the body of the marshal who

manhandled Danny. He moans but doesn't wake. The only way on to the platform is via the stage, but the stage is high, at least eight feet. I take a running jump and throw myself towards it, clinging to the scaffolding underneath and hauling my legs up. My arms scream with the effort, but I make it, panting for breath.

Silence.

I'm suddenly aware of silence.

Vibrations are no longer pulsing through my body. Warily, I pull out my earbuds. "Lullaby" has come to an end, and the arena is deathly quiet. But not for long.

Then I hear it. A mellow, melodious voice.

"Welcome, my lambs. My truth-seekers. My children."

The voice reverberates round the arena, turning my blood cold.

Adam.

Where is he? There's no sign of him on stage.

"Relax and do not fear. It's time to let your self go."

I look at Lark. I want to go to her, but Adam's words are filling my ears, urgent and insistent. My legs turn heavy, rooting me to the spot. "You have gathered here. Damaged. Lost and confused. But tonight, we will fix you. Welcome to the Community of Truth—"

And then I don't hear anything else, because suddenly Danny launches himself on to the stage next to me.

"Wren! No!" He slams his hands over my ears. "Adam's sermon. It's starting."

He's right. As I jam my earbuds back in place, I stare

346

at the silent teenagers beneath me. They make an eerie sight. Thousands of eyes glow in the light of the dying sun as Adam's toxic sermon transforms their thoughts, their values, their brains.

"Where is he? How is he doing it?"

I read Danny's lips: "… a recording … on the track…"

"He's not even here?" Fury burns inside me. It doesn't make sense. Surely Adam would want to witness this, the birth of his community?

Danny gazes up at Spinner's podium: "… try to stop … help Lark…"

He turns on his heel, gone before I can reply.

I fly down the walkway towards the platform, trying to drown out the terror in my head. Lark finished "Lullaby". She sang it to the end, like Fernanda and Anna and Mia must have done. Is it too late?

Has "Lullaby" killed my sister too?

I scramble up the steps to the platform and sink to my knees in front of her.

"Lark! Lark, can you hear me?"

Her hand is still clutching the microphone.

"Lark!" I take her gently by the shoulders. "It's me, Wren! Wake up!"

Her head lolls back, her body floppy. I lift her wrist, feeling for a pulse. *Is she alive?* It's impossible to tell. The vibrations from Adam's sermon are coursing through my body.

"Lark, I'm sorry … I'm so, so sorry." Tears are streaming

347

down my face. Cradling her body in my arms, I close my eyes.

Please save her. Please don't let her die.

I don't know who I'm praying to – not Adam, that's for sure – but suddenly, I get it, why people want something to believe in. Something bigger than themselves.

Because, otherwise, you're on your own. And what can one person do?

The vibrations stop. My eyes snap open.

Up on Spinner's podium, Danny is grinning. Beneath him, the mangled remains of Spinner's control deck and media players are smashed to pieces on the floor.

"Oh my god. You did it!" I shout, my heart lifting. I rip out my earbuds. The only sound in the arena is a fading feedback whine.

I look down at my sister. "Lark?" I shake her, gently.

Nothing.

Danny climbs down from the podium. As he replaces his hearing aids, his grin starts to fade. Lark's eyes are shut. She hasn't stirred. Spinner, too, is still hunched over. The thousands of bodies in the arena remain frozen, silent, unmoving.

"I don't understand." Dread squeezes my stomach. "Why are they still asleep?"

Danny is on the walkway. "Wren, I have a bad feeling. Adam will be coming. He'll be angry. We need to get out of here."

"And leave them all?" I shake my head. "No way."

348

I ease Lark's microphone from her hand. It falls easily from her grasp.

"EVERYBODY, WAKE UP!" I shriek into the mic. My voice bellows round the arena with a feedback squeal. I try again. "WAKE UP, PLEASE! WAKE UP!"

Screeching, then more silence.

Danny shakes his head. In my lap, Lark is a cold, heavy weight.

"No!" I wail. "Adam was creating a community. He wanted to brainwash people, not kill them!"

"I don't think they're dead…" Danny sinks to his knees beside me, staring at the unconscious crowd. "But they've been changed. The damage has been done."

I look down at my sister's peaceful, innocent face.

Is she dead or indoctrinated? Which is worse? "But we stopped the sermon," I say. "The initiation, it went wrong—"

"We need to go," Danny says again. He touches my cheek and his eyes glisten. He thinks I'm deluding myself, and maybe I am. "It's too late…"

"No." I say it forcefully. "It's not too late, it can't be." I stare out at the audience. "Look at them. They're still entranced – they're 'ready to receive'…"

A seed of an idea begins to form.

Carefully, I ease myself out from beneath my comatose sister and lay her head gently down. The idea blooming in my mind is so wild and preposterous I can hardly bring myself to think it.

Maybe the damage could be undone.

"Music did this," I say, looking Danny in the eyes. "Music was the magic. A song made them fall asleep..." I pause. My eyes flick to the instruments on the stage. "What if a different song could wake them up? A song to undo the hate—"

"Like a love song," Danny finishes. He holds my gaze. "It's worth a try." His eyes suddenly spark. "And I think I know the one..."

36

Danny places the microphone in my hands.

"What are you—"

"No time. Just trust me." He kisses me and turns, running down the walkway and across the stage. I watch as he picks up a guitar – the beautiful Les Paul that we saw in Adam's studio – and plugs the lead into one of Spinner's now redundant channels.

"I might make mistakes," he calls, cryptically. "I had to teach myself."

"I don't—"

But then he strikes the opening chords, cutting me off. Suddenly I'm speechless. The song he's playing – I know it.

It's "Song for a Sleepwalker".

My song.

A thousand thoughts flood my mind. Danny's seen my notebook. I must have left it at his house. He memorized the chords and learned my song... *He's read my lyrics, the ones about him...* My face flames and my body burns. He knew how I felt about him, before today.

"Sing, Wren!" Danny shouts, his face tight with tension. "Come on, there's no time!"

"But it won't work!" I shout back. "Nobody knows my song. I can't sing like Lark..."

"Just sing!" he shouts again. "I believe in you." He gazes at the passive audience. "What do we have to lose?"

My sister.

With a deep breath, I lift the microphone to my lips:

Everything is changing. Nothing is the same.
I don't know who to trust or to believe.
I'm scared of what I know, afraid of what I don't.
I'm losing any faith I had in me.

Of course, nothing happens. There's no change in Lark at my feet, and no change in the bodies slumped in the arena. I glance at Danny, ready to give up. Then I stop. His playing sounds amazing; powerful and confident. I can't believe he's managed to teach himself from only the scribbles in my book.

"Keep going," he shouts. His determination fills me with fire.

I move on to the next verse. The lyrics were written for Lark, but I sing them directly to the crowd.

He's going to break your heart. He's forcing you apart—
He fills you up with hateful twisted lies.
He moulds you to his whim, denies your inner fire.
He'll crush your spirit so that he can rise.

Still no reaction, but my voice is growing stronger. I move on to the walkway, pacing up and down, doing my best to project my words out to the crowds. Sure, it's not what I dreamed of – playing to a stadium of sleeping teens – but that doesn't matter. The important thing is getting the message across. I need to reach people. "Lullaby" made them numb; maybe my song can make them feel. Casting away any last, lingering doubts about how I sound, I throw all my emotion into the chorus. My song could be powerful, way more powerful than "Lullaby", because I wrote it with love, from the heart.

The Briar Arena fills with my voice.

You need to wake up.
I wish you'd wake up.
Why don't you wake up and see?
You've been sleepwalking too long,
But I'll help you find your path.
Don't listen to him. Hear me.

Down in the front row, someone stirs. One lone boy sits up and rubs his eyes. I gape at Danny. His mouth is open too. And now another boy is scrambling to his feet, pulling his girlfriend up beside him. More pairs of eyes blink awake.

Is it… working?

I open my mouth to sing the next verse, but a hideous screech of feedback turns my voice to a tiny squeak.

No!

My microphone channel has been cut.

Danny's guitar is weak and jangly. He's been cut too.

I squint. A bright light is shining from somewhere in the crowd, and I realize it's coming from the sound tower. I gasp as Adam steps into view. Even from this distance, he makes an intimidating figure, his body taut and his robes flowing.

"What a very interesting experiment." His mocking voice is amplified and it echoes round the arena. "I must say, I've enjoyed watching you make a fool of yourself, Wren Mackenzie, with your pathetic attempt to perform. It's lucky that your audience is … *indisposed*." He laughs, nastily, then his tone turns icy. "But we've heard enough from you tonight, I think. You need to stop what you're doing, or you'll endanger the lives of everyone in this arena."

"He's lying, Wren!" Danny shouts from across the stage. "It was working. We need to keep playing."

"But he's cut the PA system!"

"I'm warning you, Wren," Adam breaks in, deathly cold. "If you continue, I promise you that everyone here will die." He pauses, waiting for the weight of his words to hit me. "Terrible tragedies can happen anywhere," he continues, "even in little towns like Hamlington." He's holding something in his hand but I can't make out what it is. "I have disappeared once before. I can do it again. You can be in no doubt about that. My work remains unharmed, it can always be resurrected. I won't let another pathetic Mackenzie woman stop me."

The light extinguishes abruptly. Adam fades into the shadows with a swish of his robes.

I feel sick.

He was watching all this time, like we were entertainment, like there's no way I could ever be a threat.

I turn hopelessly to Danny. "Where's he gone? What did he mean?"

Danny shakes his head. "It doesn't matter. We can't give up. It was working!" He points to the tiny number of people in the crowd, getting warily to their feet. "Keep singing!"

"But I won't be loud enough."

Danny gestures to the audience again. "So, get *them* to sing too!"

I take a deep breath. Hesitantly, I wave my arms above my head. "Um … everyone? Anyone? Please, if you're awake, just listen to me!" I say it again, running up and down the walkway, shouting as loud as my lungs will let me. In the huge arena, my voice sounds miniscule, like a buzzing fly.

"Everyone, my name is Wren. You're probably confused and scared. You were promised a magical experience. A new dawn in a dark world." I take another breath. "You were tricked, lured here by someone who tried to do you harm. But we can undo it. You can wake your friends. All you have to do is sing."

I fill my lungs with air...

Then I launch into the chorus of my song. There's no point using my microphone so I hold it out to the crowd, hoping someone will get the message and join in. My voice warbles, thin and feeble in the vast space.

I shake my head at Danny. *This is useless. It will never work.*

Then I see someone – *Ruby?* – at the front, down near the marshals' pit. Ruby blinks blearily up at me, her face blotchy and tear-stained. Meena is crumpled in her arms, seemingly fast asleep.

"Ruby!" I cry. "Ruby, sing! Sing with me, please! Let's wake Meena!"

I start my chorus again. Somehow – somehow – Ruby joins in:

You need to wake up.
I wish you'd wake up.
Why don't you wake up and see?
You've been sleepwalking too long.
But I'll help you find your path.
Don't listen to him. Hear me.

And now Meena is blinking, looking around in surprise. I keep going, working my way across the stage. Incredibly, more and more people are singing. At first, it's the people closest to the front, the ones who can hear me best. But as others start to join in, the sound begins to ripple outwards. As the volume starts to grow, more and more people sit up and stretch, scratching the sleep from their eyes. And then they start singing too.

All except Lark.

My voice breaks as I turn back to look at her. *She sang "Lullaby". Singers don't survive that.* Shoving down the thought, I scramble back to the platform, taking her hand in mine. *Come on, Lark. Please!* Tears flow like a river down my face. I try to keeping singing but the words fail me.

The crowd sees, though. They know what to do.

"You need to wake up. I wish you'd wake up…"

Stunned, I lift my head. They're singing to me! Hundreds of voices, raised in unison, singing back my words. I blink, astonished, unable to speak.

Why don't you wake up and see?
You've been sleepwalking too long,
but I'll help you find your path.
Don't listen to him. Hear me.

And then I feel something. In Lark's slender wrist; the faintest flicker of a pulse.

My heart leaps.

Determination drives me to my feet. Maybe it's not too late after all. Maybe we can save her. But it's going to take an even bigger effort.

More magic.

"A choir!" I yell to Danny, running back to join him on the main stage. "An arena choir. Everyone singing, together. You take one side and I'll take the other. Just the chorus. I'll start first."

I lift my arms like a conductor and, unbelievably, people take notice. On my cue, they open their mouths and start to sing. On the other side of the stage, Danny works ten times as hard, watching me for cues and keeping time furiously. He brings in his section four bars later, and my heart takes flight as the harmonies soar.

The crowd responds by singing even louder. There is power in our massed voices, an undeniable momentum. Everyone can feel it. With Adam long forgotten, I move across the stage like a whirlwind, changing the dynamics and looping the chorus in a glorious, uplifting round. The sound thunders through the arena, peppering me with goosebumps from head to toe.

Music is my language. It brings me *alive*.

I gaze at all the faces filled with wonder, *enraptured* by the power of our sound. I know what everyone is thinking. We've all felt lost and insignificant. We've all wished that someone would show us the way. But we are enough as we are — and together we're spectacular.

All we need to believe in is ourselves.

I turn to catch Danny's eye, to see if he feels the same – to see if he realizes the impact he's having up on stage, playing his guitar and conducting this incredible choir.

But Danny isn't looking. His eyes move from Lark, still horribly lifeless on the platform, to a point beyond the heads of the crowd. Panic fills his face.

I follow his gaze.

That's when I see the smoke.

37

It's coming from the sound tower, right in the middle of the audience, exactly where Adam was standing only a short while ago. A thin black wisp turns into tall black tendrils, snaking up into the blood-red sky.

"The tower's on fire!" someone screams.

I stop singing and the choir fades out. A horrified hush falls over the arena.

"Not just the tower. Look!" Meena points to where smoke is rising at intervals along the perimeter fencing. A series of sudden explosions sends orange sparks flying. My heart gives a lurch, more people scream, and the crowd surges forward in fright.

"The stage!" Danny shouts, pointing upwards. Terror grips me. Huge plumes of smoke are billowing out from behind the rear wall, and a moment later I see flames – actual bright orange flames – licking the thorny framework along the edge of the dome. The fire takes hold with terrifying speed.

"The whole place will burn down in minutes," Danny moans. "Everything's so dry, and the thorns are made of wicker – it's all just wood!"

In an instant, I understand. Adam planned this. This is his escape clause, the thing he meant when he said, *"Terrible tragedies can happen anywhere."* In case something went wrong, in case there was a riot, or his horrible experiment didn't work, he needed a way to get rid of the evidence. Thousands of teens, torched alive. No one left to testify, and Adam himself long gone – some secret way out. *I bet he's miles away already.*

The crowds are in a frenzy. And when they realize all the exit gates are locked, the panic steps up a gear. People are crying and wailing, pushing in all directions, desperate to escape. The sound tower is a glowing beacon of livid orange flames, sparks flying on the breeze towards us. The heat is hideously intense.

"It's going to fall!" someone shrieks.

"We have to get out!" Danny screams, bounding on to the platform where I'm kneeling over Lark. *Why won't she wake?* Below us, people start grabbing the metal barriers from around the pit, dragging them over to the gates to use as battering rams.

"What about Lark?" I sob, my eyes foggy with tears. "We can't leave her!"

Danny drops down beside me. He's crying too. "Wren…"

"No, no – she's alive! I felt a pulse—"

My voice is smothered by an enormous crash. Somehow, one of the battering rams has breached a section of the fence and now a huge crush of people are swarming through. The arena is beginning to clear – but only just in time. With a terrible creaking sound, the huge sound tower, fully ablaze, tilts terrifyingly to one side and within seconds it falls with a thunderous smash. Waves of heat and debris fly towards the stage, scorching my clothes, my hair, my face.

"Wren, we have to go!" Danny begs.

"Help me to lift her!"

I manage to get my arms under Lark and try to hoist her up, but the chiffon of her dress is slippery. She's a dead weight, sliding out of my grasp.

A crackling sound makes me look up. The thorns above the Briar Stage are burning brightly like a hellish bonfire. We need to get out soon or we'll be trapped in an infernal cage.

A chattering sound rises on the wind. In the distant sky, a fleet of dark specks is swarming on the horizon. Adam's drones? No – *helicopters*! Still miles away but getting closer. There's no time to feel relief. Up above, a lighting rig explodes in a shocking *Bang!* and I throw my body over Lark's to protect her from the flaming shards of wicker that come raining down on the stage.

"Danny! Go!" I scream. "Get out! The whole place is coming down!"

"No way," he cries. "I'm staying with you."

"Me too." The voice makes me turn.

Spinner is lurching along the walkway towards us. In his hand is a two-way radio, like the ones issued to the marshals.

"I called for help. It's coming," he mutters, stumbling up the stairs and collapsing on to the platform. "But I'm not leaving here without her."

I blink. This is Spinner, but something about him is different, and it's not because of the ash streaked across his face or the singed fabric of his multicoloured robes.

The bravado is gone. There's no swagger. He looks young, innocent, scared.

Has my song mended the damage that was done to Spinner, too?

"Please, keep singing to her," Spinner – Evan – begs, kneeling down next to Lark and taking her hand. "Please don't stop."

Danny looks at me and nods.

So, as the Briar Stage becomes an inferno, I hold my sister tightly in my arms. And with heat searing my face and smoke choking my lungs, I sing her my love song, straight from the heart.

38

Six months later

The sun is setting beyond the gently rolling hills. The marquee is erected and the stage is set. Our instruments are tuned and ready.

I cast a last quick look over the set list, pride blooming in my belly. Ten original songs. Some new, some a little older.

All of them written by me.

I sneak a peek behind the canvas, my nerves rattling. The place is absolutely packed. This is the biggest audience we've had so far – unless you count playing on the Briar Stage at Enrapture.

But I try not to think about that.

I can't avoid it tonight though, because that's the reason we're here. Ellis and Joss organized this fundraiser, and Jim is stage-managing the gig. All my music friends from college have a slot. It's been six months since the fire, six months since we narrowly escaped with our lives, and everyone is in agreement.

It's time for Hamlington to heal.

I notice Mum and Dad at the front, holding hands, and smile to myself. Runaway Summers' renaissance is going from strength to strength. The Norwegian TV series got commissioned for a second season, and the band have decided to use the extra money to record a new album. It'll be Glastonbury next, Dad reckons.

I challenged him to a race.

Mum still feels guilty – even though we've told her a million times that it's not her fault that Adam came crawling out of the woodwork with his bigoted ideas and decades-old festering grudge. If she hadn't acted quickly, flying back from Oslo as soon as she picked up my email and alerting the police to the threat, they wouldn't have had Adam on their radar. As it was, as soon as Evan radioed emergency services, they blocked all the roads in and out of Devil's Dale, catching Adam in his Tesla as he tried to flee the site. He was charged almost immediately with breaching festival safety requirements and endangering lives – and that was before they read his notebook.

Now it's triple murder.

I sigh. It's right that Adam will be sentenced, but it's bitter-sweet consolation for the families of Fernanda, Anna and Mia.

They lost their daughters. Sofia lost her sister.

And I almost lost mine.

I close my eyes. The sight of the firefighters storming the Briar Arena is an image I'll never forget. Amid the soaring plumes of water dousing what was left of the stage, Lark was airlifted to hospital. I never left her side.

"So that's where you're hiding." Danny sneaks up behind me, making me jump. His warm arms slide round my waist. "You missed Evan's set."

"I'm sure it was great." I smile. I have nothing against Evan these days, now he's dropped his Spinner persona and removed the toxic content from his socials. He was a victim of Adam as much as any of us. He's been working hard to build up a new fan base from scratch, but I think the person he most wants to convince is Lark.

Danny nuzzles my neck. "I don't think I ever told you…"

I turn to face him. "Told me what?"

"Why Wren is a good name for you."

I snort. "Err, no. Actually, you did. I seem to remember it's because I'm small, common and generally unremarkable."

"Oh, stop fishing for compliments." He pulls me in for a kiss. I sink into it, my head spinning. Eventually, we come up for air. "Wrens are actually my favourite birds," Danny whispers in my ear, "because they're quick and clever…"

"Go on…"

"… they're tiny but they're loud…" He grabs my hand, pulling me into the marquee and leading me over to the stage. "And they're not afraid to make themselves heard." He plants my mic and guitar in my hands.

I laugh and glance over at Lark, adjusting her own mic on its stand. "Plus, you have to admit," I say, "I'm getting much better at sharing my territory."

My songs and Lark's voice.

Together they're a killer combination. We've started singing and writing together, and I'm not going to lie – I actually enjoy hanging out in the cavern with her, sharing playlists and ideas. I've even been teaching her guitar. Turns out she thought *I* was the special one. I could hardly believe it when she told me. *She* was jealous of *me*, she said, because I can play.

Lark catches me looking and flips me the bird. "Love you really, Trog."

I grin. "I know you do."

We're almost ready.

Danny dashes over to chat with Tara, who's signing the gig tonight. I watch his hands fly with confidence. His fluency in signing is growing, and so is mine, now we're both taking online classes. I smile. Finally, Danny seems to believe what I've always known deep down – that nothing about him needs "fixing". Implant surgery might be somewhere in his future, but it's a conversation for another day. For now, he lets his music do the talking.

He bounds back on stage and gives me the nod.

It's time.

Ruby's poised on drums, Jiv on keys. Lark smiles to show she's ready too.

The crowd falls silent. Beyond the marquee, dusk is falling and the sky is a purple haze. Then above the horizon, I see a shape...

No, not a shape. A swarm. I glance at Danny; he's seen it too. His eyes spark, and I remember.

A murmuration.

The swarm gets nearer. And now I see that it's dancing, twisting, turning – lilting though the sky. Rising and falling, playful and free. Thousands of tiny birds without a leader, swooping and soaring above us like musical notes on a stave. A force to be reckoned with: stronger together than alone.

I smile. *Just like our band.*

I count us in, and the sound fills the tent, as Lark's voice and mine harmonize.

Powerful, united – and filled with self-belief.

Working together to make magic.

Acknowledgements

It turns out that 'difficult second album' syndrome is real, and it applies to books as well … but I got here in the end, thanks to the help and support I've received from some brilliant people.

To my agent, Anne Clark, thanks for your wisdom and kindness.

To the team at Scholastic, it's been a dream to work with you again. Special thanks to Linas Alsenas, for seeing the potential in this story. (Sorry your excellent working title didn't survive…!) Thanks to Tierney Holm and Lily Morgan for your editorial enthusiasm; to Polly Lyall Grant for your support, and to Sarah Hall, Wendy Shakespeare,

Aimée Hill, Tina Mories, Olivia Towers and Eleanor Thomas for your individual superpowers in copy-editing, proofreading, PR and marketing. Enormous thanks to Dan Couto and Bethany Mincher for the amazing cover design.

Music has been an enduring influence in my life and a massive part of my identity since childhood. When I decided to write about book about music, I knew early on that I wanted to include a musician who has hearing loss in my story. In part, this was because *The Last Thing You'll Hear* draws on the fairy tale of the Pied Piper (in many versions of which, a deaf child plays an important part in alerting the village to the threat). But a much bigger reason was because both my dad, Michael (like my grandmother, Lillian, his mum), is a musician and music-lover who also happens to have severe hearing loss. Many people helped me with Danny's character and storyline, and I hope I've done their expertise and experiences justice. Dad, thank you first and foremost, for being on hand to answer questions on millions of subjects ranging from guitar-playing, to hearing aids, to your cochlear implant journey. Thanks to Sue Brownson at Laycock School, Islington, and to Charlie and Larissa from Creative Futures for letting me shadow your fantastic music lessons in Laycock's Deaf Provision Unit. My biggest thanks, of course, to the students O, E, F, A, M, T, M, A, B, P, A and M, for talking to me about your experiences of music and sharing your rockstar dreams! Thanks to Anna C for giving me a speech-and-language therapist's perspective, and Fi for putting us in touch.

Thank you to Neil Richardson, for consulting on aspects of audiology. Thanks to the NDCS and the BDA for all the information, and to UEA for your illuminating course on living with deafness and hearing impairment. I also learned an enormous amount from the writing and work of Rachel Kolb and Christine Sun Kim. An enormous thank you to my sensitivity readers, Jo Emmerson and Fran Benson, for your immensely helpful feedback. Fran, thank you also for sharing your important research and essay 'Where is the Deaf Representation?' (published in the *Leaf Journal*, issue 1, volume 2, 2023). I continue to learn, and any errors are of course, my own.

Big thanks to Pam and Chris Macmeikan who patiently answered all my questions about the logistics of planning a festival! For helping me navigate the murky creative waters of song-writing, thank you to the talented Neil Carter. I learned an exceptional amount from Adam White's University of Sheffield song-writing course, recommended to me by the musical Cathy Faulkner. Thank you. To all the music teachers out there – especially mine – thanks for the amazing gift you give people. And to all the choirs and orchestras I've ever joined, thanks for letting this mediocre musician feel part of something bigger and better than herself.

This book wouldn't exist without all the bands, musicians, concerts, gigs and festival experiences that have inspired me. Special shout-out to Morten Harket for the leather bracelets and multi-octave range, to Sarah Records for pulling my teenage indie heartstrings, and to Jarvis Cocker and Stuart Murdoch for writing some of my favourite lyrics. To Massive Attack and Elizabeth Fraser: forgive me for humming 'Teardrop' the whole time I was writing the 'Lullaby' scenes. Finally, Jacob Collier – you're a marvel. Thanks for being the inspiration behind Wren's arena choir.

I'm very lucky to have a host of brilliant writer friends giving me all the support. Thank you to Ali Clack, Sue H. Cunningham and Tess James-Mackey for being early readers and giving such fabulous notes. Thanks also to Annette Caseley, Rachel Delahaye, Cathy Faulkner, Louise Finch, Tia Fisher, Ravena Guron, Lou Kuenzler, Olivia Levez, Emma Perry and Nicola Skinner for your words of encouragement. Thanks to my fabulous 2023 Twitter debuts gang, and to my WM 2020 cohort, to the Oxfordshire Children's Book Award, and to everyone who supported my debut *Mirror Me*, who took the time to shout about it or write a review – your belief kept me going.

To my colleagues at HTSS in Camden – thanks – especially Luke Williams and Ledja Gashi, who endure more than their fair share of drafting drama and plot woes. Thanks also to Renaissance Learning for championing my writing, especially Cecelia Powell – world's greatest cheerleader.

To my family: the Peritons, the Dunnings, the Woods and the Rands, thank you all. Mum and Dad, you do so much for me. Helen, I promise my sibling-rivalry plot was not entirely based on us! Simon, Rowan and Meg, you're the reason I keep on doing this. I love you all. Finally, Barbara Lane and Richard Rand; this is dedicated to your memory.

"An original and layered fairy-tale thriller
that explores the dark side of the fashion
world – slick and entertaining"
Ravena Guron, author of *This Book Kills*

Winner of the Oxfordshire
Children's Book Award 2024

Mirror, mirror, on the wall, who's
the FIERCEST of them all?

Freya's quiet life is turned upside down by Bella,
the glamorous former supermodel who's about
to marry Freya's dad. But how does Bella look
so impossibly perfect, and could she be using
Freya's family for her own sinister purposes?

Freya goes undercover into the intimidating world of
high fashion, determined to stop Bella's ruthless plans…

Jan Dunning studied English and Art at university, where she set her heart on a career with words and pictures. The plot took an unexpected twist, however, when she was scouted at Glastonbury festival and became an international fashion model instead. Jan spent the next decade striding down the runway, flying around the world on photoshoots and startling her friends and family on billboards for Gucci, Garnier and Gap. Finally realizing she had more to say behind the camera, Jan trained as a photographer and art teacher and began writing fiction. She now lives with her family in Bath, dreaming up ideas in the studio at the bottom of her garden, with help from Misty, her cat.

X, formerly known as Twitter @JanDunning1
Instagram @jandunningbooks